To Lisa Kaborycha,
who has helped shape this book in so many ways.

Published by Creston Books, LLC in Berkeley, California
www.crestonbooks.co

CIP data for this book is available from the Library of Congress.

Type set in Colors of Autumn by Jonathan S. Harris, Rosarivo,
Nyala, and Kreon.
Source of Production: Worzalla Books, Stevens Point, Wisconsin
Printed and bound in the United States of America

1 2 3 4 5

MIX
Paper from
responsible sources
FSC® C002589
www.fsc.org

Caravaggio

PAINTER
ON THE
RUN

Creston Books

Caravaggio

PAINTER
ON THE
RUN

MARISSA MOSS

I

This is the low point of the story, the scene when the hero (myself, of course) has lost his home, his money (what little there was), his position, his health. All he has left is his talent. Which is all he started out with. And probably all he'll finish with.

Stuck in this hospital bed, I face long hours of nothing. No painting, no trying to prove myself as the best assistant a master could have. Instead, all I can do is think about what brought me here. Was it envy, anger, stupidity? A combination of all three? Or just plain bad luck?

I've made some mistakes, sure, but I was right to come to Rome, to try to make my name here. After all, I have to fit my talent into a huge name.

Michelangelo.

Who hasn't heard of Michelangelo? The genius who took a hacked-up block of marble, a piece everyone said was ruined, and turned it into the magnificent David. And if that weren't enough to win him fame, he went on to paint the Sistine Chapel. And then, then he took an impossible problem – how to cover the gaping hole of the too-big Saint Peter's cathedral – and solved it by designing a billowing dome.

I'm Michelangelo, but that's not me.

I'm a nobody. Perhaps even a jealous, foolish, hotheaded nobody. It's the year of our lord 1592 and I've reached the age of twenty without a good set of clothes or a major position.

So far, mostly I've painted fruit.

There's a ranking for paintings, as if they were part of an army, going from lowly foot soldier all the way up to king. The most important pictures tell the stories of Christ and His followers. Below everything else is the absolutely lowest form of painting – the miserable still life. Grapes, peaches, plums, a thorny rose or two.

The kind of thing I paint.

But Rome promised more than that. Yes, I started out in a miserable studio, with a miserable artist as my master. A painter with a name as awkward as his brush, Anteveduto Grammatica. When I first met him, I didn't know where to rest my eyes. On the bulbous nose with a large mole tucked in the corner of one nostril? Or on the eyebrows that sprouted wildly, giving him an expression of perpetual surprise?

Anteveduto means "seen before" or "déjà vu," the eerie feeling that you're experiencing something that has already happened. Grammatica, of course, means "grammar," so together it makes "Seen Before Grammar." I'm not sure what that means as a name. Maybe he should have been a Latin teacher?

In any case, I never called him by either name. To me, he was and always will be Mister Salad. Because that was all he fed us. Every meal consisted of a big salad, nothing else.

At least Mr. Salad gave me a place to sleep, conveniently near Saint Peter's, like a promise of where my art would one day hang. It was also close to Castel Sant'Angelo, the prison that houses the condemned before they're executed, often in the piazza right in front. Their heads are left to rot on the bridge that juts from the piazza over the Tiber River. Stuck between heaven and hell, the people in the neighborhood joke, with God on one side and the devil on the other, and sometimes it's not clear which is the devil.

I didn't mind the flocks of cardinals, the herds of monks, the gaggles of nuns. I didn't even mind the rotting heads. In fact, they were useful models since I couldn't pay people to sit for me. Besides, the heads didn't move or spoil the pose. What I did mind was salad for breakfast, lunch, and dinner.

And I minded having to paint the same heads or half-length figures over and over again. True, it wasn't fruit, but only barely.

The other assistants seemed content to work on the same old tired themes – Merchant with Scale, Saint Praying (eyes rolled upwards, of course), Fishmonger Displaying Fish. All the assistants except one.

Mario was also new to Rome. He came from Sicily, not the north like me. So he should have been temperamental. I should have been the calm one. Instead, he was like a soothing breeze to my quick fuse. I enjoyed his stories of home, his silly jokes about our stupid pictures, his love of all things Roman. So when I decided to leave Mr. Salad, I asked Mario to come with me.

"There's no point working with another mediocre master," I told him. "We'll go right to the best, the man who receives the most prestigious commissions, who paints for the pope himself. That's the way to get noticed."

Mario nodded sleepily. "Come on, Mario!" I shook his shoulder. "I'm going. You can come with me or stay here, starving on salad."

That woke him up. He pulled on his clothes, swiped his fingers through his thick curls, and was by my side, striding out the door.

"Well, now," said Mario, gulping down the fresh morning air. "Where are we going? Who is our new master?"

"Only the best – Cesare d'Arpino. I've asked around and he's our man. Everyone says he's the artistic heir to Raphael."

"Oh, really?" Mario yawned. "And he's hiring?"

"He has so many assistants, what are two more?"

"You mean, how can he resist your charms?" Mario teased.

"No, how can he resist my talent?" I led the way across the bridge over the Tiber and followed the narrow streets that led us to Piazza Navona, a large oblong piazza following the footprint of an ancient chariot racecourse. On the western side, the small dome of Sant'Agnese echoed the much bigger one of St. Peter's further west. I stopped to admire the young girls pouring into the church to pray that the martyr would reveal their future husbands to them. The daughters of the noble and wealthy were there, dressed in brilliant silks like tropical birds, followed by the simple cottons of the less fortunate. I was drawn to one face in particular. The eyes were dark and large, the mouth full over a sharp chin, the red hair piled up on top, tucked into a cap. The girl sensed my eyes on her and turned to look at me. I smiled, took off my hat, and gave an elaborate bow. Her cheeks glowed pink and she lowered her eyes, hurrying into the church.

"Do you know her?" Mario asked.

"Not yet," I said. "But I will."

We crossed to the other side of the piazza to Pig Street. Maybe in ancient times, there was a pig market here. Not just a regular street with a ridiculous name.

When I thought we were close, I stopped and asked a fruit seller where d'Arpino lived.

The fruit seller, a skinny young man with an Adam's apple so large a real apple could be lodged in his throat, pointed to a building across the way. Not an ostentatious palazzo, but wealthy, no doubt about it.

"We're home," I said and rapped loudly on the door. Mario stood behind me, as if afraid to show himself. We didn't look like anyone you'd be eager to open your home to. But I had faith in my silver tongue to win over d'Arpino. A little flattery works marvels.

An old woman opened the door a crack and blearily gaped at me. "What business have you here?" she rasped in a voice as warty as her chin.

I wanted to say: "No business with you, old witch." But if I did, she'd slam the door in my face and probably spit at me, too. I've learned you attract more flies with honey than vinegar and this old servant was about as close to a pesky fly as you could get. In fact, in my mind, she assumed the form of a giant horse fly with her whiskery face and bony arms.

So instead, this is what I said: "Gentle goodwife, can

you kindly let your master know we are two modest painters, our hearts burning with ambition to learn from the greatest artist in Rome. We have left the studio of a mediocre talent in order to profit from his genius and to serve him as best we can."

The woman's jaw worked as if she were a cow chewing her cud. She stared at me from my muddy boots to the worn hat on my head.

"Humpff!" she snorted, but she opened the door and gestured for us to enter. Still glaring at us suspiciously, she led us to a sitting room.

"Wait here," she snapped and scuttled off like the insect she was.

I perched on a chair, my hat in my lap, like the gentleman I aim to become. The room was filled with ancient sculptures. I admired an elegant bronze figure of a woman wrapped in a cloak, twisting within the cloth so that it swirled around her in a great spiral.

"What is it?" Mario whispered, following my gaze.

"Nothing an artist today could do," I whispered back. "Isn't it perfect, how it catches the motion of both the body and the fabric?" I was both in awe and jealous. But then, I'm not a sculptor, so of course I couldn't even begin to come close to such artistry. Could I do it with paint? I promised myself I would one day.

I heard his footsteps before I saw him and leapt up from the chair, head bowed in a falsely submissive pose. He was slighter than I expected, with a sharp beard and wisps of hair fanning out over his ears. His eyes were bright and piercing, intelligent and shrewd. I hadn't counted on d'Arpino being smart. Still, even clever men like to be flattered.

"You are interested in joining my studio?" The voice was refined, confident.

"I want to study with the best." I quickly summarized my training until then and pulled out from my bag the small sample paintings I'd done to prove my abilities. "I've heard that you need painters to handle the flowers and fruit in your great altarpieces. As you can see, I'm more than competent."

I wasn't actually asking to paint fruit. But if it took fruit to avoid salad, then so be it.

"Hmmmm." D'Arpino picked up a painting of grapes in a basket, a simple thing I labored many hours over. "Yes, I'd say you're quite good. And you're right, I need more hands – or should I say, brushes – for my many, many commissions. What about your silent friend over there?"

I jostled Mario with my elbow and he stepped forward with an awkward bow.

"Mario Minniti." His voice cracked from nervousness. He brought out his own samples, admittedly not as accomplished as mine, but serviceable enough.

"You'll do," d'Arpino said. "Beatrice will show you your room. Put away your things and come to the main studio. You begin at once."

We'd done it! We'd gotten places in the best studio in Rome. I even felt a twinge of affection for old beetle Beatrice, the whiskery woman who took us to drop our satchels in a cramped room beneath the roof and then to the high-ceilinged studio, a large, open room with high windows pouring in light like golden honey.

Canvases in different stages of completion stood on easels. Young assistants mixed colors, finished landscapes in the background or sketched in still lifes in the foreground while the master went from picture to picture, correcting, directing, adding a brushstroke here, another there, before he returned to the largest canvas of them all and started sketching in the composition in light ochre tones. There was an energy to the room, a hum of artistic enterprise that made me itch to hold a brush. This wasn't a dreary factory of saints' heads, but a center of culture, of art. Exactly how I'd always imagined a great studio would be.

D'Arpino set me to work painting a basket of fruit and a vase of flowers. Yes, fruit again. I had to prove myself, so I took extra care with every dewdrop on every leaf, every reflection on every grape. I hesitated when I come to the water in the glass vase. I wanted to show my mastery, but also leave my mark on a painting that would be presented as done by the master, Cesare d'Arpino.

I glanced around the room. Nobody was watching me. Why should they, after all? So I painted a reflection into the glass, oh so faintly. My own face looked back at me from the shimmering glass. I was there, captured in paint and light. Too bad no one would ever notice but me.

Dinner that night was sausage and polenta, a feast after our months of salad. Just as nourishing as the food was the company. There was Floris Van Dyck, a Dutch painter, a master at flowers, as his first name suggested. If he'd been named Cheese or Salami, he would have gone into a different sort of business altogether. His Italian was limited, but he managed to get across his ideas with the few words he had and an expansive range of gestures.

"How long in Rome?" he asked me.

"Six months now," I said. "And you?"

He held up two fingers. "Months?" I guessed. "Years?"

He nodded and pointed to d'Arpino, then patted his heart. Was he telling me he was in love with the master? Saying he was loyal to him and had been for two years?

Francesco Zucchi sat on the other side of me. He painted faces made out of squashes, garlands of fruits and flowers. One of those stupid fashionable styles from Milan that was too trendy for my taste. A face should be a face, a squash a squash, and that's that. But maybe with a last name that means "squash," you'd be fated to indulge in that kind of visual pun. I took it as an odd sort of sign that I was flanked by artists who were named for what they painted. What did that say about me? I wanted to be as famous, but the only Michelangelo I wanted to paint like was myself.

"You're from Milan, aren't you?" Francesco asked me, his nose reminding me very much of a zucchini.

"Yes." I'd lie, but my Lombard accent gave me away.

"Then you must know the work of Arcimboldo? I admire his painting very much! Don't you think his visual riddles are extremely clever? Peaches for cheeks, corn for necks, peas in a pod for teeth! I hope to be the Roman Arcimboldo!"

I busied myself with eating so I didn't have to say the mocking words running through my head – "Just what this city, what every city, needs!" Instead I nodded in seeming approval. Yes, by all means, follow that path. At least if you paint that garbage, there will be one fewer artist to worry about snatching my fame from me.

As if he could read my mind, the assistant across the table from me said the words aloud. "You can have your Arcimboldo! That's a fad that will soon fade."

"Said like the hack you are, Prosperino," Francesco responded. "I'm looking forward, to new art styles. You're stuck in the past!"

"Isn't that where Rome's glory lies?" Prosperino smirked.

"Which past are you talking about?" I asked. "The glories of Raphael and Michelangelo?" Everyone wanted to paint that well. But who could really live up to such geniuses? Which one of us around this table, I wondered.

"I specialize in 'grotesche a la romana.' You know, the kind of thing that decorated ancient Roman villas, strange figures that are part beast, part man, part god, part vegetation. You can see some of my work in the Scala Santa in San Giovanni nel Laterano."

"That's an impressive commission!" I wasn't jealous of him for painting such odd figures. In fact, from that description, I'd already dismissed him as a possible artistic rival. But the Lateran was a major coup, the pope's newest, greatest church.

"It's fresco," Mario piped up. "Not the kind of thing you do." He'd read my mind, knew how envious I was. But he was right, I didn't do fresco. I needed the time that slow-drying oil paint allowed.

"It's not my commission," Prosperino said. "It's the master's, of course. I'm merely an extra hand."

"A hand that's getting noticed, I'll warrant." The lump of bread stuck in my throat. Was I really that jealous? I preferred to think of it as ambitious.

"As will yours. I saw your painting today. You won't be stuck painting fruit for long."

"When I do figures, I want to paint from life." I shouldn't have admitted it, but the wine and sausage relaxed me to the point of honesty. A dangerous place to be.

"No one paints people from life, unless you mean someone sitting for a portrait." This from a large man sitting across from the master at the other end of the table. He was well dressed and from the size of his belly, well fed. Not your average assistant.

"Who is that?' I whispered to Francesco the Squash.

"Bernardino, the master's brother. He's a painter himself, but mostly he runs the studio. And the picture dealership, as well. He organizes the commissions and sells the paintings the master collects."

"Master Bernardino," I called out across the long table. "A pleasure to meet you, though I must disagree with your opinion." Now that I'd said it, I'd stick to it.

"It isn't opinion, it's an observation of fact. Art comes from ideas, from classical models, from refined drawing, not from looking at actual things. Isn't that so, my brother?" Bernardino took a generous gulp from his goblet.

"My art does," affirmed d'Arpino. "I can't speak for this fellow's. Remind me of your name, young man."

"Michele," I said. "Michelangelo Merisi da Caravaggio."

"Michele it is, then," d'Arpino repeated, ignoring the rest of my name. "You're new here, to both the studio and the city, so perhaps you haven't heard of the Council of Trent, the Church's decree of what does and does not make fine art. In this studio, we obey those strictures. It's part of being a member of the Accademia of San Luca, the painters' guild. We follow God's direction and we'll paint masterpieces. We don't, and we'll end up with mud."

I pasted on a fake smile to cover my disgust. More lists of what makes good painting! And who made the lists? Not artists, but the Church. What did cardinals know? But I didn't want to argue on my first day. There would be plenty of time for that. Instead I raised my glass in a toast, changing the subject entirely.

"To masterpieces!"

A chorus of voices chimed after me. "To masterpieces! To Art! To Painting!"

"To Cesare d'Arpino," some toady of an apprentice called out. Naturally, we all followed suit.

"To Cesare! To Cesare! To Cesare!" It was like the ancient Romans, calling to Caesar to take the crown, to be king of the empire. And like his famous namesake, d'Arpino pretended modesty, then accepted the acclaim as his due, lifting his glass above us.

"To continued success!" he offered.

I imagined him crowned with laurel leaves, the idol that everyone adored and admired. My stomach curdled. I couldn't deny he was talented. A little. But a king among artists, a genius equal to Raphael or Michelangelo? Ha! His figures lacked blood and muscle – they were pure thought. And now I understood why. He was following Church doctrine, a sure way to suck the life out of anything.

Still, his studio was a good home until I made my own way. And in the meanwhile, there was plenty to eat that wasn't salad.

II
Cesare d'Arpino
Personal Journal, April 1594

That new apprentice, the one with the cocky attitude and the swaggering brush, he's a problem already. If he didn't paint so well, I'd throw him out into the street. True, during the day he works hard, and I admit he's quick. He can paint a magnificent still life in less time than it takes that dundering friend of his to paint six mediocre ones. But at night, ah, at night, he's a terror. I hear him gathering up a group of my assistants and heading for the taverns as soon as supper is over. They don't come back until the first cock crow, stumbling and retching from all the drink they've had. It wasn't like this before he came. My household was orderly and quiet. And the way he talks about painting – it's practically heresy! I won't have those ideas spread, not here, in my studio. Fine painting comes from drawing, from ideal concepts, not from looking at real, earthly things. Who wants an apple with a bruise or a worm in it? We crave perfection, the divine. That's what art is for! If only his grapes weren't so beautiful. . .

III

When we first came to d'Arpino's studio, I took him for a stuck-up snob. Turned out, he was even worse. Bad enough he belonged to the Accademia di San Luca, the boring painters' guild that laid out strict rules for what to paint and how to paint it. He was also a member of the Accademia degli Insensati, the Academy for Those Without Senses. Really, that's what they called themselves. It sounded like an organization for idiots, those without an ounce of common sense. But d'Arpino explained that its purpose was to support its members as they starved their senses. Which sounded even more ridiculous! They fasted, abstained from drink, denied themselves all earthly pleasures so they could focus on the divine.

"It grants me clarity so I can see how to paint these important religious subjects," the master explained as he sketched out the composition for an altarpiece.

"God's wounds!" he raged, throwing down his brush. "But not clarity enough! See what a botched job that is, what a clumsy mess I've made!"

The composition wasn't brilliant, nor imaginative, but perfectly serviceable – for d'Arpino. In fact, it was exactly what I expected from him.

"Maybe if you turn that figure's head to the left there, you'll have more movement," I suggested.

"Don't offer me your ignorant advice!" d'Arpino raged. "I'm the master painter here, not you!"

"I meant to help, not offend." I bowed my head. Not because I was sorry, but to keep myself from saying, "That's what you get with your senseless nonsense!" The best way to deal with the master's many tantrums was to let them blow over, like a smelly, but harmless fart.

I left him to scowl at his hash of lines and went back to my own painting. I'd been at the studio long enough that I was allowed to work on my own pictures when I'd finished my assigned work.

My first models had been the heads of criminals left as warnings on the bridge in front of the Castel Sant'Angelo. And they were still my models, probably always would be. Those severed heads, each with its own story to tell, fascinated me. But I didn't want to paint a dead head with bulging eyes and grimacing mouth all the time. They were useful for biblical scenes of decapitation like Judith and Holofernes, David and Goliath, and Salome and John the Baptist, but I needed to broaden my range. I didn't want to be known as the Severed Head Painter the way Floris was known for flowers, Zucchi for fruit-and-vegetable portraits, and Prosperino for his grotesques.

So I needed a model and being too poor to pay for one, had limited possibilities. The most obvious one was my own face, using a mirror. I'd been told I was handsome, but staring at my own features for hours left me all too aware of every fault. My snub nose, my broad forehead, my absurdly round eyes. The only way to stand it was to mock myself, both my features and my ridiculous ambition.

I started by making myself a scrawny, yet muscular Bacchus, wrapped in a sheet that faked a toga-like garment, with leaves circling my head, and a fistful of grapes. The expression on my face warned the viewer not to take me seriously. I certainly didn't. I was playing dress up, a painter playing at a mastery I didn't yet have. I felt slightly queasy exposing myself that way at first, but there was something hypnotically powerful about the challenge. As I shaped my eyes, shadowed my nose, traced the line of my chin, I was both claiming and creating myself. It was an odd kind of intimacy. Especially since I was doing this in a large, open studio, surrounded by dozens of other painters, every single one of whom must have thought I was some kind of lunatic. It was like one of those dreams where you're naked in a gathering of clothed people, all staring at you.

Except for Mario, who got the joke and laughed along with me. "I like it," he said, looking over my shoulder as I perfected the apricots in the foreground. "You've definitely captured your essence – you're a drunk pretending to be an artist, not an artist pretending to be a drunk."

"Come on now," I protested. "Bacchus isn't a simple sot. He's the god of wine, a king of pleasure, the opposite of Mister Deprive Your Senses d'Arpino."

Mario smiled. "I see – this is a sly slap at our master.

How very politic of you. Has he seen it yet?"

I nodded. "He says the drawing of the hand is awkward and the perspective of the table is off. But he likes the fruit. Of course."

Mario squinted his eyes. "Well, he may have a point."

"What?!" I roared, suddenly furious. "You agree with him?"

"No, no, of course not! It's a fine picture. Paint me next."

The anger ebbed as quickly as it rose and I paused to consider Mario's face. I'd love to paint him, actually. He was a few years younger than me, only sixteen, and had a round chin, girlishly full lips, dark eyes with brows arching smoothly over them.

"Mario, you're ideal!"

Mario strutted like a rooster, his chest puffing out with pride. "I'm that handsome, am I?"

"You're exquisite, and I'll make you even more so." How had I not noticed before how perfect his face was? I'd prove how real people could be a worthy subject for pictures. "I'll bring out the blush in your cheek, the ripeness of your lips, the soft welcome of your eyes."

"Ripeness? I'm not a peach!"

"No, you're not, but I want people to see you as alluring, as vividly alive. I'll have the rich and powerful lusting after you, or at least your likeness." The more I thought about it, the more the idea appealed to me. What better way to prove that even a young apprentice was a worthy subject, so long as you did it well? I'd look to nature as my master, not the antique statues that everyone else slavishly copied.

As I painted Mario, the picture changed. I wasn't

painting him so much as responding to what was forming on the canvas in front of me. The more alluring I could make him, the more powerful the painting would be. I wanted patrons to lust after my brush, after colors, shapes, and light. The picture was no longer a portrait of Mario at all, but of something else altogether. It was a portrait of the sensuality of painting, as full of life as I could make it.

It was the first painting I made that really mattered.

IV

I posed Mario holding a big basket of fruit. Yes, there was that fruit again! But this time, it was my choice, not my master's. Mario offered the cherries, peaches, apples, and grapes the same way he offered his shoulder, his dreamy gaze, his upward tilting lips. It was every bit as sensual as I'd hoped, proof of how much we need our senses, how they enrich us, rather than weaken us.

D'Arpino hated the picture. "This is shameless pandering. You're trying to titillate, not uplift! What have I taught you? Have you been listening this past year or stopping up your ears? The worst is the fruit! It's so fresh, so perfect! If only you'd painted simply that." He would have shown me the door except for that fruit (another reason I included it). It was a reminder of my talent, of what I was worth. To d'Arpino, that is. To the rest of the world, it was Mario's face that would matter, his inviting look that would linger in the memory. If anyone got a chance to see it. D'Arpino threatened to burn the painting, to cut out the basket of fruit from the canvas and throw away the rest.

I waited for him to stop railing and finished the highlights on the weave of the basket, touching up a leaf here and there. It was my painting, my talent, and I'd do what I pleased, no matter how much the master bellowed like a constipated bull.

I glanced at d'Arpino to see if his tantrum was over. His lips were flecked with spittle, his eyes bloodshot, a vein in his neck pulsed threateningly. In fact, he looked like a demon painted in a fiery hell and I could imagine a pitchfork in his hand instead of a brush, goading sinners on to eternal torment.

"Michele, do you hear me? I won't have my studio tainted with the stink of a street corner tavern!"

I laid down my brush with deliberate calm. "I've painted a boy with a basket of fruit. I've painted God's creation as I see it. Are you calling that foul?"

Mario made a clown's face, grinning foolishly with goggly eyes. How could anyone think him a seducer?

D'Arpino snorted and stomped off, looking to vent his fury on some other hapless assistant. Mario giggled.

"He's gone, Michele. You can finish painting."

"I'd finish no matter what." And I would, though I'd probably pay the price when d'Arpino assigned me some horrible task with obvious spiritual overtones, like painting lilies as symbols of purity, a punishment meant to purge me of my sins. Or he could send me to clean chamber pots. I wasn't sure which would be worse.

I was cleaning my brushes, putting away the colors

when Bernardino came up to me.

"I've heard you had a bit of a scrap with my brother," he said. Not as an accusation, but as if he were mildly amused by my stupidity and d'Arpino's temper. "I know a way you can make it up to him, get on his good side again."

"What do I have to do?" I asked. "Take a vow of senselessness?"

"Now, now, don't be silly!' chuckled Bernardino, as if we were old friends.

I said nothing, waiting to hear Bernardino's offer. The silence between us thickened, turned gray and muddy with all that was unsaid. It was like one of those staring contests children play at, seeing who will break off their gaze first. Too bad for Bernardino I was a master at those games.

I turned back to my brushes, humming softly to myself.

"Well, aren't you curious, not even a spark?" Bernardino snapped, losing the contest.

"Hmm?" I forced my lips into a thin line, trapping in the gleeful smile underneath.

"How you get back into Cesare's good graces – don't you want to know? Don't you care?"

"Oh, I'm sure he'll forget about his little fit today," I drawled. "He does rely on his assistants, after all." He might punish a lesser painter for months for a clumsy remark, but my talent was too big for d'Arpino to waste like that. He depended on my vases of flowers, my baskets of peaches, apples, and grapes.

"Don't flatter yourself," Bernardino taunted. "Nobody is essential to the master. None of you matter more than his own vanity."

That was probably true.

"Why don't you join us tonight? We're going to some taverns, playing some cards, maybe we'll get into a scrape or two – the kind of evening that relaxes my brother." Bernardino smiled. "He may have renounced his senses, but he's still no saint, thanks to me."

I'd heard the stories, how Bernardino liked to brawl, how his best friends outside of the studio were brigands, how he'd sent men to the hospital. There was even a rumor that he pushed one fellow off a bridge, both of them roaring drunk, and the hapless idiot drowned in the Tiber. Not Bernardino, the other one.

"I love a good fight as much as the next man," I said, "but I can't imagine the master wants my company."

"Come as my guest." Bernardino faked a friendly smile. "You'll impress him with your drinking, your wit, your quick reflexes. All will be forgiven and forgotten."

I should have been wary, given how hard he was pressing, but I finally agreed because, well, why not?

"Well done!" Bernardino clapped me on the back. "We'll have ourselves some fun tonight, you'll see."

As soon as he'd left, Mario walked up to me.

"What was that all about?" he asked.

"You were eavesdropping," I accused.

"How could I not hear? We all work together in the same room. It's not my fault if you didn't notice me in the corner cleaning my brushes."

"Fair enough," I admitted. "Anyway, it's not a big secret. In fact, I'm sure you can come with us if you like."

"No, thank you! I don't like that Bernardino one bit! He can be nasty, especially when he's drunk. I've heard that while d'Arpino might not brawl himself, he does nothing to stop his brother. Maybe it's entertainment for him. Do you want to be the butt of one of their pranks gone awry?"

I rolled my eyes. "I can take care of myself. We'll drink, we'll be loud, and that will be it."

After supper I waited by the front door, trying to look nonchalant. Which turned out to be tricky. Should I lean against the wall or stand with my arms crossed? What posture spelled out "I-don't-care-if-you-like-me?" I settled on stroking my chin as if deep in ponderous thought.

I assumed there would be a big group, the master surrounded by his devoted assistants, the ones who usually went drinking with me, but as the bells in the nearby church clanged ten times, only two figures descended the stairs, d'Arpino and Bernardino.

"Ah, there he is!" Bernardino threw out his arms in a gesture of welcome. "The very talented Michele! Soon to be the toast of the town and we can tell everyone he cut his teeth here, learned the tricks of the trade from the best and the brightest!"

Every word out of his mouth was a cliché. I glanced at d'Arpino. He couldn't be pleased to hear this kind of praise about a miserable assistant, especially one he was furious with.

In fact, his mouth was tight with annoyance and he raised one elegant eyebrow in that way he had. I realized too late that this must be a trap. Bernardino wasn't trying to get me back into the master's good graces – he was trying to get me in trouble, worse trouble than I was in already.

I tried to smooth things over. "I'm a mere painter of flowers and fruits and still have much to learn."

The words hit their mark. D'Arpino's mouth relaxed. He allowed himself a stingy smile. "And tonight I hear you're studying drinking with us. Is that so?"

"Well, that's one thing I dare say I don't need lessons in, but I'm flattered to share your company."

"Better than that, we'll enlighten you! We're meeting a group of painters tonight and it's not just wine that will flow, but ideas about art. We're restoring painting to its noble place among the arts, above sculpture and architecture, the best way to open people's eyes to the spirit of Christ."

I swallowed a groan. I'd thought I was going to a tavern, not a church! I cursed Mario for abandoning me. I'd considered him so loyal and true! Though clearly not enough to suffer the boredom of this evening with me.

And really, who could blame him?

Bernardino grinned. "Cheer up, Michele! It won't be all dull moralizing, not when I'm around. There's fun to be had tonight, I promise you!"

I didn't believe him, but I followed the two of them to the Piazza di Spagna where we squeezed our way into the noisiest, darkest, most crowded tavern in the neighborhood. It reeked of garlic and bad wine, but the company seemed cheery enough. Bernardino shouldered his way to a large table where a roar of greeting exploded as soon as he loomed into sight. D'Arpino and I plowed behind him, enjoying the wake of empty space created as his stomach led the way.

"More wine!" a flushed fellow called, thumping the table.

"Ho, there, Baglione," Bernardino bellowed, louder than the table-pounder. "The evening is young yet. Why the hurry to get drunk?"

"The sight of you drives any man to drink!" Baglione retorted.

Ah, so this was the famous wit d'Arpino had described. I really was in for a treat. Bernardino introduced me to the man with the heavy fist as a fellow painter. In fact all the men at the table were artists and they were discussing how art could inspire virtuous behavior, how artists were more spiritual than priests and had a moral duty to lead the illiterate to heaven. Blah, blah, blah.

"You don't agree?" D'Arpino turned to me. "You haven't said a word yet."

"I haven't had much chance," I protested. Everyone was talking over everyone else, each anxious to be heard, none eager to listen. Not that I blamed them. I didn't want to listen to this drivel either. I did think painting was noble, but not in the stupefyingly boring way they meant. I didn't want to moralize or preach. I wanted to open people's eyes, to help them see themselves, this world, in ways they'd never imagined. I wanted to get at the essence of things, to make vivid and real what seemed faded and musty. To make the ordinary seem extraordinary.

I wanted to paint something important, not just fruit.

"That Baglione's nothing but a blowhard." D'Arpino lowered his voice, though there was no chance of Baglione hearing him over the din of voices, laughter, clattering plates, and clinking mugs. "His figures have as much spine as a limp noodle. His compositions are hackneyed, his colors simplistic. All in all, thoroughly third-rate."

I nodded, though I hadn't seen his work or known of his existence, for that matter, before that night.

Suddenly d'Arpino burst out laughing. The sight was so odd I wasn't sure whether he was amused or having some kind of fit. "Is something the matter?" I asked. "What's so funny?"

He wheezed with gasps of heee heeee heeeee, his eyes crinkled, his hands holding his sides. I looked around for Bernardino, for someone to help with my apparently dying master. D'Arpino held out his hand as if to stop me.

"Ho, ho, ho," he chortled. "It's just too funny! I have the perfect idea!"

"Ah," I sighed, relieved that he wasn't dying after all.

"And you'll do it for me, won't you? It's just too perfect!"

"What?" I asked. "What will I do? What are you talking about?"

"The joke, the one we're going to play on Baglione."

I didn't have anything against Baglione, but I'm always open to pranks. And this seemed like a painless way to get back into my master's good graces. Seemed, I emphasize now.

"Count me in!" I said. "What are we doing?"

D'Arpino dug into his pockets and pulled out a tattered paintbrush. "I knew I kept this for a reason. We'll tie it to the tail of Baglione's nag, the bay horse tied up outside. It'll look like the animal is pooping out art or pooping on it, which is exactly what his owner is doing!"

"He has a horse?" Not that artists didn't own horses – well, most didn't since they were an expensive extravagance – but why bother when you could walk across the entire city in an hour?

"Pretentious little snot, isn't he? Acting the gentleman! We'll show him how refined he really is!" D'Arpino started chortling again.

"How would you rank painting?" A bearded man across the table leaned over and yelled into our faces, interrupting our little plot. "Orazio is arguing that religious scenes are at the top, but Caio says that historical ones from classical literature rank above those. I say, what's higher than God and His Word? Nothing!"

"I'm with you!" D'Arpino lifted his glass. "To Divinity and Divine Works! Nothing else is worth painting. That's what assistants are for."

I gritted my teeth. I was relegated to painting the unworthy bits of pictures. Except I didn't agree that a still life or scenes of everyday people were less inspiring than biblical stories.

But if I said that, no matter how many brushes I tied to horses' tails, my master would despise me. So I said nothing and drank my watered-down wine.

The conversation swirled around me, everyone arguing over whether saints mattered more than the Virgin Mary and which scenes from Christ's life ranked the highest. Most voted for the Crucifixion, though a few argued for the Resurrection. What a stupid waste of time! It was like one of those silly arguments you had when you were a kid – which was worse, being deaf or blind? Dying by drowning or in a fire? Being kicked in the head by a mule or a horse? It was all a kick in the head, a colossal waste of words. They should have been asking which was worse, a bad painting of the Virgin and Child or a brilliant picture of a loaf of bread?

I'd forgotten about the prank and was calculating how I could sneak out when d'Arpino jabbed his elbow in my ribs.

"So, will you do it?" He shoved the paintbrush at me and a fistful of string he'd somehow got hold of.

"I thought you'd changed your mind," I said.

"No, no, of course not! You go on. I'll wait here. When you come back, we'll all go out and have a good laugh."

I was only too happy to oblige, to get away from the idiotic conversation, out into the fresh, cold air. I'd take a horse's ass over a table full of human asses any day.

Outside the tavern there were three horses and one mule tied up. There was only one bay, though, so it was clear which one was Baglione's. I tied the brush to the string first, judging how far I wanted the brush to hang below the horse's tail. Not too close, not too far, the perfect length to make the statement the master wanted.

"Now, there, horsie, this won't hurt a bit," I crooned as I walked up to the horse's rear and leaned over to loop the string under its tail.

And thud! I was thrown onto the ground, my chest burning in agony – the beast had kicked me! I lay there a minute, gasping for breath. My head throbbed where it had hit the cobblestones. But the worst pain was in my side where the hooves had punched me.

I tried to stand up, but I wavered, toppling onto my hands and knees, retching in agony. I curled up in misery and waited for the pain to ease. Voices from the tavern wafted outside, the argument still going on. Other voices drifted on the wind from across the piazza. One of the horses snorted. Probably the bay, laughing at me.

I couldn't bear the thought of anyone seeing me like that. I forced myself to stand, then hobbled slowly away, stopping often to lean against walls and catch my breath while the ache pulsed through me. It took me hours to get to Santa Maria della Consolazione, a hospital that offered consolation as well as healing for the poor. I banged on the front door and collapsed, huddled in the doorway.

I pounded on the door again and again. "Open up!

Open the blasted door!"

An eternity passed until the massive door creaked open and a young nun poked out her head.

"Help me," I croaked. "Please."

The girl leaned down and lifted me up. She had the face of an angel and the strength of an ox. She wrapped one of my arms around her neck and walked with me leaning against her until we came to a room with rows of cots. She set me down on one and left, but came back quickly with a basin of water. She washed my face and hands, pried off my boots and washed my feet as well. Then she covered me with a thick wool blanket. All in silence. Her face was a shining calm moon, her touch gentle and sure.

"Thank you," I whispered and then the moon was eclipsed in darkness and I fell asleep.

V
Mario Minniti
Private Journal, April 1594

Usually Michele comes home just as the sky lightens with the promise of sunrise, but not this morning. I knew I should have gone with him. What a coward I am! He's my friend and here I've let him down. Bernardino probably threw him in the Tiber. He's dead and drowned, all because of me.

I should have told him my suspicions instead of keeping them to myself. I see how the master looks at Michele, like his liver is being gnawed by a bilious green monster, a fiend of jealousy. He sees Michele's talent, how can he not? And it tortures him. He hates that someone he despises should paint so well. Because he does despise Michele. He hates his loud, boisterous energy, the way the other apprentices listen to him, the way he fills a room as soon as he enters it.

That's the magic of Michele. He walks into a tavern and the festivities begin. He turns a boring, drab evening into an exciting adventure. Like the time he had us all swimming races in the Tiber under a full moon. Or the time we milked the cows hobbled in the forum at night, spraying white froth into each other's faces. Or the time we tried to climb the bell tower of Sant'Andrea.

Rome was boring, tedious work before I met Michele. What will I do now that he's gone?

VI

And here I still am. Adding up the moments of my life and not happy at all with the sum.

After that first night, a doctor bandages my ribs, doses me with something to dull the pain, and prescribes rest and food. I'm happy to obey, but I know Mario will be wondering where I am.

When a boy comes in to empty the slop jars, I offer him a penny to get word to Mario that I'm here. It isn't long before Mario rushes to my side, his face tight with worry.

"Michele, what happened?" he cries, seeing my chest swathed in bandages. "I warned you about Bernardino!"

"Mario!" I grin. "It's good to see you, my friend! Yes, yes, you were right and I should have listened to you, but it wasn't Bernardino who got me into this mess. It was the honorable Cesare d'Arpino himself." I tell Mario the whole story, admitting my foolish willingness to do whatever the master told me to do. "I mean, it seemed a simple enough prank. How hard could it be to tie something to a horse's tail?"

"Well," says Mario, "that depends on the horse." He pulls up a stool and sits down beside my cot. "I can't stay long. The master doesn't know I've left, but I'll come back tonight. What can I bring you? What do you need?" He scans the room. There's not much in it. The thing that takes up the most space is the smell. The man in the next cot reeks of rotting flesh. The old woman across the room stinks of onions and sour urine. Only the poorest wretches are here, lying in their own filth and contagion. Those with the means and money suffer at home, attended by physicians with milky soft hands and an array of potions. This place is for those like me, paupers with nowhere else to go.

"Can you sneak out a canvas, brushes, and colors?" I ask. "The doctor says I may be here a while and I'll go crazy with boredom if I can't do something."

"Of course," Mario promises. "And I'll pose for you, too, if you promise to make me less pretty than last time. You know, the other apprentices have a nickname for me now – Amoretto, like a little love." Mario shakes his head. "They're not saying it as friends, either. You're my only friend. If you're not going back to the studio, I'll leave, too. We can find a new place together."

"I didn't say I wouldn't go back. I don't know what I'll do yet." Though Mario's right, how can I face d'Arpino after failing him?

"But they treated you so badly! Look what d'Arpino asked you to do. Sure, it's an insult to Baglione, but it's an insult to you, too. He was probably hoping the horse would kick you."

"So the master hasn't asked about me? What about Bernardino?" I thought my talent actually mattered. What had Bernardino said, something about being able to brag that I had studied in their studio? Didn't that mean they expected me to make my name one day and that my glory would reflect on theirs?

"Neither of them mentioned anything about you," Mario says. "They have a couple of important commissions right now and that takes all their attention.

What a fool I've been! Mario is right – d'Arpino doesn't give a fig about me.

"If they want to know how or what I'm doing, they can visit me here. Tell them that," I say, but I already know they won't ask. They won't come.

Mario nods. "I'll tell them you have a long recovery, but you'll work from here."

"Don't say that!" I object. "I'm on my own here and I'll paint what I want, subjects that matter to me."

"Fine," says Mario. "I'll just tell them you're here after being badly injured by a certain bay horse. Maybe they'll offer to have you treated at the studio instead of leaving you in a Church-run charity. I'll tell them the man on one side of you is being eaten up by the pox and the one on the other suffers from his toes rotting off. Maybe that will prod them into taking care of you the way they should."

"Maybe," I say, not believing it.

"Is there anyone in your family I should contact? Maybe someone who can pay for a doctor?"

"No one."

"There must be somebody." Mario's brow crinkles in worry.

"When I was five, the plague ravaged Milan, killing all the men in my family in one brutal week – my father, my uncle, my grandfather. Only later, when I was ten, did I start hearing the whispered rumors about my true father."

"Your true father? Who?"

I don't admit this claim easily. I don't want to be mocked. But I trust Mario. "The man who gave me his name, Fermo Merisi da Caravaggio, married my mother when she was already pregnant with me, but he wasn't really my father. My mother – and Fermo – worked in the palace of the most powerful family in Milan, the Sforzas. Everyone knew the rumors about the great lord, Francesco Sforza, how he slept with any serving maid who caught his eye. Which my mother did. And then once she grew round with me, Francesco married her off to his steward, Fermo."

"You're the bastard son of Federico Sforza?!" Mario squeaked. "You're a nobleman!"

"But how to prove that? I waited for my real father to claim me, but then he, too, died, when I was twelve. My mother, also dead, would never admit to anything. And the half-brother and -sister I have know nothing of all this." I sigh. "The only way to prove my greatness is through my brush. And not by painting fruit!"

"Don't worry, I'll bring you everything you need tonight." Mario hesitates, as if now that he knows the story of my birth, he should treat me differently. "I could tell there was something great in you." He bows his head and gets up to go.

"Mario!" I call after him. "Thank you! You're a good friend." And he is, better than I knew.

Days stretch into weeks and I wait for Cesare or Bernardino to send for me, visit, or at least ask about me.

Nothing. Not a single flicker of interest, according to Mario. My smoldering resentment stokes itself into a blazing rage. No matter what, I won't return to that cursed studio. I'll starve first.

Anyway, I've turned a corner of the hospital into my own studio. I've chosen a place between two windows, giving me cool fresh air and warming light. I can't avoid the moans and groans of the suffering, but at least I can breathe. The kind nun, Caterina, and Mario pose for me in the evenings, when both have finished their duties. When I first asked Caterina if I could paint her, she blushed more shades of red and pink than I knew existed. If I could have painted her cheeks right then!

"I'm not worthy of a portrait." She lowered her eyes. "I'm a simple nun."

"To be honest, I'm not going to paint you as yourself, not as Caterina, not as a nun. You'll be dressing up, as will my friend Mario, playing a part."

Caterina raised her eyes, now glittering with interest. "Like a play? Like someone on stage?"

"Exactly!" I said. "You'll be a gypsy fortune teller and Mario will be the wealthy young man you're lying to, telling him all kinds of silly things you see revealed in the palm of his hand while you pick his pocket."

"A gypsy!' she gasped. And then her lips broadened into a sweet smile.

For a devout nun with a farmer's strength, she's really just a young girl. If Caterina had been born into a different family, she'd spend her days embroidering or playing music, not washing bloody wounds, cooling burning foreheads, cleaning bedsores. Posing for me will give her a break from all that, a chance to play a little make-believe.

We start that night. Caterina ties a tablecloth across her shoulder, wraps a shawl around her head, and just like that, is transformed into an exotic gypsy. Mario has brought clothes, a sword, a feathered hat, soft suede gloves from the studio to dress the part of the young fop. The two make a charming couple. Caterina surprises me with her knowing, sly look. Mario has no problem appearing innocent and credulous. I'm so excited to be painting a picture of my own conception that I work quickly, blocking out the composition, the darks and lights. The pair stand in a nondescript space – inside a tavern, in front of a wall, on the street. It doesn't really matter. I think only of the right color to set them against, a warm ochre with tinges of gold, a swath of light, a swoop of dark.

Now the painting is almost done and a crowd is drawn to our little silent drama. Other patients come to look. Nuns, doctors, even the prior in charge of the hospital, all have an opinion. The prior is so pleased, he offers to buy the picture even before it's finished. But I'm not ready to sell.

"I've never seen anything like it!" he says. "So fresh, so full of life!"

"It's a great work of art, definitely!" a deep voice chimes in. I look up from the canvas, sure I recognize that baritone.

"Prosperino!" It's the painter of grotesques from d'Arpino's studio.

"Mario said I'd find you here. You know, the studio isn't the same without you, though d'Arpino and Bernardino will never admit that. But why bother with them? You're talented enough on your own."

"But once I leave here, where will I live? How can I set myself up as an independent painter with no connections, no commissions, no money?"

"I'll help you with that," Prosperino offers. "My brother, Aurelio, is secretary to the powerful Farnese family. If he recommends you, you're bound to get work, prestigious work. And if you paint a few more pictures like the one you're working on right now, I can vouch for you myself."

Prosperino leans forward, scrutinizing the painting. A smile plays on his lips.

"I know it's an odd subject for a picture," I say, warding off the barbed joke I feel coming.

"It's more than odd," says Prosperino. "It's brilliant! How did you think of it? You'll start a new craze for this kind of art, I'll wager. I should follow your trend and give up grotesques as sadly old-fashioned."

"But this kind of subject doesn't fall in the Academy's hierarchy. It's not historical, not religious, not a still life, not a landscape. It's not at the bottom of their scale – it's off the scale." I wave my paintbrush at him. "No wonder d'Arpino forgot I exist – I'm lower than the lowest, according to his system."

Prosperino turns to me, his eyes gleaming. "You've created a whole new system. Bravo! Bravissimo!"

Mario leaps out of his pose and starts applauding. "Bravo, Michele, Bravo!"

As soon as I've laid the last brushstrokes on the canvas, we have an impromptu celebration. The prior bustles around the room, handing tankards of wine to everyone. Caterina has slipped out of the tablecloth and run to the kitchen for a loaf of bread and a generous wedge of cheese.

My ribs still ache and deep breaths are painful, but I feel light, giddy almost. I was proud of Mario's portrait, but this painting is something else, something new that I've created. I've found my style and subject matter both at once, the here and now, the people around me, the light that both reveals and hides. I believe in the divinity of it all!

"To art!" I toast. "May it bring us to the deepest parts of ourselves and to the light of others!"

Mario gapes at me. "Michele, you're more of a poet than you let on! I thought your brush was the delicate visionary and you the simple brute who wielded it."

I burst out laughing. And even though it hurts, I don't stop.

"Once again, my friend, I've underestimated you! Mario, you should be a philosopher. You're far too wise to be a painter."

Mario doffs his hat and gives a graceful bow.

"To the master!" he says, lifting his own wine. "To Michelangelo Merisi da Caravaggio, a name soon to be known to all!"

But for once I don't care about fame and fortune. I've finished my first great painting. Without one bit of fruit in it!

VII

I refuse to go back to d'Arpino's, so I pack up my canvases, paints, and brushes, and walk out of the hospital a free man. A homeless, poor man, but free to paint whatever I choose. Mario walks with me, carrying both of our satchels of meager belongings, as we did together that day long ago when we knocked on d'Arpino's door.

What have I gained in the meanwhile? I take stock as we walk aimlessly across Piazza Navona toward the Pantheon. I've painted a few pictures that got left behind in d'Arpino's studio for him to hack up as he pleases. I've given away a couple – to the prior whot wanted to buy *The Fortuneteller*. He couldn't pay the price I want for it, the price I'm determined to get, so I painted two smaller pictures as thanks for healing me.

I've met many artists, some interesting and talented, some bombastic and boring, a mix of all kinds, two of whom have become good friends, Mario of course, and Prosperino.

I've explored Rome from the ruins on the Palantine to the catacombs along the Appian Way. I've graduated from painting fruit and flowers to painting people in subjects of my own choosing. The past three years have not been wasted after all.

As we cross in front of the church of San Luigi dei Francesi, a shop window catches my eye. Paintings are propped up for view, some still lifes, a landscape, an Adoration of the Magi. None of them are very good, but they're not bad either. Competent, I'd say.

I nudge Mario. "Let's try this place. We might be able to sell our work here."

Mario examines the wares in the window. "Do we really want our pictures next to these?"

"Normally I'd agree with you, but I can't afford to be so proud right now. And maybe there are better things inside."

"Could be," Mario says. "Though it's an interesting strategy to show off the mediocre stuff and hide the quality goods in the back of the store."

I roll my eyes. Mario's made his point, but I'm not wrong, either. We need to make money any way we can. And we need a place to stay.

I open the door, setting a bell to jingling. A man emerges from behind a curtain in the back.

"Constantino Spata at your service." He looks us over. We're not the most promising clientele. We look like we could barely afford a roll of bread, much less a work of art.

"Signore Spata." I bow, a grandiose gesture to make up for my ragged clothes. "I'm Michelangelo Merisi da Caravaggio and this is my friend and colleague, Mario Minniti. We're both painters, with Cesare d'Arpino for the past couple of years, now setting up shop on our own. We wondered if you'd be interested in selling our pictures."

"Could be," the man grunts. He cocks a critical eye. "Show me what you have."

I unwrap the paintings I've been carrying. One is the fortuneteller scene. The second is another canvas I finished at the hospital, a scene of two young men playing cards while a third man signals to his partner what their victim holds in his hand. Mario modeled for the two card players – his face seen three-quarters from the front and then again from the back in a one-quarter view, so altogether there are all four quarters of his face, just not in the same person. I've lightened his hair and sharpened his nose so the figures look different from the fop with the fortuneteller. The older man with the beard and mustache gesturing with his fingers behind the mark's back is Prosperino. D'Arpino criticized the perspective of the table in the self-portrait I did as Bacchus, but this table, I'm proud to say, is perfect, covered with a richly textured rug holding a backgammon board as well as cards. It's the most complicated piece I've painted – three figures from three very different angles, strong light raking across the faces, the hands, the edges of the cards tucked in the waistband of the cheating player.

"These are good, very good!" Spata looks hungrily at each picture. "Much better than anything else in this shop." He hurries over to the window and takes out the paintings on display there, stacking them on a table. Instead he angles in my two canvases, so big they take up the entire window.

He turns back to me. "Leave me your address. I'm sure they'll sell soon and I'll fetch a good price for you, I promise."

"I don't have an address at the moment, but I'll check back with you every few days to see if they've sold."

"No address?" Spata furrows his brow. "There are monasteries that will take you in if you're desperate. Or perhaps an artist friend?"

"Don't worry, I can take care of myself." We set off the jingling bell again as we leave. I take it as a good sign, a cheery promise that money will soon be in my purse.

Mario hasn't said a word the entire time in the shop. "Is something the matter?" I ask. "You're usually not so quiet."

"You're better than this, Michele, selling at a cheap store like that. I hate to see you sink so low."

"Oh, you've seen me much lower!" I chuckle, thinking of our nights together in taverns. "This is business, plain and simple. I'll find a patron, commissions, fame and fortune. But right now, I'd settle for a bed and a full belly."

"You know we can always stay with Prosperino. He said so. Why not spend a few nights there?"

I'd rather find rooms of our own, someone who will rent to me on the promise to pay soon rather than cold, hard cash right now. Given how suspicious landlords are, that's unlikely. I'd have better luck with a landlady, a woman who can appreciate my charms. Better still, a lonely widow who might value a different kind of payment, one I'd gladly provide with no waiting necessary.

"Michele, are you listening to me?" Mario's voice intrudes on my daydream of a merry widow inviting me to stay with her and warm her bed.

"Yes, yes, I hear you." As enticing as my vision is, it's only a fantasy. Mario's right, as he so often is, to my continual surprise. "We'll go to Prosperino's then, but only for a night or two. We have to find something ourselves. You know the old saying, houseguests, like fish, stink after a few days."

"There's a better saying, a Sicilian one, that there are three kinds of truth – one you tell the tax collector, one you tell God, and the one so terrible, you tell no one, not even yourself."

"Interesting," I say, "But what does that have to do with me, with Prosperino, and with finding a place to stay?"

"You're not facing the third truth, the one you can't admit to yourself," says Mario.

"What truth is that?"

"That you need help. You can't always do everything on your own. Sometimes you need other people. Tonight we need Prosperino. And we may need him still tomorrow and the next day and the next."

"You're wrong!" I snap. "If I had to, I'd sleep in the gutter, on the floor of a tavern, in a garbage-strewn alley. I've done it before. I can do it again. I need no one!" I'm roaring now, the fury growing in me as I speak. I stop in the middle of the street, put my head back and yell, "I'm Michelangelo Merisi da Caravaggio! I DEPEND ON NOBODY AND NOBODY DEPENDS ON ME!"

Someone throws a moldy cabbage out of a third-story window as an answer, but it splats beside me harmlessly. The anger in my chest drains out of me, leaving me panting and hollow.

Mario stands beside me, patient as ever. He's familiar with my fits of anger. My black spots, he calls them.

"Personally, I prefer a bed." Mario's voice is mild, as if we're having an ordinary conversation. "So to Prosperino's then?" He heads toward the crowded rooms that our friend calls home.

I sigh. "To Prosperino's." Only for a day or two, I

promise myself.

It's actually on the way to Prosperino's that we stumble onto our new home. We're walking past the Pantheon when I recognize the slim shape of a young girl, her red hair coiled on top of her head.

I nudge Mario. "It's the girl from Sant'Agnese – remember? The one who turned and smiled at me."

Mario shakes his head. "I don't know who you mean."

True, it was a few years ago, but it's her, I'm sure of it. I hurry after her as she ducks into a house. Before I can think of what I'm doing, I knock on the door.

The woman who answers is older than the girl, but must be her mother since her hair is equally red and there's something familiar about her features.

"Forgive me for the intrusion, but I was told you have a room for rent. Is that so?" The words tumble out of my mouth. Why am I saying this? Do I know this woman is a landlady? Do I know anything about her or her supposed daughter?

The woman studies my face. "We were hoping to rent to a woman."

My gamble has paid off! She is actually renting, and she looks lonely enough to appreciate a man's company.

"I would think you would prefer a gentleman," I say. "Someone who can protect you should there be any trouble. Someone who can take care of you." I give her my sweetest look. The one that works with servant girls, with young nuns who feel trapped by their vows.

She laughs and instantly looks years younger. "Prefer a man?" she hoots. "That's a good one!" Mario looks hurt and I'm puzzled myself.

"Come in, let's talk," she says, still chuckling. She leads

us into a room with a fireplace, a table, and some stools. She sits on one and gestures for us to sit where we like.

"This is a brothel, if you haven't guessed already. There are only two girls right now, my daughter and my niece. We'd like a third one to help with the trade. But since no one's come yet, I suppose there's no harm in the two of you taking the room. If another girl shows up, you're out, you understand. And no helping yourself to the merchandise. If you want a girl, you pay for her."

Now Mario really looks offended. "We're honest men, signora."

"Of course you are. All men say so." Her eyes mock us. She's clearly seen her share of honesty.

"Signora, we're painters, poor men ourselves. I can't pay the rent up front. I'm waiting on the sale of some pictures." I try to look upstanding and worthy.

She snorts loudly. "I always take payment first. It's a whore's first rule of business."

"But this isn't whoring business, it's room rental. I swear I'll pay you twice over."

"Two times nothing is nothing. Even I know that," she scoffs.

"I'll pay you for the room," I promise. "And I'll pay your daughter to model for me."

The woman's eyes flash angrily. "My daughter may be a whore, but she has her standards. No posing naked for filthy pictures to be made into those nasty books smuggled past the censors."

"I'm not talking about pornography!" I protest. "I want her to model fully clothed as the Virgin Mary herself. This is an honor, not an attack on her virtue!"

The woman leans back, her mouth tight. She thinks I'm making fun of her.

"Signora," my voice is urgent. "You must believe me. I saw your daughter three years ago in Piazza Navona and I knew then that I wanted to paint her. She has the face of an innocent, of one truly blessed by God. Let me show the world that face, her goodness, the blessings she carries within her. Please, signora."

The shrewd gray eyes soften. The woman sighs. "I shouldn't believe you, but I'll give you a chance. The room is yours for a week. If you haven't paid your month's rent by the end of it, you're out. As for my daughter, she'll pose for you for nothing, so long as her clothes stay on and you give her the dignity she deserves. And of course, you paint her only when it doesn't interfere with a paying customer."

"Of course, signora. Thank you, thank you very much. I promise you won't regret it." I clasp her hand and bring it to my lips, kiss it as if she were a noblewoman, a bishop, a patron. She is. This brothel madam is my first patron, giving me a room and a model on the faith of my talent. I smile at the thought. Better than a stupid, fat cardinal, even if the pay is lower.

"You see." I turn to Mario. "We're home."

VIII
Mario Minniti
Private Journal, July 1594

I miss our old attic room, the three solid meals, the company of other painters. But I don't miss d'Arpino or his loutish brother, Bernardino. When I ask Michele if he wishes we were back in the grand studio, painting unimportant parts of important commissions, he laughs at me.

"I like living in a whorehouse. I can watch the customers and get ideas for new paintings. And if I want a drink or a tumble, I don't have far to go. I'm exactly where I belong."

"I suppose that's an advantage," I grumble. "If we had the money to pay for either. Which we don't."

"Not yet, but soon."

"And if the paintings at that hack store don't sell?"

"Then we try another brothel. There are plenty of them in the city, all with cheap rooms. Stop worrying, Mario."

I wish I could, but I can't stop thinking of my father, how he urged me to make a name for myself when I left home, how I'm supposed to become a fancy painter in this fancy city, then go back to Sicily and set myself up as a master, like d'Arpino, someone with a great studio, a small army of assistants, a constant stream of commissions. Thank the saints my father can't see me now, living in this wretched place, not even studying with anyone, just painting my own miserable little canvases.

I watch Michele paint and that makes me feel better. He's the reason I gave up my position at d'Arpino's and I can't regret that. I learn more from his brush than from that arrogant fool anyway. And at least for the week we have a place to stay. I'll worry about next week when it comes.

IX

When Anna comes down to breakfast that first morning, her eyes widen when she sees me.

"Michele," I introduce myself. "We've met before, in front of Sant'Agnese a few years ago. I don't suppose you'd remember."

Her face flushes and a dimple winks from her cheek like a second smile. She lowers her eyes modestly. She may work as a prostitute, but there's an innocence about her.

"Actually, I do remember," she murmurs.

"You do?" It's ridiculous how pleased I am to hear it.

"You bowed to me very gallantly, even doffed your plumed hat." And now she raises her eyes to meet mine. "A girl doesn't forget that kind of gesture."

"Does the girl have a name?" I ask.

"Anna Bianchina," she answers. "A pleasure to meet you. Mother tells me you're our new tenant and that I'm to pose for you." Her name is a perfect fit – "little white one." Her cheeks are pale marble, framed by russet hair, her hands small and delicate.

"If you wouldn't mind. It would be an honor to paint you."

"Excuse me," Mario interrupts. "I'm sitting here too, you know. It would be nice to be included in this little conversation."

"Oh, Mario, forgive my rudeness. I was so taken with Signorina Bianchina, I forgot my manners."

"Clearly," he remarks dryly.

"Anna, this is Mario, my loyal friend, fellow painter, and roommate. Mario, this is Anna, our landlady's daughter and the perfect model for my Virgin Mary."

Mario says that using a real person as a model for the holy Virgin is a way to make the sacred seem more human, less distant. That's not my intent at all. Just the opposite. I want to show the holiness of the human, the natural, the real. I want the world to see Anna as I see her – pure and blessed.

That first painting of Mario showed the sensual appeal of a common person, not an ideal. This new painting will prove the holiness of an ordinary woman. What matter if she's no virgin, capitalized or not, if in fact she's a prostitute? I look into Anna's sweet, tired face and I want to restore her faith in herself.

Anna gapes at me. "I'm posing for the Virgin Mary, the Blessed Mother of Christ Our Savior?" I can see the capital letters as she speaks.

"Certainly," I assure her. "You're absolutely ideal. I want to paint the Rest on the Flight to Egypt." I'm using my own capitals now. "You know, when the Virgin, Saint Joseph, and the infant Christ are fleeing from King Herod's orders to kill all the baby boys born to the Jews."

"I know the story. Everyone knows the story." Anna's voice is full of wonder as if she can't imagine herself playing such a part.

"Who will pose for Joseph, for the baby?" Mario asks.

"Good question." I turn to Anna. "Do you know of a baby we could borrow, one you wouldn't mind cradling for several hours?"

"The woman next door has a young daughter. I suppose it doesn't matter if the baby's a girl, does it?" Anna asks.

"Not at all! What matters is whether it's a pretty baby or one that looks like a little old man with big ears sticking out."

"This baby is beautiful, with golden wisps of hair, a sweet round face. She looks like an angel, truly." Anna says.

It's settled then. Anna will offer to mind the neighbor's baby in exchange for allowing it to be painted into a sacred scene. What mother could object to that? And Mario will ask the old man down the street who sells wine if he'll pose for a while in exchange for a nice hot dinner.

"Good!" I'm satisfied that the most important roles have been taken care of. "But I need one more model, a young boy. Younger than you, Mario. And fairer. I'd like a young blond, if possible."

"What for?" Mario asks. "You have all the main characters – the Virgin, Joseph, and the Christ Child. Who's left?"

"I want an angel in this picture." I can see the scene in my head now. It's more than a family at rest, it's a concert, a moment to nurture the spirit as well as revive the body. The angel will have its back to the viewer, playing a violin and reading the sheet of music that Joseph holds up for him. On the other side, Mary will sit with the baby, lulled to sleep by the violin's song.

I begin by blocking out the part with Anna and the baby. I'll paint Joseph when Anna's busy working. And I'll fit in the angel once I've found him. For now there's a column of light where his body will be.

I pose Anna holding the baby, her cheek resting lightly on the babe's head. Her every line is tender, but also weary. Here I am, finally painting a "high" subject, a biblical story, but I'm doing it my way. First by showing Anna in all her basic goodness. I dare anyone to look at this portrait of her and label her a sinner. She's a woman, nurturing her child, a sight as holy as can be.

Anna is right – the baby is pretty. She sleeps peacefully the whole afternoon, nestled in Anna's arms. The young girl I remember from Sant'Agnese is so still, I think she's napping as well. Even with her eyes closed, her face looks sad and worried, as if she knows her child's fate. Her hands are gentle, the slope of her neck innocence itself. When Mario comes bustling into the room, Anna blinks sleepily and looks up at me, embarrassed.

"I'm sorry, I didn't mean to ruin the pose," she says.

"You didn't ruin anything. You're perfect."

Mario stands behind me, studying what I've done so far. Tears well up in his eyes.

"Mario, what's wrong?" I put down my brush and turn to my friend.

"It's just as you said – perfect," he whispers. "You've made them holy."

"No," I say. "I've allowed you to see them as they really are, that's all. God made them holy, not me."

Mario nods, drags a sleeve under his nose. "I'm sorry to interrupt, but I found your angel. He works at the tavern across the way. He's busy at night, and can come by in the morning. But we have to pay him."

"Pay him?" I object. "With what? How?"

"I have a few coins saved, enough to satisfy him," Mario offers.

"That's too generous of you. And then we'll both be broke." Mario knows I don't take charity.

"You'll pay me back when you sell one of your paintings. We should go by the shop tomorrow. Who knows, you may be rich and not even know it!"

I don't want to accept, but I need my angel. "Thank you, Mario." The words aren't easy for me to say.

"Now go back to work," says Mario. "That baby won't sleep forever."

I manage to get a good bit done before the mother comes for her child. She stops to look at the painting. Anna studies it, too. And so does her mother who comes in with the day's shopping. The silence is so thick, I feel it choking me.

I stare at each of their faces, but they don't notice me. They're drinking in my picture as if it were fresh, cool water. Anna's eyes are soft, her mouth open in wonder. The baby's mother is smiling as if she's been told a secret. And the signora, Anna's mother, is crying, silent tears silvering her cheeks.

I stand stock still, frozen by their reactions, until the signora turns to me, her lips curved in happiness, her eyes shining. "Bless you, my son," she says. "You've seen my girl, seen her as she really is. I didn't believe you, Lord knows I didn't believe you." She shakes her head, laughing now. "What woman believes anything a man says?"

"Mama, isn't it wonderful?" Anna asks, squeezing her mother's arm. "Isn't Michele wonderful?" She turns to me, her big eyes drinking me in the same way they took in the painting.

"It's not finished, barely started. . ." I mumble. I start washing brushes, busying myself. I need fresh air. I need a drink. I need to get away. "Mario, let's go," I call gruffly, pull on my coat and stride out the door.

Mario races to catch up with me. "Is something wrong?" he asks.

"No, of course not!" I snap. I should be happy with the signora's praise. Instead I feel oddly responsible, like I've taken on a duty toward her, toward Anna, one that I might not be able to fulfill. I shrug off the nagging discomfort, focusing instead on the violet shadows sliding down the ochre walls of the church as the sun sets.

"I thought we should check on the shop, like you said, maybe pay Prosperino a visit."

"Good idea," Mario agrees. "This time I'll leave him some of my pictures, too." He's carrying some small canvases tucked under his arm.

"Which ones?"

"A couple of still lifes, thanks to d'Arpino, and that small *Adoration of the Magi* I did, you know, the one you said was good."

I nod. It is a good painting, cozy and domestic. Not great, but certainly solid, worth a decent price. "So you've changed your mind about Spata? You're willing now to use him as a dealer?"

Mario shrugs. "You're right, what choice do we have? Anything is better than nothing, and I can't eat a still life, no matter how deliciously I paint it."

When we reach the shop, I notice right away that *The Fortuneteller* isn't in the window anymore. Mario and I exchange a smile. We'll eat tonight!

I push open the door, setting the bells chiming. Spata comes out from the back right away. He beams when he sees us.

"You see your painting is gone, don't you? I told you I could get a good price." He pulls out his purse, pours out some coins, and counts eight scudi into my hand. It's not a fortune, but it's by far the most I've ever been paid. "And a couple of gentlemen have expressed an interest in *The Cardsharps*. I'm sure I'll have sold it by the end of the week. Do you have anything else for me?"

"I'm working on something right now," I say, collecting the money. "And Mario has brought some pieces for you."

Mario spreads out his canvases on the table. Spata examines them carefully.

"Not as good as Michele's. And they're smaller, so they won't bring as much. Still, I'll sell them." He arranges three of them in the window where *The Fortuneteller* was.

Mario stares at the floor, miserable. "Thank you," he mumbles.

"Yes, thank you," I echo. We go out the door and I link my arm in Mario's, pulling him close. "Don't worry about what Spata says. You're a fine painter. Your pictures are smaller than mine, that's all."

"That's not it at all," Mario sniffles. "And you know it.

I'm competent, nothing more. I should paint wedding chests or decorative panels for cupboards, not works of art. Who am I fooling?"

"Don't be so hard on yourself! You're younger than me. Give yourself time to become a great artist."

"Not everyone is a great artist. In fact most artists aren't. Remember all the ones in d'Arpino's studio, all his friends, all the members of the stupid Academy of Senselessness?"

"You're not like them!"

"Yes, because I admit my limitations. I'm too Sicilian to lie even to myself."

"Mario, we should be celebrating! Come on," I urge. "Where do you want to go?"

Mario waves me away. "Just be quiet for a minute, Michele. Let a man feel sorry for himself. No girl will ever look at me the way Anna gaped at you."

"Is that what this is about? The admiration of a girl? I've seen plenty of girls ogle you – you're much better looking than I am." That's not empty flattery – it's true. I exaggerated a bit in the portrait with the basket of fruit, but not by much. Mario has the kind of face women dream of, soulful and sweet. I look like a snuffly-nosed dog in comparison.

"That's not what I meant," Mario snorts, though he can't help smiling. He knows my weak spots as well as I do. "She was looking at you like you're a genius."

It's what I've dreamed of, how I want the whole world to see me, but now there's a heaviness to my ambition. The burden of living up to Anna's goodness, of being able to protect her from the criticism that will surely come. But that's not what Mario means and not what I want to talk about.

"Would you rather be a genius or an Adonis?" I ask,

reminding Mario again of his own gifts.

"Personally, I'd like both."

"And which is Prosperino, I wonder." I lead the conversation further away from myself.

"He's a tough case – neither attractive nor supremely talented. I mean, he paints well, but only one thing."

"Grotesques!" we both hoot at the same time.

Mario is back to his cheerful self by the time we reach Prosperino's. He's eager to tell our friend about the sale, about our new place, about the painting I've started. Prosperino has news for us, too. Cardinal Francesco Maria Bourbon Del Monte has heard of me and is interested in my work.

"Heard of me? How?" I ask.

"This is Rome. People talk. That picture you did of Mario at d'Arpino's studio and *The Fortuneteller*, everyone's talking about them. Michele, you might be the new sensation this city has been waiting for."

X

Prosperino Orsi

Personal Journal, September 1594

It's good to see Michele again, to go out and get drunk with him like old times. The studio is dull without him. No one swims races in the Tiber any more, no one clambers up the columns in the Forum, bellowing songs to the stars, and no one sweet-talks a gaggle of serving maids into playing tag with a gang of tipsy artists. Instead we eat our supper and go to our rooms, silent, bored, and grumpy.

During the day, we paint. And sketch. And paint some more. D'Arpino tries to inspire us with lectures on the Ideal and the Divine, on how we should breathe life into drawing. But all our painting seems dead to me, dry and still. I used to love drawing, the line a muscle has, the tension, the vibrancy, but Michele showed me something different. In his pictures, I saw light and shadow in a way I never had before. I saw something deeper than lines: colors that were light and airy, rich and buttery, heavy and coarse. I could feel the texture of his images. I could breath the air captured on his canvas. And now my grotesques seem flat and soul-less, truly grotesque.

But what else can I paint? These half vegetable- half human faces are what I know how to do. I can admire Michele's skill, his vision, but I can never paint like him. A man has to make a living, after all.

At least I can still drink with him, be his friend, stride through the streets of Rome, howling songs to the moon and telling stupid jokes. Tonight was like that, like the old days. We started at a tavern over by Augustus' mausoleum and ended up sneaking into the church of San Pietro in Vincolo, admiring the statue of Moses that Michelangelo sculpted. Michele ran his hands all along the marble, playing with Moses' stone beard, the small horns sprouting from his head, the handsome fingers, the muscular thighs.

"I'll make my own Moses!" he yelled into the empty church.

And he probably will.

XI

The boy –he's called Giovanni – is perfect for the part of the angel so long as he keeps his mouth shut. He has long golden curls, slender hips, and muscular arms. Standing with his back to me, he holds a borrowed violin. I add great gray-feathered wings and a swirl of white cloth billowing across his legs as if blown by the breath of God. Silent, he looks like the Holy Spirit glows within his skin, and his feet lightly touch the earth as if he's weightless. Then he speaks, cracking a joke in thick Roman dialect, and the angel vanishes.

Anna adores Giovanni. She laughs at his stories, teases him about posing nude for me when everyone else is clothed, even the baby. I'd be jealous, except Anna adores me even more. As does her mother. The signora doesn't complain when, after tending to her customers, Anna slips into my room and spends the rest of the night with me. In the morning I paint her as the Virgin Mary. At night, I hold her as a woman.

Fortunately for Mario, not every night. He shares my room, after all, but when Anna's there, he leaves without a word and sleeps on the bench in the kitchen. A true, loyal friend, as I've said before. He seems happier these days because he's found a new focus for his painting. Instead of trying to invent scenes out of his imagination, he copies my pictures. He's made two versions of *The Cardsharps* already.

"What market is there in fake Caravaggios?" I tease him. He's working on his third *Cardsharps* while I finish up the *Rest on the Flight to Egypt*. "I haven't sold the original yet," I remind him.

"But you will. I've heard the talk in the taverns. Everyone says you've created a new style, a new subject matter. I bet d'Arpino is sick with envy."

"If I'm so beloved, why am I still so poor?" The money I got for *The Fortuneteller* has long been spent on rent, food, Giovanni and, finally, fine clothes for myself and Mario.

"I saw Spata the other day. He said there's a bidding war for *The Cardsharps*. That's why he hasn't sold it yet. He's waiting to see which collector will offer the most. When I told him I've made copies, he was thrilled. He says he can sell as many as I make."

"Really? Does that mean I'll get paid soon?"

"By the end of this week. That's the deadline Spata gave for the final bids."

"Good timing! It's been a while since we could afford a night of drinking." I'm done with the figures now and am painting the landscape in the background of the picture, using color sketches I made along the Tiber River. My holy family is resting in Rome on their way to Egypt. After all, isn't Rome the center of the universe?

I set down the wooden board I use for a palette. I'm pleased with the finished picture. Every rock and leaf is lovingly detailed, but I'm especially proud of the angel. I think I've breathed sanctity into all the figures, even the moist-eyed donkey looking over Joseph's shoulder, but the angel, ah the angel, is truly divine.

"That Giovanni," I murmur. "I could almost fall in love with him."

Mario laughs. "You mean your image of him! The Giovanni I know is about as far from godliness as you can get."

I shake my head. "I don't care what he does or how foul his language. In my picture, he's an angel, holy and pure." I stare at the white rock I painted in front of Joseph's feet. "Like that simple rock. It's not a lump of earth, but something magnificent."

"Yes!" Mario throws his arm around me. "Because you've painted it that way. And do you mean to compare Giovanni to a stone?"

"You know that's not what I mean." I wipe my brushes on a rag. "I'm talking about the miracle of painting. Of showing how marvelous our world is, down to the magic of a donkey's nose or a pebble in the dirt."

"If only my painting could be a miracle! I sweat blood for every inch I paint. It's such an effort, my muddy handprints are everywhere. I suppose that says a lot about how different we are as artists. You're a genius. I'm a hack."

"You're no hack," I protest.

"You're too kind," says Mario. "Now that your painting is finished, shall we take it to Signore Spata? See how much he can get for this beauty?"

"Not yet. It needs to dry and that takes days. But we

can visit Spata anyway, find out what's happening with *The Cardsharps*." I put on my new black cloak, handsome and elegant. Now I look the part of a court painter. Or my clothes do. My hair needs trimming, as does the beard I've grown. My eyes are red from lack of sleep, having spent long hours on the painting. But as soon as we walk outside, the crisp fall air and buttery light fill me with energy. I love this time of year when the light is golden, the days have begun to get cooler and the city is at its most welcoming. It feels good to stretch my legs and take in the bustle around me. Hawkers call out their wares while men sit at tables outside, drinking and arguing about politics, that favorite Roman topic. When we come to the piazza where the Pantheon stands, I take Mario by the elbow and steer him inside.

"This is my favorite building in the city," I tell him. I gaze up at the dome, soaring over our heads with quiet dignity. Those ancient Romans knew how to build. The colored marble is more luscious than any painting could be, the geometry of it all so harmonious, the very air inside feels purer, cleaner than ordinary air.

Mario stands beside me, admiring the play of light and shadow on the coffered ceiling. "So this is where you find your inspiration? Your sense of light and dark?"

I sigh and head back into the bright daylight. "More likely in the world of taverns, the shadows of the night, the real world all around us. But I can still admire ancient perfection."

The bell jingles merrily as we open the door to Spata's shop. He's standing behind the counter talking to a heavy-set man dressed in fine robes with the soft hands and face of nobility.

"Ah, and here's the artist himself!" he calls out. "Just

the man you wanted to see!"

The man scours me with his eyes. His gaze is piercing, intelligent, and something else I don't understand. "Michelangelo Merisi da Caravaggio?" he asks.

I nod, intrigued. "And my friend, Mario Minniti."

"Prosperino Orsi and his brother Aurelio speak highly of you. And I see myself that you're a man of great talent." His voice is a deep bass, as mesmerizing as his eyes. Hearing it is like drinking thick chocolate. "I'm Cardinal Francesco Maria Del Monte, the fortunate collector who has just purchased *The Cardsharps.*"

"Ah, so it's been sold at last."

"And I think it's your copy of *The Fortuneteller* I've also bought," Del Monte says, turning to Mario. "Alas, I missed getting my hands on the original, but I'm pleased to have your copy."

Mario grins at me. So we've both made a sale. We'll definitely celebrate tonight.

"I would like to make you an offer," Del Monte continues, "and I hope you'll seriously consider it."

"An offer?"

"It would be a great honor if you would join my household. You would have your own room, be well fed and clothed, and naturally be free to take any commissions that come your way. But you would also paint for me. Perhaps you would even allow me to suggest subjects that particularly interest me."

He's offering to be my patron? To support my painting?

"My palazzo is just around the corner. And of course your friend Mario is also welcome."

Now Mario is staring at Del Monte, too. We stand

there, gaping like a pair of wide-mouthed fish.

"What are you waiting for?" Spata asks. "Say yes to the cardinal! You'll never meet a finer patron. In his palazzo you'll meet artists, musicians, philosophers, poets, great minds all. A far cry from living in a brothel, wouldn't you say?"

I'm stunned. Could the years of poverty be over so quickly? I shiver with the enormity of it. This is the true beginning of my fame, my fortune. It all starts here, in this dingy shop, in the shadows.

XII

"I don't believe it!" Mario gasps as we head back to pack up our meager things. "Cardinal Francesco Del Monte! I've heard of him – he's famous!"

"Then why don't I know him?"

"You don't pay attention when people talk about cardinals or the nobility. I've seen your eyes glaze over. It all bores you. But you might have heard what a generous patron of the arts he is, how he supports musicians, poets, scientists as well. That Pisan, Galileo Galilei, the one who studies the stars and planets with that device, you know the one, the telescope? Del Monte tried to get him a position at the university in Florence."

"How do you know all this?" I think of Mario as a fair painter, a good drinking partner, a gripping storyteller, but now he's also a source of information about Roman society?

"I pay attention!" Mario is excited at the thought of

being connected to such a great man. "He's a Venetian – you might have guessed from his accent. From a very important family. You know who attended his baptism?"

"Of course I don't. But I'm guessing you do." I can't help feeling irritated at his being such a know-it-all.

"Only the most important men in Venice!" Mario brushes off my annoyance with his enthusiasm. "Pietro Aretino, the great poet and playwright, Titian, the most admired painter in Venice, and Jacopo Sansovino, the architect and sculptor. Del Monte drank in culture with his wet nurse's milk!"

I'd be thrilled if only Mario knew less and allowed me to learn these things myself, directly from Del Monte. Now I'll just be intimidated by him. No, I promise myself, I won't. I belong in that kind of esteemed company!

"And there's more. He's a close friend and advisor to the Grand Duke Ferdinando de' Medici, the one who lived in the Villa Medici here in Rome until his brother and wife died. Poisoned so the rumor has it. He had to rush back to Florence to take up the title of Grand Duke. Don't you see, Del Monte is the political agent of the Florentine Grand Duke and his artistic advisor! That's why he lives in the Palazzo Madama. It's a Medici palazzo." Mario pauses to catch his breath. "Talk about power, influence! He has it all. It's even been said he would have been named pope, except. . . "Here Mario drops his voice, which has been loud enough before that everyone in the neighboring buildings could hear him. "Except. . ." He's whispering now.

"Except what?" I yell, furious at the games he's playing. "What?!"

Mario looks around as if spies could be following us.

"Except he sleeps with men. No one would dare accuse him to the authorities, but it's too well-known a fact to allow him to be pope."

"That's ridiculous!" I snap. "He wouldn't be the first pope with those inclinations. Nor the last! No one actually expects popes – or cardinals or priests – to be celibate. It's a concept, not a practice."

"Still, it's politically tricky these days, with the Protestants talking about Church corruption. Appearances must be kept up, no matter what the reality may be. And it's one thing to look the other way with a courtesan – sex with a woman may be a sin, but it isn't a crime. Sex with a man is."

"Who cares who the man sleeps with!" A man threading his way through the puddles turns to look at me. I forget how my voice carries, but I've had my fill of gossip. What matters about Del Monte is that he's a man of taste and intellect. In his home, I'll meet interesting people and I'll be one myself. And if he's close to the Medicis, he could even introduce me to Pope Clement, another Florentine, and get me a commission to paint something for Saint Peter's. I glare at Mario and don't say anything else. Let the streets find their entertainment in someone else's rumors.

We're back home now and Anna runs up to greet us. "I see you've finished the painting," she says. "It's beautiful, Michele. It'll make your reputation."

"It's already made!" Mario is bursting with the news. I try to stop him, but he blurts out, "We're moving to the Palazzo Madama today! Cardinal Francesco Del Monte is Michele's patron!"

Anna looks flustered, not as happy as Mario foolishly thought she'd be.

"Anna, cara," I soothe, holding her to me. "I'm still yours. I can visit here or you can come see me there. This changes nothing between us."

"Oh." Mario finally realizes his gaffe. "I'll just start packing," he mumbles as he heads upstairs to our dark little room.

Anna sits down on a stool, her face a blank mask. "You're leaving."

"I'm not leaving you, only this house." I lift her chin with my finger, forcing her to meet my eyes. "Promise me you'll still model for me."

She bursts into tears. "What will I do without you? I thought you loved me, you swore you loved me!"

"I do love you," I gather her into my arms, rock her back and forth. "I'm not leaving Rome. I'm moving five minutes from here. I'm making my career. Don't you want me to do that?"

"Of course I do." She sniffles, wipes her eyes, and sinks into my chest. "I'm being silly and selfish. Forgive me."

"Shhh, there's nothing to forgive." I kiss her forehead, then her lowered eyelids, finally her mouth. "Can't you see how I love you?"

She nods.

Mario creeps down the stairs, carrying our two satchels. He stands there awkwardly a moment, blushing with guilt. "What about the painting?" he squeaks.

"Leave it here until it's dry," Anna suggests softly. "It will be safe, I promise."

Mario nods. "Anna, I'm sorry. I was an oaf."

"It's nothing," Anna snorts. "As if I haven't seen my share of men acting like donkeys."

Mario smiles. If she can insult him, she must be feeling better.

"I'll be back tomorrow," I say and kiss her again.

"Tomorrow," she agrees.

And then we go. It takes us until we've rounded the corner for Anna's sorrow to stop weighing on us. Then we bounce on the cobblestones, light as feathers, as we head for our new, noble home.

"Wait a second," I tell Mario and duck into the tavern where Giovanni works. I find him sweeping the back room. "Come with me," I say. "I can offer you better work, better pay, a better place to stay."

"Where? What are you talking about?"

"Do you want to be the manservant of a famous painter, living in a fine palazzo, eating a feast every night?"

"Of course!" Giovanni blinks his eyes. "Who's the painter?"

"Me!" I laugh. "Me! I'm coming up in the world and I need a servant."

Giovanni drops the broom, grabs his coat off the hook and doesn't look back for a second. "I'm with you! Let's go!"

So now it's the three of us making our way to the Palazzo Madama. Mario's grinning so widely he looks like he's swallowed a sliver of the moon. Giovanni's smile is just as broad. And me, I'm striding down the street as if I own it.

XIII

Rome is a big city, but I seem to stay in the same small section of it. Palazzo Madama is around the corner from San Luigi dei Francesi. One side even faces onto its piazza and looks into the window of Spata's shop. On the other side of the palazzo, across the street, is Piazza Navona, where I first glimpsed Anna on the steps of Sant' Agnese. Walking from there toward the Tiber is Campo dei Fiori, the big fruit and vegetable market, beyond that lies the Forum and its marble ruins. In the other direction across the looping Tiber swells the Dome of Saint Peter's. I'm in the heart of Rome, which is itself the center of the world.

A servant shows us to our rooms on the top floor. There's one for me, one for Mario, and even a small cupboard-sized one for Giovanni. We're told to put away our things and find the master, that is Cardinal Francesco Maria Del Monte, in the music salon when we're ready.

I tell Giovanni to wait in his room. I'm not sure what I need a servant for yet, but my higher station demands one; that much I know.

"You have no idea why you hired him, do you?" Mario mocks me. "Yesterday you were practically a beggar yourself and now you need a servant!"

"Yes," I insist. "I'm Del Monte's painter and from all you've told me about the man, that's a high position indeed. If you're worried about the money, I'm sure I'll have plenty as soon as Spata gives me my share for *The Cardsharps*."

Mario brushes off his sleeves, suddenly nervous as we near the music room. "Do I look presentable?" He bares his teeth, pushing his face toward mine for inspection. "Is there anything stuck between my teeth?"

"You look fine," I snort. "And in any case, you're not the one Del Monte is interested in."

"I know, I know." Mario blushes, embarrassed. "But I still want to make a good impression, to be worthy of being your friend."

Now I really laugh. "Even with a crust of bread between your teeth and sauce smeared on your chin!"

A servant opens the door and ushers us into a large, light-filled room with high windows and an elaborately painted ceiling. A harpsichord stands in one corner, a viola da gamba, three lutes, and several violins are set against the walls or lie on tables. Shelves stacked with music and books line much of the walls, a backdrop for the brocaded chairs and settees that are interspersed with finely carved tables. There are three men besides Del Monte, and the chatter of conversation abruptly stops as we walk in and the door is shut behind us.

Mario turns a deep scarlet. Perhaps because he is so

embarrassed, suddenly I'm not. I stride toward Del Monte, bow my head quickly while waving my plumed hat in an exaggerated arc, and look my new patron in the eyes.

"Michelangelo Merisi da Caravaggio, at your service."

"Michelangelo!" Del Monte claps his hands together. "Delighted to see you here so soon. Sit, sit, take a chair. And your friend, too. It's Mario, isn't it?"

"Your grace has an extraordinary memory," Mario mumbles, his cheeks mottling pink and deep scarlet.

"It wasn't that long ago that we met!" Del Monte chortles. "Now let me introduce you to Nicolas Cordier, a sculptor from France, Ottavio Leoni, who's working on a series of portraits of famous men for me. Perhaps he'll even do yours. And Vincenzo Giustiniani, not artistic at all, except in the sphere of money and banking and his own art collection. There, he's very creative indeed."

The sculptor has bright blue eyes and a sharp chin, his skin as pale as the stone he chisels. I dislike him immediately. Leoni is a different story. His round face is open and warm, his fingers stained with ink. He has the air of a craftsman about him, someone who knows his trade and is devoted to it. The two are an interesting study in contrasts. Del Monte is clearly a man of broad tastes, in people as well as everything else.

The third man, the banker, has a fierce intelligence in his dark eyes and broad forehead, but a surprising sensitivity to his mouth and hands. Not a coarse financier, but someone finer, more astute. It's an unusual grouping, and Mario and I only make it more so.

"We're sorry to have interrupted your discussion. It sounded like a topic of much passion and interest." I say, sitting next to Leoni, the friendliest of the lot.

"Yes, we're all men of strong opinions, so any subject is bound to be heated," says Del Monte. "And this time we were talking politics – the French faction versus the Spanish and which the pope should support."

"Which do you prefer?" I ask, ignorant of the merits of either. They're all the same to me, foreigners who feed off of Rome's greatness, who squabble over territory from Sicily to Milan, with Spain by far the more powerful. Perhaps that's reason enough to root for France. Someone needs to put the Spanish in their place.

"Do you really want to know?" Del Monte leans back in his chair and smiles. "Now that you're here, we should talk about more interesting things – your vision of the natural world, for example. I'm struck by the way you exalt the everyday, the ordinary, the focus you give to each detail. My friend, Galileo, is like that. He had me pierce a hole in the ceiling of one of the rooms in my villa outside the city. That way he could use his telescope to observe the stars and planets. He left me a telescope so that I could continue his observations, but I don't have his patience. I like to look, but not to study."

"As do I. For me painting is a form of looking, of understanding what I see."

"A form of owning it, I wager," says the sculptor. His voice is as pinched as his nose. "You capture something on canvas and it's yours."

That's not at all what I feel. Just the opposite! What I paint creeps into my blood, my bones, my spirit, becomes part of me. The painting owns me, not the other way around.

"You deny it?" the sculptor presses.

I'm lost in my own thoughts and don't notice his words at first.

"Well, do you?" He's as insistent as a horse fly buzzing around a pile of manure.

"Yes," I answer slowly and deliberately. "Yes, I do deny it. That's not what happens at all. Perhaps you are talking about yourself, what you feel when you sculpt something?"

"Absolutely not!" snaps Cordier. "I don't make art out of the sorts of things you do. I take Platonic ideals and give them physical form. I'm a neo-Platonist."

I almost blurt out: "Is that an arrogant ass? Because you're acting like one." But I don't want to start a fight the first day I'm here. Fortunately I don't need to respond at all. The banker fellow changes the subject to music, how it exalts the senses in a way literature and art don't, how eager he is to hear a concert by some singer who is also staying in the palazzo, an event planned for later in the week. The conversation wends its way from music to alchemy to the essential properties of things and back to art again. I detest every word Cordier offers, but I have to admit the whole thing is fascinating. I've never heard people talk like this before. It's like watching a group of people unwrap a package of strange objects and then try to figure out what each part is for, how it behaves, where it comes from. It's not the sort of gossip and story-telling you hear in a tavern, not the sort that artists trade when they're amongst themselves, arguing over subject matter and styles. It's a kind of probing, a curiosity about the world.

I stare at Del Monte as the words weave their complex structures around me. He's clearly so much more than Mario's description – a man of keen understanding on an incredibly broad range of subjects. I'll never meet anyone as intelligent again, I wager, or as compassionate, because there's that too.

The next few days only deepen that initial impression. The more time I spend with Del Monte, the more I respect him. I've already started on a couple of paintings for him, both featuring musicians. It seems a way of combining his passions for art and music. And since the musicians are all alluring young men (Mario models for me again), I'm also catering to his third passion.

But the painting he admires most is the one I fetched from the brothel once it dried, the *Rest on the Flight to Egypt*.

"Of course I want to buy it," he says as soon as I show it to him. "You've even included music, as if you had me in mind." He bends over to peer closer at the book Joseph holds open for the angel, then starts humming a few bars. "I know this motet," he says, turning back to me. "A lovely piece by Noel Bauldeweyn with lyrics from the Song of Songs. Interesting choice, Michele." He raises one thick eyebrow. "I think you're ready for more serious commissions. This painting proves it."

St. Peter's, I think, my heart hammering wildly. He's going to get me a commission to paint for the most important church in Christendom.

"Let me talk to some people, sort out the details. In the meantime, you keep painting."

"Of course, your grace," I say, but my mind is far away from the unfinished canvases of lute players in my studio upstairs. I'm thinking of the great dome of St. Peter's, the huge columns inside the basilica's vast space. And in one of the side chapels, a painting by me. I shuffle subjects through my mind – a Death of the Virgin, Deposition from the Cross, Martyrdom of St. Peter? What do I want to paint for such an impressive site?

I'm too agitated to think calmly, so I do what I normally do when I feel my blood start to boil. I go to a tavern. I have plenty of money to spend now, my patron sees to that. I wear good clothes. I even have aservant and when I enter a restaurant, an inn, or a tavern I expect good service and now I get it. Mario's not around this evening, but I have new friends, artists, writers, architects I've met at Del Monte's, so it's a large group of us that ends up weaving through the streets, loud and drunk and a bit belligerent as well. We pick a few fights, belt out some badly sung tunes, and head home as the sky turns pink with dawn.

I've said good bye to Onorio, the last of the pack, so it's just me and Giovanni as we pass in front of San Luigi de' Francesi, where I hear a whimpering from the doorway.

I almost don't bother to look. It's probably one of those annoying beggar women who post themselves at the entrances to churches, their callused hands held out like scoops as they whine, "Signore, signore, per pieta, per pieta, have pity, have pity," like a high-pitched mosquito you want to swat to make it shut up. But it's too early for one of those nasty crones, so I walk up the steps and peer into the doorway's shadow.

It's a puppy, a small black puppy, whimpering from cold, hunger, loneliness. I lift him up and try to warm his shivering body with my own.

"Poor little one," I croon. I remember what it's like to sleep on the streets, to have no one to protect you. "I'll take care of you." The puppy licks my finger. He believes me!

When I crawl into bed that morning, the puppy sleeps by my feet, and I dream of painting great things, masterpieces so brilliant that all the world comes to praise me. Standing by my side is a strong, jet-black dog wagging its tail like a triumphant banner. It's my puppy all grown up, licking my hand in devotion.

XIV

Cardinal Francesco Maria Del Monte
Notes to Biographer, February, 1595

I've taken in many artists, always adding to my collection, but this Caravaggio is different. I knew it from the moment I saw that painting of his, The Cardsharps. It was like finding an undiscovered work by Leonardo da Vinci or Michelangelo di Buonarroti, a true masterpiece. I could feel it in the pit of my stomach. I was looking at artistry of such a high level my mouth felt dry and my pulse pounded in my temples.

And to think it was sheer chance that I glanced in the window of that small, common shop on my way home. But for that, I never would have known such power and beauty could exist. The day was dreary and gray, my mood gray to match. Then I saw it, a vision that glowed in that oh-so-ordinary window. An image that was like nothing I'd ever seen before, a completely new kind of painting. Suddenly the day was filled with a divine light, my heart lifted, and a strange joy suffused my body.

I'd felt something similar when Galileo showed me the stars laid out like a carpet of wildflowers in a pitch-black field and pointed out the moons of Jupiter. A trembling awe at the majesty of the universe, the smallness of men. But with Caravaggio's painting, it was the divinity of man that struck me, the blessings our lives can be.

I couldn't wait to show Vincenzo Giustiniani. I sent for him as soon as the picture was delivered and I could see from his trembling fingers, the utter stillness of his face that he felt the same way I did.

"Who is the artist?" he said when he found his voice again. "Where does he come from?"

"His name is Michelangelo Merisi da Caravaggio. The picture dealer didn't know much about him other than that he's living in a brothel. But not for long. I intend to invite him here."

"If you feel your household is too crowded, I can happily find a room for him."

"Vincenzo!" I laughed. "You're already trying to steal my artist? Let me enjoy his talents for at least a month before you poach him from me."

Vincenzo ducked his head, ashamed at being caught out. "I'm sorry, Francesco. It's just that I've never. . .I mean, to know someone like this. . ."

I nodded. "He's a treasure, isn't he? One I'll gladly share with you. I don't mean to own the man or his brush. I just want to be near, to support this genius any way I can."

"And to own as much of his work as you can." He grinned, meeting my eyes. "Can't blame you for that."

"No," I said, scouring the painting with my eyes once

again. "Who wouldn't want to be in the presence of such powerful beauty? Who wouldn't fall under his spell?"

XV

Now that Mario spends hours with some secret mistress, Raven, the dog, is my constant companion. I named the puppy that because of his black fur, so black it's almost blue. Of course, ravens, the birds, are black, but raven is also an alchemical term. I didn't know anything about alchemy until Del Monte explained it to me. He has a room devoted to special tools and vessels for his alchemical experiments, but when I asked him what he actually does there, he launched into a long speech that touched on minerals, plants, the alignment of the stars above, herbs grown in moonlight, metals changing shapes and form.

In alchemy, raven is the name for melancholy, and since black is the color of sadness, the name fits the dog in both ways. After all, it was his miserable whimpering that brought me to him. He follows me through the streets, sniffing at beggars, chasing cats, snuffling up crumbs under tables. He goes with me when I visit Anna as soon as I finish my musical paintings for Del Monte. I want her to pose for me again. This time just her alone, her and her sadness.

Anna jumps up when she sees Raven and rushes to pet him.

"What, no kisses for me? All your love goes to the puppy?"

She lowers her eyes, rubs the dog's belly, and ignores me.

"Anna, love, are you angry at me?" My voice is gentle now. No more teasing.

"You haven't been here in over a month." Her lower lip trembles and her chin crumples up into the very shape of misery.

"I'm here now, aren't I?" I pull her into my arms, leaving Raven to scour the floor for tidbits left by last night's customers.

Later, after I've proven my devotion to her, I tell her that Del Monte is negotiating a major commission for me. "I'll have something in Saint Peter's soon. I can almost see it there already. I'll paint an enormous picture of the Death of the Virgin and you can be my model."

"Hush, Michele, that's not funny!" She turns away from me, curls up into a question mark on the bed.

"I'm not trying to be funny. You think it's ridiculous that I could paint something for the pope's church?"

"No, no. Of course you could have a picture there. But me, a model for the Virgin, in Saint Peter's?" She shakes her head. "It's one thing painting me as the Virgin in a picture that won't be in a church. But what you're talking about – it's blasphemy."

"It's no such thing!" I glower at her small form, shrinking into itself as I yell. "Why can't a real flesh-and-blood woman pose for the mother of Christ when she herself was a real flesh-and-blood woman? Nonsense!"

I leap out of bed, pull on my clothes, and stomp down the stairs. I can hear Anna crying softly behind me. I thought she believed in me, in my talent, but she's just as narrow-minded as d'Arpino, as foolish as the French sculptor, Cordier. I've had enough of those idiots, the ones who think ancient sculptures are the best models for figures, dry drawings the only basis for a painting. I have no patience for limp lines, pallid sketches. I want rich colors, deep dark shadows, brilliant raking light.

"Come, Raven," I bark at the dog. "We're going home. I need to paint."

I don't think before I start this picture. I let the brush think for me. I paint Anna as I remember her, curled up and sad on the bed. Only on the canvas, she's sitting, her hands folded in her lap, her head lowered in misery, a single tear staining her cheek. I try to soften her sorrow, make it more pensive, dreamier. I make her as noble as I can, not just in the rich brocade of her dress, the lace trim on her blouse, but in the quiet dignity that pervades her grief.

This time she's herself, a prostitute, and another whore, a spiritual one, Mary Magdalene. I paint her after she's met Christ, realizes the sins in her life and chooses to follow Jesus as his true disciple. She's cast off her jewels and perfumes and I paint them discarded on the floor. This is who Anna really is. A prostitute who wants to be a saint. If only she knew how.

It's not a complicated picture. There's only one figure.

The background is dark except for a slanted beam of light in one corner, like the echo of a halo over Anna's bowed head. Still, I'm pleased. It's my last gift to Anna. I won't see her again, but at least I can make sure that the rest of the world will see her as she really is.

There's a knock on my door just as I'm finishing the sheen on the pearls cast onto the ground.

"Enter!"

Mario pokes his head in. "You're painting. Something new, is it?" He knows I've finished *The Musicians*, *The Lute Player*, and *The Bacchus* (another one, not with my own crude face, but a softer, exaggerated version of Mario's). My last painting was something Del Monte specially asked for – flowers in a glass carafe. He wanted a painting of light itself, transparency, reflection, refraction. In the glass vase, I caught the reflection of other objects in the room and behind them, a window, so there's a reflection of a reflection. On the flowers, every dewdrop is a miniature mirror, capturing a tiny image of the surrounding room. It was a masterful study of light, something I wouldn't have painted on my own, but once I understood what Del Monte wanted, I threw myself into the task, savoring the subtle plays of light.

But this painting of Anna is different. I'm still painting surfaces, but now I'm trying to evoke what lies beneath them – the thoughts that cloud Mary Magdalene's brow, the regret in the set of Anna's chin. Mario sees right away it's a personal image, not something done with Del Monte in mind.

"You're painting Anna even though she's not here?"

"I can see her well enough in my mind's eye."

"You? The great advocate of working from nature, of painting what you see right before you?"

"They're my rules, I'm allowed to break them," I snap. "I know every inch of that girl. I could paint her blindfolded." I set down my brushes. "But you're right. I won't do it again. It's time to look for a new model."

"Oh, I see." Mario stares at Anna's sad face. "No wonder she looks so miserable." He bends down to scratch behind Raven's ears. When he stands up, his voice is bright and cheerful. He's forgotten Anna already. "If that's the case, I have someone for you to meet. Tonight?"

"Who?" I ask.

"Not a prostitute, oh no, a courtesan." Mario is triumphant.

"Big difference!" I scoff.

"But there is, there is," Mario insists. "Courtesans are high-class. They're educated, skilled musicians, masters of intelligent conversation. They nurture the spirit as well as the body. Just meet this woman. If nothing else, I'll wager you'll want her to pose for you."

"You know I can't say no to that." I turn the painting of Anna to face the wall. Now that I've said good-bye to her, I don't want her downcast face reproaching me.

"Who else is coming tonight?" We travel in a pack these days. Onorio Longhi, the architect, Andrea Ruffetti da Toffia, a literary scholar, Nico Eritreo, a collector of anecdotes and epigrams, and Lionello Spada, a scientist/inventor who designs machines to explore the bottom of the sea or hear a human voice at a great distance. My friends are interesting people, the sort of men Del Monte collects. We drink together, share ideas, play tennis and cards. Like that first day in Del Monte's music salon, we create intricate structures of conversation, building on each other's ideas.

It's a fellowship, we're brothers. So if I'm to meet a new model, possibly a new lover, naturally we'll all go. Our motto is "nec spe, nec metu," which Onorio translated for us. In Italian, it's "without hope, without fear." For if you have no hopes, there's nothing to fear. And fear is something I absolutely refuse to feel.

"Andrea and Nico are busy, but Onorio and Lionello are coming. Probably Prosperino, too, though he may be with his brother tonight." Mario counts them off on his fingers. "There should be at least four of us then, plus your servant, Giovanni, and Raven. We'll make a definite impression on Fillide."

"Is that her name?"

"Yes," Mario nods. "Fillide Melandroni. She's from Siena but don't hold that against her."

"I wouldn't!" I object.

Mario snorts. "You're telling me you don't mock the Tuscans constantly? I've heard you. You think they all have uppity airs."

"Only because they do. Have you met a Tuscan yet who admits to NOT knowing something? According to them, they're all experts at everything. And they think they're the only ones who speak properly with their breathy Florentine dialect. Ridiculous!"

"Go ahead, be snide now," Mario says. "Then when you meet Fillide you won't have to bite your tongue. You can be sincerely polite."

I'd be angry, but Mario knows me too well for me to argue. Besides, he's right. When we're ushered into Fillide's salon later that night, the impulse to tease her for any reason vanishes in the light of her beauty. She's absolutely exquisite.

I want to paint her immediately. We're sitting in a room rich with tapestries, knick-knacks, porcelain figurines, and I itch to be back in my studio, surrounded by nothing but paints and brushes with Fillide before me, posing.

Onorio is telling some lewd story about an abbot and some nuns. Fillide lowers her eyes demurely as if she's a chaste maiden innocent of such goings-on. Prosperino interrupts with his own gem about a cardinal letting rip an enormous fart during an audience with the pope.

"And you know what his Holiness said?" Prosperino hoots. "He said, 'Indeed God works in mysterious ways.' Mysterious? I'd say smelly myself!"

"That's not funny," Lionello objects. "You can't even tell a good story, Prosperino. Now, this is a good story. . . " And he launches into his own anecdote about a donkey, a rotten turnip, and a farmer. My friends are at their crudest tonight, falling over themselves to impress this woman.

Myself, I say little. I drink her good wine and watch her. I notice how her auburn curls frame her cheeks, how the light falls on her bare shoulders, how the creamy skin of her neck melts into the creamier skin of her breasts, cinched tight in her bodice. I don't know yet how I'll paint her, but I'm certain I will. She feels my eyes on her and her lips curve in a slight smile. From across the room, she looks back at me, and when our gazes meet, the rest of the room falls away. The chatter of my friends is a dim buzz. I see nothing but her, hear nothing but the breath rising and falling in her chest.

It's Mario who breaks the spell, pulling on my arm, shouting in my ear. "It's late, Michele, time to go. The lady needs her beauty sleep." The others have already shuffled off into the entryway, retrieved their cloaks and hats.

I take Fillide's hand, bring it to my lips, our eyes locking again. "Tomorrow?" I ask.

"Yes," she says. "Please come tomorrow. Alone."

"Alone." I press my lips to her hand again, then turn to go.

Out on the street, in the cold winter air, the magic of the moment, of the woman, drifts away. Onorio shoves me, part in play, part in anger. "Do you have to take them all, Michele? Leave some for the rest of us."

"You can always go console Anna. She's in need of a good man now."

"Mario's already seen to that!" Prosperino says.

"What?" I turn to my friend. "You have? Without even a word to me?"

Mario blushes. "I didn't think you'd mind."

"Of course, I don't. But I'd like to know." I'm happy for Mario, for Anna, too. "Should we celebrate? Find a tavern somewhere? The night is still young!" I'm not ready to go home yet, but the wind is too biting to stay out in the streets. It's rained torrents the last few days and the water in the Tiber is so high, it looks ready to leap over its banks. A few more days of rain and it will flood the streets, the shops, the piazzas of the lower parts of the city.

"Someplace warm then," says Orazio.

"I know just where to go!" Lionello puts one arm around Onorio, the other around me, and off we stride, Prosperino, Mario, and Giovanni, my servant, behind us. The stars glitter coldly over us and the city is quiet in the dark, until we come to a street that's lively all night, the taverns at their busiest. Lionello steers us toward the most crowded one. I take a last look up at the black sky, so empty and cold above us, fill my lungs with a breath of the night's chill, then dive into the warmth, the noise, the sweat of the tavern.

XVI
Fillide Melandroni
Private Journal, June 1597

I heard he was a rising star in the art world, a genius like Michelangelo, Raphael, Leonardo, the kind of artist this town hasn't seen for decades. All Rome is gossiping about his pictures, his temper, his tavern brawls. And every courtesan is out to hook her nails into him. Lucia had the gall to warn me not to even try to seduce him.

"He's mine," she hissed. "You have that silly magistrate. You don't need anyone else."

"Has he even met you? Does he want you?" I snapped my fan shut, sealing the argument. "No and no. It's no business of yours if he prefers my company."

"He won't!" Her voice shrilled in panic. Obviously no man with decent eyesight would choose her over me. She's longer in the tooth than she's willing to admit, and no amount of powder can hide the creases in her neck, the dullness of her skin.

It was easier than I thought to arrange. I sent a note to his friend, the Sicilian boy, and he answered right away. I dressed with special care for that evening, chose the most delicate of my perfumes, the simplest of my jewelry, the better to show off my natural charms.

He wasn't at all what I expected. I thought he'd be a wet-behind-the-ears country buffoon, but as soon as he strode into my sitting room, I saw my error. He filled the space as no man ever had, without saying a word, just sitting there. And he held me with those masterful eyes. I thought I would be the one controlling him, making him serve my every whim. As usually happens with men. But his gaze was so intense I melted and all I wanted was to be his forever.

XVII
Onorio Longhi
Private Journal, June 1597

Of course she only had eyes for Michele. He let Prosperino, Lionello, and me all blather while in his silence he held her gaze. I can be charming, witty, am certainly handsome. Michele is none of those things. Instead he's like a coiled serpent, mesmerizing in his dangerous allure. There's no way to compete with that kind of attraction. I can't even be angry with him about it. After we left Fillide's house, he led us drinking and turned the damp night around from sodden failure to exhilaration. That's the magic of Michele. I find myself doing things I never thought I'd do before, like sneaking into churches to admire art – who does that? Or clambering up the arcades of the Colosseum to serenade the monks who live there. Or riding sheep in the Forum.

It's not that Rome was boring before I met him, but it's definitely more interesting with him as a friend. Still, I can't stop thinking about the lovely Fillide. Ah well, the city is full of beautiful courtesans. There's always Lucia.

XVIII

Anna Bianchina

Personal Daybook, June 1597

I know he's not coming back. He always was too good for me. Anyone could see that. But I miss him, oh how I miss him. When he looked at me, I felt like I was really being seen for the first time in my life. He was such a forceful personality he could be frightening. But he also saw who I really am and he loved me the more for it. It was like being touched by God's grace. In his embrace, I felt truly blessed.

Now I'm back in the shadows. Not seen by anybody. Lord help me now.

XIX

Rome is a city of gossips and sensational murders are especially popular subjects. The Massimi murder trial fueled conversation for months. There were the usual elements of class and money – brothers murder their peasant stepmother (they're acquitted for this) and then attack each other to claim their father's inheritance (convicted for that). Which just goes to show that if you're going to kill someone, choose a poor wretch with no powerful protectors and you'll be fine, so long as you yourself are of a high enough class or have your own influential patrons.

Now the talk is of the Cenci family, an even more lurid story, and Fillide is the biggest gossip of them all. Like everyone else, she's obsessed with the fate of the beautiful, wealthy, noble Beatrice Cenci. When I'm with her, I have to endure at least an hour dissecting every element of the case before I can finally take her to bed.

When the gossip is as alluring as Fillide, it's a small price to pay. And I confess I find the drama as compelling as everyone else. In fact, I'm tempted to paint scenes from it, but that would be considered provocative propaganda. Still, if I'm clever enough, there might be a way to cloak the whole thing in religious allegory.

Tonight Fillide is actually tearful on the subject. "I hear they're going to torture her, torture a noblewoman! I thought that wasn't allowed. Is nothing sacred anymore?"

"In Rome of all places, you ask that?" I raise an eyebrow. "The pope can do whatever he wants. And what he wants is the Cenci fortune. If Beatrice, her stepmother, and her brothers are all found guilty, who gets their lands and chests full of gold?"

"Oh, Michele, you're so cynical," sobs Fillide. Not gulping sobs of course, but delicate, sweet, feminine gasps of sorrow. She's such a masterful courtesan, she makes even crying seductive. That's a rare talent indeed.

I don't think I'm being a cynic, just a realist. No matter how innocent the people of Rome say Beatrice is, no matter how loudly they clamor for her pardon and release, the choice for the pope is simple: the love and approval of the population or vast properties in Rome and outside the city, as well as a treasure-trove of gold. Hardly a decision at all, I'd say, and it's clear which way the pope will go, but that only makes the clamor in the streets more strident. Pasquino, the armless statue in the piazza behind Piazza Navona, sports nothing but commentary on the case now.

The statue has stood in the corner of the square for centuries, a place where the public posts grievances against the pope, cardinals, lords, ladies, taxes, the tavern down the street that waters its wine too much. Crude poems and pictures, savage tongue-lashings, displays of wit are tacked to the statue for every passer-by to read, a kind of public newsstand, a soapbox for anyone with a pen and paper. Today when I walked past on my way to Fillide's, this is what I read:

"Shall the pope shed the blood of an innocent maiden to get his greedy claws on her gold?"

"If a wolf is killed to protect the sheep, is that a crime? Punish the real criminals and let the innocent go free!"

The postings only get cruder from there. There's something about anonymity that allows ugly truth and just plain ugliness to flourish. The basic story, unadorned by politics or dramatic flourishes, and far too long to fit on Pasquino, is this:

A very wealthy and domineering old man, Francesco Cenci, lived with his wife, two sons, and a daughter, Beatrice, in a grand palazzo in Rome along the Tiber. When wife number one died, Francesco promptly remarried, but because of some nasty business, he was forced to move to La Petrella, the family fortress outside of the city. The nasty business? Well, it gives you an idea of Francesco's character. He was accused of raping the stable boys and servant girls so savagely he almost killed one. To escape the death penalty for sodomy, he paid an exorbitant fine (or bribe, if you like) – 100,000 scudi according to some sources, 250,000 according to others – and left the city. La Petrella lies deep in bandit territory, basically sealing the two women, his new wife and teenage daughter, behind its high rock walls. Beatrice was so miserable in her isolation that she wrote to the pope, begging him to force her father to marry her off or put her in a convent, anything to free her from her prison.

Pope Clement, naturally, didn't answer. A father has the right to do what he will with his daughter, even a father as bestial as Francesco. Alone in his fortress, the old buzzard raped his wife in front of his daughter, tried to sodomize his 15-year-old son, and brutally assaulted Beatrice. Who knows how long this family torture continued until the children decided they'd had enough? Beatrice plotted with her brothers and stepmother to drug and murder the tyrant, throw his body outside into the brambles, and accuse the bandits who swarm the hills of the crime. With the torturer dead, the family hurried to bury the old goat and rushed back to Rome, to freedom, to civilization. Or so they thought. All that haste aroused the suspicions of the local priests and they got to sniffing around. They found no evidence, nothing to prove anyone's guilt. Except for a confession tortured out of a servant, but since the man died from his injuries, it isn't enough to convict Beatrice or anyone else in her family.

Up to now, that is. As Fillide says, the rumor racing through the city is that Pope Clement is going to grant dispensation for the torture of the whole family, all of noble blood. If he wants to send a message that even nobility have to obey the laws, it would be a novelty indeed. After all, Papa Francesco broke plenty of laws and simply paid to have the pope look the other way and grant him absolution. Too bad his family isn't as fortunate.

Fillide is sniffling into my neck now. "Oh, Michele, it's too horrible. Something should be done! Beatrice was only protecting herself and her family. She's a hero, not a villain!"

A hero, not a villain, yes, that's exactly who she is and it's how I'll paint her.

"Fillide, you're a genius!" I kiss her forehead. "I've been

wondering how I wanted you to pose for me, and now I know! It's going to be magnificent!"

I want to start right away and once I've whispered my idea to Fillide, so does she. I send Giovanni for my paints, canvas, and easel, and start setting them up, right there in the bedchamber. Fillide's old cook will play the role of servant. Fillide and I will take the other parts. I haven't painted myself in a while and I smile, thinking of the position I'll be putting myself in.

By the end of the day, I've blocked in the lights and darks, found the composition I want, fleshed out Fillide's powerful arms, her hand tense on the sword hilt as she cuts off the villain's head. I'm painting her as the biblical heroine, Judith, slaying the evil Babylonian general, Holofernes, after getting him drunk in his tent. An ancient crone of a servant, Fillide's cook, stands behind Judith, her gnarly hands clutching a cloth to wrap the enemy's head in. Judith pulls on the man's hair with one hand, severing his head with a sword with the other, her brow knitted in fierce determination. She's not angry or crazed, but firm, as if she were Justice herself. I'm painting Judith, but also Fillide, and Beatrice, and every woman who's suffered at a man's hand.

And who poses for the dying general? I do, using a mirror. I look up in horror and surprise as the blood gushes out of me. Go ahead, Fillide, chop off my head, I deserve it. I'm a brute toward women, even if I don't beat them. I think of Anna's tearful face and feel like I've avenged her – on myself.

When Mario sees the painting, he's appalled. "How can you paint yourself like that?" he asks. "You're comparing yourself to a monster!"

I shrug. "You've often called me a beast, especially

when I'm in one of my black moods. Anyway, someone had to pose for Holofernes. Why not me?"

"Couldn't you make it a little less obviously you? Change the nose, lighten the hair?"

"Is it a good painting?" I ask.

Mario stares at the large canvas. The background is blacker than a starless night, broken by the whiteness of the bed Holofernes lies on and the deep red cloth of the tent pulled back over his head. A golden light rakes across his twisted arm and shoulder, his grimacing face. Judith emerges from the darkness like a vision of Purity and Right. The profile of the old woman behind her accentuates Judith's youth and beauty, so that the girl is framed between the twisted evil of Holofernes and the wrinkled age of the servant.

"It's more than good," Mario says. "It's brilliant! Everyone who sees it will think of Beatrice Cenci! This painting says more than all the notes on Pasquino, all the tracts being handed around the city, arguing for the family's innocence. If the pope saw it, even he would be convinced of the girl's righteousness. Which is exactly why you can't show it to anyone."

"I don't understand. Why not?" Mario follows the gossip, especially about the pope, far more closely than I do, so I know there's a reason behind his words. I just can't guess what it could be.

"If the pope allows Beatrice to be condemned and executed, as is highly likely, your picture will be seen as inflammatory criticism of his blessed wisdom. You're betting on the wrong side to win here, Michele. And if Beatrice loses, so do you."

I throw my brush down. "I'm not betting at all. I'm

painting the truth as I see it. It's a picture of a biblical subject, not a contemporary crime. If people see Beatrice in Judith, is that my fault? If the pope doesn't like it, what's he going to do, throw me in prison?"

"Don't be an idiot! He could do exactly that! Do you want to end up in Tor di Nona or Castel Sant'Angelo along with the Cenci family?

The anger boils through me and though I try to contain it, I can feel it surging up my throat, raging to pour out of me.

"I'll paint what I please! Always have, always will! Pope Clement should be glad it isn't his old, wrinkled face I've put on Holofernes!" I stomp out of the room, slamming doors on my way. Giovanni and Raven run to keep up with me as I tear through the streets, thudding anger with every step. I find the nearest tavern and it isn't until my third glass of wine that my heart stops pounding, my blood cools to a simmer.

"Blast that Mario!" I mutter through clenched teeth. "I paint the most important thing I've ever done, the best thing, and he talks politics!" Two more glasses and I'm feeling calmer. I leave some coins on the counter and walk out into the evening. The sun has set, but the streets are still full of people, the chatter and noise of daily life. I walk toward the Tiber. Now that the waters have receded, the people in the flooded homes are drying things out. Quilts, blankets, drapes, tablecloths hang from windows and balconies as if everyone chose to do their wash on the same day. The neighborhood that was worst hit is naturally the poorest, the Jewish ghetto alongside the southern curve of the river. Dominating the dark, cramped homes is a large, elegant palazzo, totally out of place in the midst of the hole-in-the-wall stores and down-at-the-heel poverty. It's the Palazzo Cenci. I walk around the impressive façade. Not a single light burns in any of the windows. It seems shuttered, mourning for the family that may never return.

The night air clears my head and I'm not angry anymore. Not even drunk. I'm inspired. I'm painting Fillide again, as soon as I finish the *Judith and Holofernes*, and I'll make her a symbol of Beatrice Cenci once again. May the pope choke on it!

XX

Fillide's tears prove prophetic. It takes a while, but months later the pope grants the unheard-of permission to allow nobility to be tortured. So it's done. All of the Cenci family are given the strappado, that is they're hung by their wrists for nine, ten hours, until their shoulders tear from their sockets. The two boys and the stepmother confess right away. Pain will do that to you – you'll say anything to stop it. But not Beatrice. Even with the strappado, she refuses to admit any guilt. A young woman, not yet twenty-two, five years younger than me, and she stands her ground. I knew I'd captured her strength in that Judith!

All of Rome erupts when word of the torture gets out. People pour into the Ara Coeli, the ancient church on the Capitoline hill, praying for Clement to show mercy. It's all people talk of at Del Monte's. He meets constantly with princes, ambassadors, cardinals, all trying to convince the pope to pardon the family. Del Monte confides that Beatrice has written to Cardinal Pietro Aldobrandini, her godfather and the pope's own nephew, to intercede on her behalf. But he remains stonily silent. In fact, he passes laws forbidding anyone to mention the Cenci family, to "use vile tongues in public places" in discussing the subject. If you speak too loudly, you risk being handed over to the Inquisition.

Does that silence the Romans? Sienese maybe, possibly Venetians, but Romans – never! They're not the kind to quietly bow their heads and obey stupidity. They don't want to be arrested, no, but they won't shut up. Pasquino is covered in angry curses, so many they spill onto the wall behind the statue. Anonymous tracts paper the city, decrying the injustice about to be done. Nightly in every tavern angry arguments erupt over how to save this girl whose only crime has been to save herself from a tyrant. She's a symbol of liberty, of the courage to fight back against cruel injustice. And now the ultimate injustice will be done to her. The city holds its breath, waiting for the inevitable, the declaration of guilt and the death sentence that's bound to follow.

While I wait like everyone else, I paint Fillide again, this time as Saint Catherine, sitting next to the wheel that martyred her. On the face of it, the painting is in honor of Del Monte's sister, named for the saint. But the look of fierce pride, the deep sense of herself and the rightness of her cause is more than Catherine's – it's Beatrice's. It's her I think of as I paint Fillide, her spirit I strive to capture. I've never seen Beatrice, but I've heard all the stories. Cardinal Aldobrandini is a close friend of Del Monte, a frequent guest, and he's described how even as a little girl, Beatrice had a spark, a fire inside her.

"She needed it to stand up to that monster of a father,"

Aldobrandini says. "He had a soul like a lump of coal, the meanest brute I've ever met. But she, she was nothing like him. She was light and sweet, charming and smart, smarter than a girl should be." He sighs and his hands tremble as he thinks of her fate. "I've tried, Francesco. I've tried everything. Clement won't hear me. He won't hear any of us. He says it's God's will."

Del Monte pounds the arm of his chair with his fist. "His will is not God's will and if he doesn't know the difference, he shouldn't be pope."

A heavy silence falls. He's gone too far and he knows it. But he's in a room with friends. Not a word of this will be breathed outside these walls. Still, he should be more careful. I may paint allegories that are pointed, but the allegory provides a mask. Del Monte's naked words are much more dangerous.

"Enough," murmurs Giustiniani, the banker from that day so long ago when I first came to the palazzo. "We're none of us happy with the situation but we can't change it."

"Is there really nothing to be done?" Del Monte's eyes are red with sorrow and frustration.

Aldobrandini sighs again, more loudly this time. "There's one thing I can ask for that he may grant."

"What is it?" Del Monte asks.

"A quick death. I can ask for a swordsman to behead her rather than the torture of being quartered or clubbed to death."

Giustiniani grimaces. Del Monte looks even more pained. Myself, I want to howl at the horror of it all, but I clamp my mouth shut. I'm here to listen, nothing more.

The following week all Rome knows of Clement's decision. A Mass is said for the souls of the condemned and their execution is set for the next day. I hope that it's quick, as Aldobrandini suggested.

September 11, 1599 dawns bright and mild, the sky a brilliant blue with great wisps of clouds. The air is apple crisp, the light that shimmery gold of autumn, too beautiful a day for the ugliness that will happen. The battlements of Castel Sant'Angelo are already crowded with spectators. People mob every window, rooftop, balcony, or loggia with a view onto the piazza in front of it. The bridge over the Tiber is packed while police strain to keep the passage clear for the procession. Del Monte has reserved a prime viewing spot for me among the cardinals and other high officials.

Executions are popular with artists, good sketching opportunities for those bloody subjects like the Beheading of John the Baptist or Judith and Holofernes. Along the bridge I see Mario, Prosperino, Onorio, Giovanni, even my old masters Cesare d'Arpino and Anteveduto Grammatica. Usually the mood of the crowd at an execution is festive. It's entertaining and satisfying to see justice done, evil punished. But no justice will be done today. The people are somber, as if holding their collective breath, praying for a miracle that won't happen.

First we see the procession of officials. There's the clergy, the sbirri – Rome's notorious police force – and the pikemen whose job will be to display the heads once they've been torn from their bodies. Then come two open carts followed by women weeping and wailing. The first cart carries Beatrice's two brothers, Giacomo who's eighteen and Bernardo, a mere boy of fifteen. Giacomo is stripped to the waist and as the cart wheels forward, torturers tear at his bare skin with red-hot pincers. He moans but stands as proudly as he can. He may have confessed under torture, but now he looks determined to die with as much dignity as he can muster. The poor boy has no idea how savagely he'll be killed. There'll be no quick death for him, that's for sure.

Young Bernardo is really here to watch his family being executed. He's fully dressed and has been spared a death sentence, at least an immediate one. Instead, he'll be sent to the galleys, chained to a ship where he'll row until he dies from exhaustion and starvation. It is in fact a fatal condemnation, but the pope can feel merciful in sparing the youth his brother's gruesome death. Now the boy stands still and silent, his eyes squeezed tight shut.

The second cart holds Beatrice and her stepmother, Lucrezia. The older woman is shaking and limp, her face whiter than a newly bleached bed sheet. Every time she sees the flesh torn from her eldest stepson, she cries out and tears streak her pallid cheeks. Behind her stands Beatrice, the calmest of them all. She carries herself like a saint facing martyrdom. We've all seen that determination, that righteousness before. Not in real life, but in countless pictures of Saint Catherine, Saint Lucy, Saint Ursula, Saint Cecilia, Saint Theresa, so many others. And now here, Saint Beatrice.

The wheels grind to a halt at the end of the bridge. A device called the Halifax Gibbet looms in the piazza in front of Castel Sant'Angelo. It's a wooden frame that holds a heavy blade raised on a pulley. The criminal's head is set in a hollow below the blade, the pulley is released, allowing the blade to whoosh down, chopping off the condemned head neatly at the neck. It seems the pope is a man of his word after all and has kept his promise to his nephew, Cardinal Aldobrandini. Death, for the women at least, will be quick and merciful. Not a swordsman, but still, a quick, clean cut, thanks to the Scots who invented the cruelly effective machine centuries ago.

Lucrezia, as the oldest, most responsible member of the family, is the first to die. Her legs collapse in terror and she has to be carried up the scaffold to the blade glinting evilly in the morning light. She's shoved into a kneeling position, her neck forced into the hollow where a basket lies on the other side to catch her lifeless head. Usually the crowd would be roaring, jeering, laughing at this point in the gory ritual. Instead it's eerily silent except for murmured prayers and stifled sobs. Then whoosh, thud, and the deed is done. Lucrezia's grimacing head is lifted up by a pikeman, thrust out for all to see. There are no derisive hoots. Nothing is thrown at it. The mood of the crowd is one of deepest mourning, as if we're at a funeral, and I suppose we are.

It's now Beatrice's turn. Unlike her stepmother, she climbs the steps herself, pulling away from the executioner's hands. She stands before the crowd and calls out in a clear, firm voice.

"God will avenge me against Pope Clement. He refused to listen to me or hear my defense, but God sees all and knows my purity. I die with a clear conscience." The silence deepens. We're all stunned by her composure, her strength of will, that at this last moment, she can stand so strong, defending herself against the monstrous injustice about to be committed. Even the priests and torturers are shocked into shame. Unable to look her in the eye, they move back respectfully as she lowers her own neck into the bloody hollow. And thwack! It's done.

The crowd erupts in one long, wild wail. It's the most soul-wrenching sound I've ever heard. Hundreds, thousands, of people keening in grief, all at once. The very heavens must weep to hear it. But the pope is locked away in his palazzo, his ears stopped up with gold.

The city itself cries out, wracked by howling sorrow. Every face is contorted with sobs and tears, hands beat breasts, pull out hair. I've never seen such a vision of intense mourning. I pray I never will again.

But it's not over. It's Giacomo's turn. He's dragged from his cart, pushed up the scaffold, but he's not allowed the mercy of the blade. The executioner clubs him fiercely with a mace, and as his body crumples, blood spurting from the splintered skull, the torturer leans down and slashes off his head. A pikeman spears the head to display it alongside Lucrezia's and Beatrice's. But the executioner isn't finished, oh no, he's just starting. He hacks at the lifeless body, quartering it, flaying it, hanging up pieces on the scaffold. It's a hideous display and Bernardo, who has been silent in shock up to now, faints at the gruesome gore. His part is done anyway. He was just there to witness the pope's power. Now he's taken away in his cart, carried off to his fate as a galley slave.

The killing over, the priests, sbirri, torturers all leave. The scaffold stays, as do the heads and bodies. And now it's the people's turn. They surge forward, toward the grisly stage, leaving flowers, wreaths, saints' medallions as offerings to the departed souls. The piazza has become a shrine and throughout the day, the heap of gifts grows. It seems as if every single person in the city has something to give. There are rosary beads, ribbons, ladies' fans, charms, amulets, and candles. I feel moved to leave something myself, but I'm not sure what. Del Monte has brought a single lily, the symbol of the Virgin Mary. I watch as Giustiniani lays a bouquet of wildflowers. Mario weeps loudly as he gingerly puts down a pink silk ribbon, something he must have bought specially for the occasion. Fillide wipes tears from her eyes as she takes the silk shawl from around her shoulders and drapes it artfully among the offerings. If she could take off her dress, her shoes, she would. Nothing feels like it's enough. There's no way to bring solace to the murdered family. For that's what it feels like – not justice, but cold-blooded, officially sanctioned murder.

I take off my hat and lay it next to Fillide's shawl, but my heart feels no lighter, so I search for something, anything, else. Tucked into my belt, my fingers find the fine suede gloves I bought so proudly weeks ago. There's no pride now, only sorrow as I add them to the shrine.

Before I go, I study Beatrice's face. This is the only time I've ever seen her, in her last hours of life. She was as noble, as holy, as pure as I imagined. Even in death, her features are calm, restful. She's in a better place now, where she belongs after her ordeal on earth, first with her evil father, then with the pope.

I race to my studio, the image seared into my eyes, and paint a quick sketch, both to capture the horror and to drain it out of me. It's not a finished picture, just a study of light and dark, good and evil, pain and oblivion. I want to paint justice. What I paint is martyrdom.

Del Monte's palazzo is a house in mourning, draped in black crepe. All afternoon and evening people come to pay their respects, to grieve together. Cardinal Aldobrandini is here, as is the envoy to the Medici in Florence, both of whom tried everything to intercede on the Cenci's behalf. Artists come, too – musicians, poets, writers, philosophers. But for once the conversation isn't lively. A thick blanket of sorrow lies over all of us. Finally Del Monte can stand it no more and he orders some musicians to play. The sweet strains of the lute, the low breathy notes from the horn and flute, the contralto's clear voice carry away our sadness. We're left hollow and empty, exhausted from it all. Tonight is not a time for taverns. Mario and I both go to bed before midnight for once.

My dreams are far from peaceful, however. I thought my brush had emptied the image from my mind, but over and over, I see the sharp blade fall, hear the thud of the head rolling into the basket. I've seen plenty of deaths. Why have these affected me so? It's because of Beatrice. She's touched us all, moved a whole city to compassion. It was a horror to watch, but also somehow a privilege. I witnessed sainthood today, as close as I'll get. Through a young woman, I feel I've seen God's hand, heard His whisper in my ear. And I'll never be the same because of it.

XXI

Cardinal Francesco Maria Del Monte
Private Letter, September 1599

The Musicians, The Lute Player, The Bacchus —
everything Michelangelo has painted for me so far has been
full of life and joy. So I was surprised that he was so excited
when I told him about the new commission, the gift I wanted
to send to the Grand Duke Ferdinand I de' Medici. I expected
an argument from him, a lecture about appropriate subject
matter for a leader as powerful and important as the Grand
Duke. He is an argumentative sort, that Michelangelo, never
accepting anything at face value. He walks through life with a
swagger, as if daring someone to attack him. Naturally, that
leads to precisely that, constant petty fights and squabbles.

But in this instance, he eagerly snapped up the subject
matter. Perhaps he was drawn to the unusual form. I wanted
the painting to be on a canvas that was set on a rounded
wooden shield to complete the trompe l'oeil effect. That way
the painting would look like the actual object on an actual

shield — a clever gift that Ferdinand would appreciate.

And what was to be painted on the shield? The decapitated head of Medusa. Snakes coiling like locks of hair around the head, blood spurting from the neck. It was a perfect symbol of courage defeating monstrous enemies, the kind of bravery in battle, facing terrible, ugly odds, that Ferdinand exemplifies. I knew he would understand the meaning as well as savor the visual pun.

When Michelangelo presented me with the finished shield, I was stunned. Of course the painting was gorgeous. The mouth frozen in a hollow death cry, the eyes bulging in terror, the brows frowning in anguish. Caught at the moment life poured out like the blood flowing from the neck. I would have been entranced except the face was Michelangelo's. He'd used his own features as a model, painting himself as a monster, an evil creature framed in sinister snakes.

I stared at him, but couldn't bring myself to ask why. The minds of artists are often beyond the understanding of men such as myself, no matter how learned. Michelangelo is stranger than most, an extravagant imagination, moody and dark. And brilliant.

XXII

I've painted Fillide several times now while I wait for the big church commission Del Monte promised me. He's asked me to paint several small things for his personal collection, but not a word about St. Peter's. I pace around my studio, around the entire city, waiting for my chance. Mario says I'm impossible to be around. Fillide is losing patience with me. Even Raven whimpers now when he hears me stamping around in my boots. Have I ruined my chances for a papal commission with my *Judith and Holofernes*, my *Saint Catherine*, my Martyrdoms of Saint Beatrice?

My foul mood is echoed throughout the city. The Romans are still grieving for the Cenci when Pope Clement VIII declares 1600 a holy jubilee year. As if he's making up for how unholy 1599 was!

It's good news for the churches, which will be crammed with pilgrims eager to make the rounds. If you go to all the pilgrimage churches in the city, ending up with the biggest and best, St. Peter's, you'll earn a crisp, clean piece of paper, an absolution, excusing you from all your sins. No matter what you've done, you're white as snow, pure as a baptized baby. At least until next year.

It's bad news for the rest of us. Clement wants Rome to be pure, pure, pure. He's cracking down on prostitution and has proclaimed that no sex is allowed on Fridays and Saturdays. I'd like to see him enforce that one!

At least when I pace the streets I can now do it in style, with a sword, thanks to Onorio. He's a talented, proud swordsman himself and says all of us in our band of friends should be as well – as quick to draw a blade as a cat arches its back. He takes me to an armorer he knows, a Milanese, of course, since the finest swords and suits of armor come from Milan – and Toledo.

"I bought my own sword from Signore Andrea, see?" Onorio unsheathes an elegant, supple sword with a handsomely decorated handle. "You really can't walk the streets without something like this. After all, you belong to a noble household now, you have the right, nay, the duty to carry a sword." He slides the blade back into its sheath. "Besides, when you're used to wearing a sword, even when you don't have it with you, you walk like an armed man and no one will dare attack you."

Signore Andrea's shop gleams with swords, rapiers, sabers, shields, helmets, suits of armor, all made with the expert flair of a master craftsman. I want to use him and his shop as models for a painting of Vulcan at his forge, but he waves away the idea.

"I don't have time to look pretty for a picture. I'm not

the sort of thing people paint," he says.

"It's the sort of thing I paint," I insist. "I'm not like other artists."

"It's true, Signore Andrea, you can take Michele at his word for that. He's dressed up prostitutes as the Virgin Mary. Why not dress you up as well?"

"I'm not a prostitute and I don't play make-believe," he growls.

I jab Onorio with my elbow. "It's fine, signore, I don't need to paint you. What I need from you is a sword, and that, I'm sure you can help me with." I look around the shop and point to one with a black curved handle, metal laced like wicker. It's gorgeous, far finer than a man of common blood deserves. Then I think of my real father, Francesco Sforza, and I feel in my gut that's the sword for me.

"You have a good eye," Signore Andrea grunts. "That's a real beauty. Go ahead, pick it up. See how it feels in your hand."

I fold my fingers around the haft, balance the weight of it in my hand. It feels as natural as a paintbrush. I slice the air in front of me, feint with a suit of armor in the corner. The sword is neither too heavy nor too light. It has just the right amount of resistance, just the right amount of give. Holding it, I feel as powerful and blue-blooded as my father. I may not have an official title, but I carry one inside myself. And with a sword like this, everyone will recognize my status.

"So that's the one?" asks Signore Andrea. "You hold her well enough. But you should practice with Onorio here. If you know how to bear a sword, you will know how to bear yourself."

Onorio bows and gives a sample of his quick swordplay.

"See, Michele. That's how to hold yourself like a man. How to move so that no one can surprise or defeat you. It's a skill that can mean the difference between life and death."

And that's our first lesson, though I'm sure there will be many others. Just as I've named my dog, I give a name to my sword – Vengeance. For Vengeance is mine and will serve me well whenever I'm in need of her.

"Come, Vengeance," I say, tucking her into the sheath I now wear around my belt. "Let's show you to Mario, see what he thinks."

That very night, walking home through Piazza Navona after an evening of cards with Onorio, Mario, Giovanni, and my dog, Raven, a couple of sbirri accost us.

"You there!" the shorter one shouts. "Do you have a permit for that sword?" He points to me, then to Onorio.

Onorio lifts his goateed chin high, the better to look down his nose at the policeman. "I'm a nobleman. That gives me permission to wear a sword."

"Oh yeah, what about your friend? He don't look so noble. His clothes could use a good wash."

I wear fine clothes, but I admit that I tend to keep them until they're filthy and ragged. Then instead of doing laundry, I buy new clothes. It seems far simpler that way. And I can afford it now, so why not? The suit I'm wearing today has certainly seen better days, but still the stupid sbirri should be able to tell quality, even with a few wine stains and ragged edges.

"I'm part of a noble household, that of Cardinal Francesco Maria Del Monte, and that gives me the right to wear a sword as well," I declare.

"We'll see about that." Each of the sbirri grabs one

of my arms, holding me firmly between them. I gnash my teeth and try to pull away from them, but they hold me all the tighter. Raven growls, but a vicious kick from one of the sbirri dissolves him into a whimpering coward.

Giovanni curses them. "Leave my master alone! And don't touch his dog, you foul-breathed, worm-eating, mangy-eared cur!"

"Should we arrest you too?" the fatter policeman growls.

"That's enough." Onorio pulls Giovanni away. "I'll take care of Giovanni and Raven, Michele. Go with these boobs for now. I'll talk to the cardinal. He'll have you out in no time."

So I'm arrested for wearing a sword without a permit. The sbirri drag me to Tor di Nona, the notorious prison where the Cenci family rotted away before their execution. Part of me is curious to see the place where they were held, to hear the echoes of their cries and moans in the thick stone walls. The other part of me is outraged to be treated like a criminal. It's my first time being thrown into a Roman prison, but I have a feeling it won't be my last.

XXIII

Mario Minniti
Personal Journal, October 1599

For all the stones Michele's thrown, windows he's broken, knuckles he's bruised, faces he's spit in, all the many times he's lost his temper, he's never been thrown into prison. I watched the whole thing frozen. I didn't argue with the sbirri. I didn't try to pull them off my friend. I stood and watched in horror. Ashamed of myself.

He hadn't even done anything wrong for once! True, he's not nobly born, but as part of Del Monte's household, he's earned the right to wear a sword. His genius buys him that honor. Besides, he told me the secret of his birth, who his real father is. If anyone deserves a title, a sword, it's Michele. His little toe is more noble than all of Cesare d'Arpino!

XXIV

It's impossible to sleep in the chill stench of the dark cell. It reeks worse than the fish market, a blend of rot and piss that combines into its own distinctive perfume. I stare at the solitary high window, waiting for the blackness of night to give way to the cold light of dawn. When the first streaks of pink and gold tinge the sky, there's a creaking rasp at the door as a heavy key jiggles the ancient lock.

I hold my breath, waiting. There's a shuffling noise, the clank of iron keys, then the thick groan of the door as it inches open on weary hinges.

"Michelangelo Merisi da Caravaggio?" a wizened old man asks. He looks as old as the prison, as gray and soul-less.

"Who else?" I mock. Don't the sbirri keep track of those they lock up?

"Just want to make sure I'm freeing the right man." The old man's jaw moves like he's chewing on the words.

"I'm free? I can go?" I leap up from the filthy straw scattered on the hard stone floor.

"Yup. By order of. . ." the man pauses, searching his cobwebbed memory for the right name. "By order of Cardinal Francesco Maria del Monte. And I'm told to return your property."

He hands me my belt, sheath, and beautiful sword. My fingers are numb from the dank cold, but I manage to buckle the belt and put my sword back where it belongs.

"Next time carry a note saying you are del Monte's man. That's what they told me to tell you. Save us all a lot of trouble."

"So sorry to inconvenience you!" I snap. "Those idiot sbirri should apologize, they should polish my boots, they should darn my socks, they should eat –"

"Calm down now, youngster!" The old man has probably heard the same curses countless times before. "Best you get out before you're arrested again for that temper of yours. Follow me and no more guff, you hear!"

I clamp my lips shut and clamber up the narrow spiral staircase behind the old man. We walk down dark corridors, climb another staircase and weave through yet more barren halls until we come to the massive front door. It's so large a smaller door is carved into one side and it's this door-within-a-door that the old man opens.

I push myself through it into the bright Roman morning. The air is so deliciously fresh I gulp huge mouthfuls, fill my lungs and nostrils, clearing away the lingering dungeon stench. I stare as a shadow detaches itself from the building across the street, moves toward me, and takes on a recognizable form.

"Mario!" I call out, flinging my arms wide in welcome. "My faithful Mario! Have you waited for me all night?"

Mario clasps me in his arms, then pulls away, holding his nose dramatically.

"You need a bath! And new clothes! You're thoroughly disgusting, you know!"

"What do you expect after a night in there?" I jerk my thumb toward the prison where the small door has shut behind me.

"Come, let's go home. The cardinal has news for you."

We walk through the early morning streets, just beginning to stir with the life of the city. Carts deliver freshly baked bread to inns, street vendors lay out their wares, old women hurry to morning Mass, eager to start the day with pure souls.

"What's the news? Do you know?" I ask.

Mario shakes his head. "No. I only know that Del Monte sent me to have you released as soon as possible this morning."

I stop. Mario takes a few more steps before he realizes I'm not moving, then he too stops, turns around, and looks at me.

"Michele, what are you waiting for? Let's go! The cardinal wants to see you – after you've washed and changed, of course."

"You came for me this morning, first thing?" I ask.

"Yes." Mario looks puzzled. "Is something wrong?"

"You liar! You said you waited all night for me!" I fling myself at him, throwing us both onto the ground.

"Michele! Stop! I didn't do anything! What's the matter with you?" Mario writhes underneath me, trying to block my fists from pounding on his head and chest.

We've attracted a small crowd, even this early. It's always amusing to see a street fight and a special novelty to see one where the combatants aren't drunk.

Satisfied, I get up, dusting the fresh dirt off of me, leaving Mario lying on the cobblestones with a bloodied nose lying on the cobblestones. "Next time," I warn, "tell me the truth."

Mario stumbles to his feet. "What do you mean? What are you talking about?"

"You didn't wait for me all night, like the loyal friend I thought you were. You slept like a babe, enjoyed your breakfast, then took a leisurely stroll to fetch me."

Mario gapes at me. "I never said I'd waited all night for you."

"But you let me think it. That's the same thing. Anyway, it's settled now and I'm sure it won't happen again. "

Mario heaves a dramatic sigh. "You're right, Michele, it won't happen again. I'm sorry if I led you to think I'm a better person than I really am. Not like you – you're perfectly clear about your faults."

I put my arm around him. "Forgive me, Mario. You know I have a temper. I truly meant you no harm."

"I suppose I should count myself fortunate then. But next time I'll send Giovanni to fetch you from the prison."

"There will be no next time," I insist.

Mario laughs. "With a temper like yours, of course there will."

He's right and we both know it. If only I could be as easy-going as Mario. We walk the rest of the way in contented silence, close friends once again.

After I've scrubbed every speck of prison filth off of me and put on fresh clean clothes, I look as noble as Onorio. Now no fool sbirri would think me a low-life. I'm fit once again for the household of the honorable cardinal.

I head for the music room as the most likely place to find my patron, but no one is there. I try the library next, but still no luck. I decide to go back upstairs to the alchemy study on the top floor. If Del Monte's not there, I'll have a hearty breakfast and search for him later. My stomach growls loudly as I knock on the narrow black door, almost hoping now that nobody will answer.

Naturally, that's when somebody does.

"Enter," Del Monte calls out.

I push open the door and walk into the long narrow room filled by an enormous table. It's covered with beakers, glass tubes, jars of herbs, mortars, pestles, all manner of strange contraptions, including the telescope that the cardinal says was given to him by the professor from Pisa, Galileo Galilei.

"A new discovery, your grace?" I ask.

Del Monte looks up from the lens he's been peering through. "Ah, Michelangelo, home again, I see. None the worse for your little escapade?"

"Maybe a louse or two, but nothing serious."

"So you're rested up, ready to work then?" A smile hovers around the edges of his lips, his eyes sparkle with excitement.

"Is there work to be done?" I ask. "Something specific you have in mind?" My stomach pitches and churns. Is it the commission at last, the commission for an altarpiece in Saint Peter's?

"Not for me, something a bit more official." Del Monte pauses for an eternity.

I just stand there, silent, trembling.

"An altarpiece – no, I'm sorry – it's two altarpieces."

My knees start to shake. This is it, the commission I've dreamed of all my life!

"For a church," continues Del Monte.

"For a church," I repeat.

"For the Contarelli chapel. My nephew, Contarelli, left a large sum to have this chapel decorated in his memory. He's been dead now for years, but the chapel languishes unfinished."

"Ah!" I nod. "The Contarelli chapel! Of course!"

"You know it?" asks Del Monte.

"No, not exactly, but it sounds like an important commission. For an important church." I hesitate. Dare I say it? "For the most important church."

"It is a major commission. One that will make your name, I dare say. And it is an important church, though perhaps not the most important church."

"Not the most important church?" My voice comes out in a squeak. "Not St. Peter's?"

Del Monte reads the crushing disappointment that oozes out of my every pore. I slump down into a chair. Put my head in my hands.

"Not yet, not yet, but the Contarelli chapel isn't a trifle. It's a great honor."

"What church?" I manage to ask though I feel like retching.

"San Luigi dei Francesi, just around the corner, very convenient, really. A church close to my heart, where I plan to be buried. And I think you'll be more eager about this once you learn the history of the chapel."

I nod my head numbly.

"The ceiling has already been painted and the two altarpieces were commissioned from the same artist for the generous sum of 400 scudi. However the committee has tired of waiting for the work to be finished and has taken my recommendation to give the work to you instead – and for the same handsome price."

My mind stops following his words after 400 scudi. That's a fortune! A princely sum that only a great artist could command. It's a balm that almost heals the searing shock of the church not being St. Peter's.

"Cesare d'Arpino."

"What?" I ask. The name of my old master catches my attention.

"I said d'Arpino painted the ceiling, but he took so long with the altarpieces, they agreed to take away the commission and give it to you instead. D'Arpino was going to paint al fresco, directly on the walls. Since you don't do fresco, you'll make the paintings on panel and then install them on the two side walls. A sculptor will do something for the central altarpiece."

This is even better than a commission in St. Peter's! I'm snatching major work away from d'Arpino, that old hack, and what I paint will put his ceiling to shame. I'll show all of Rome who's the better artist!

"Saint Matthew," Del Monte is saying now.

"Yes. Saint Matthew?"

Del Monte smiles. "Michelangelo, your thoughts are elsewhere. I'm trying to tell you the subjects for the altarpieces.

One is to be The Calling of Saint Matthew. Facing it, will be The Martyrdom of Saint Matthew. Naturally because of the Jubilee, they want everything done yesterday, but I'm sure you'll get to work quickly and have something to show the entire city soon, no?"

"My brush will fly!" I promise. I take my leave and rush down the stairs, on fire to get started. I grab my cloak and hat and hurry out of the palazzo, around the corner, up the steps of San Luigi dei Francesi. I slow down inside the church, pace up the nave until I find the chapel with d'Arpino's smudges on the ceiling. I'd know that vapidly idealized style anywhere.

I study the space, measuring the walls with my eye. It's a dark corner but I'll have it blazing with light. Thick with black shadows, too, the better to contrast with the cutting light. I stand there, letting the image come to me. Then I go back to my studio and start to paint.

XXV
Cesare d'Arpino
Personal Journal, November 1599

I heard the rumors but I couldn't believe they were true! I knew I'd lose the commission – too much work, too few apprentices – Del Monte said they'd waited long enough. I told them you can't rush genius, that great artistry takes its time, but in the end I didn't care enough about the chapel to keep it. After all, I'm painting for the pope himself, for the biggest, most important churches of the city. Who cares about a little church dedicated to a French saint?

I didn't, until this! Until I hear whom they've given my commission to! That stupid assistant from years ago, the one who encouraged my apprentices to reject my teachings and paint from life instead. That vulgar Caravaggio who's more known for prodigious feats of drinking than painting.

I still have those two horrible canvases he did while he was here. One is a sneering self-portrait of the artist as Bacchus, perfectly fitting! The other is of his foolish friend,

Mario, holding a basket of fruit. I'd slash the two to rags except something stops me. Maybe some day I'll be able to sell them for a decent price or use them as leverage with their maker.

Blast him! I'll show him who's the better artist! Everyone will have eyes only for the ceiling – my masterpiece, all the more divine above his heavy-handed, earthy figures.

XXVI

I've never worked on such a large canvas. The size alone is intimidating, as are the far-too-explicit instructions left by the dead Contarelli. For the Martyrdom of St. Matthew, he directs that the saint be shown murdered by an executioner sent by the evil Ethiopian king in "a suitable architectural setting with a crowd of on-lookers appalled by the pagan brutality." I'm shackled by his details. The devil only knows what Ethiopian buildings look like! But looking at the ceiling painted by that arrogant fool d'Arpino, I get what Contarelli means. He wants an idealized version of the story. Women and men wailing under great classical arches as Matthew is slaughtered and made a martyr.

I try, I really do, but the composition feels choked by the arches and pilasters, the figures small and unconvincing. I don't even feel like myself as I paint. I'm too busy trying to be the artist Contarelli imagined for this story. Mario keeps me company as I sweat to give life to something so weak and pallid.

"This doesn't look like your style, Michele," he remarks. "What are you trying to do?"

"I want to be the kind of painter that gets commissions for St. Peter's! I'm trying to paint what that old buzzard Contarelli wanted!"

"Contarelli's dead, don't worry about him. Del Monte chose you to paint this. He wants you to paint it your way."

"But I've never done anything this big and complicated I don't know what my way is!" I slash through the milky figures with a great brushstroke of black. "There, that's better!"

"Michele, stop! You're ruining it!" Mario tries to hold back my brush.

"No, I'm fixing it! It needs life, blood." I slather black over everything, erasing the botched mess. "You said it yourself – this isn't my style."

I face the canvas to the wall. The Calling of Saint Matthew will be easier. I can picture it as a larger, more elaborate version of The Cardsharps. Maybe by the time I finish it, I'll figure out how to deal with the Martyrdom.

Once again Mario models for me, from the front and back, playing two young fops counting coins in the custom house. Lionello takes the part of Matthew, called to serve Our Lord, and Onorio stands dramatically as Christ. He laughs when I give him his role, saying it's as close as he'll ever come to being pure.

"No one has ever said I look like Jesus before!" he says. "I've been called a lot of things, but never that!"

"Don't flatter yourself," Mario says. "He'll alter the nose, the eyes, something to turn you into Jesus. You're just clay for Michele to shape as he will."

"That's not true!" I object. "I've painted you faithfully several times now."

"Mostly," agrees Mario. "But you've changed my nose sometimes, made me much handsomer others. I'm not complaining! I'm just honest enough with myself to know the difference between how you paint me and what I really am."

My friends are right, I'm using them, but I need still more models. This will be the most complicated picture I've ever made, with seven people in it. Each one turns, leans, hunches differently from the others. I want a play of heads and hands, looks and gestures, to flow through the painting like currents of air.

I borrow some servants from Del Monte's kitchen to complete my cast. Then I add something else to the scene. I lend my new sword to Mario to wear, giving it pride of place, the object closest to the viewer, the only thing seen in its perfect entirety. Everything else emerges from the thick shadows or is swallowed up by them, but the sword is seen whole.

"Anyone who looks at this picture will see I have the right to wear such a sword!"

"Maybe," Mario smiles. "But as elegant as your sword is, I doubt that's what will attract people's attention."

Of course he's right. Who's going to notice a minor object in a grand story? But I'll know it's there. It will be a kind of signature.

Days I work feverishly on the painting. Nights we all need to clear our heads with fresh air and then fog them up with plenty of wine. I don't have time for Fillide anymore. As a courtesan, she expects certain rituals, like long dinners, intimate concerts, entertainment that ends in bed.

One night after a full day of work, we're walking to our favorite tavern when we cross paths with three sbirri making their noxious rounds. Perhaps we've already had too much to drink. Or we just hate the sbirri, which is perfectly understandable, since all they do is pester ordinary, innocent folk. I don't remember who throws the first stone, but one of us does – maybe Onorio, he's always ready for a fight. Anyway, we're hailing rocks on the miserable police, cursing them as colorfully as we can. The prize goes to Lionello who calls them "rats suckling on the teats of Rome."

Naturally, they start threatening us with a cold night in jail. But there are three of them, six of us – six and a half if you count my servant, Giovanni. Six and three-quarters if you count Raven, though he's such a coward, he may be a zero. Doesn't seem like a fair fight, does it? Except we never get the chance to try. One of their ugly lips pierces the night with a whistle, like calling a dog, only he's summoning other sbirri. Before we can melt into the darkness, we're surrounded and dragged to the Tor di Nona. Everyone except Giovanni and Raven, who are allowed to go home.

At least this time, we're all thrown into the same cell, so it's not lonely and miserable, just beastly uncomfortable.

"Some Jesus you are, Onorio! You're supposed to turn the other cheek, not cast the first stone," Lionello growls.

"Well, you're no saint, either!" Onorio barks. "You kicked that beanpole officer, the one with the hairy wart on his chin."

"He should be arrested himself for ugliness, for being a blight on our beautiful city!"

We argue like that all night and it helps the time

pass. In the morning we're let go, thanks to Del Monte's intervention.

While I'm working on *The Calling of St. Matthew*, I spend two more nights in the Tor di Nona. Once, for coming to Onorio's rescue in a fight and whacking his attacker with the flat of my sword. Note that it was the flat side. I didn't pierce, stab, or slash the bastard with the blade. Still, I'm sent to "cool off" in the by-now-familiar dungeon. The next time was after I threw a plate of steaming artichokes into a rude waiter's face. Apparently I was guilty of assault with a deadly vegetable.

The old wrinkled jailer knows me well now, knows I never stay long. It's almost a joke between us, with the punchline being whatever charge I'm facing. Naturally, he liked the artichoke attack best. But I tell him I'll come up with something even better. Maybe grievous belching or felonious farting. The sbirri take any chance they can to lock me away, so I really don't have to do anything except stand on the street corner and breathe. They hate that they can't touch me – not really. They can throw me in prison, but Del Monte always gets me out.

He needs me to finish the commission, he says. He can't have me wasting my time in jail. After the artichoke incident, he calls me into his alchemy lab and asks me to kindly avoid the sbirri if at all possible.

"Don't give them the opportunity to lock you up, Michelangelo. Be a good boy."

"What does that mean?" I snort. "You want me to act like a monk? I work hard all day. I've earned the right to play hard all night. And since when is drinking illegal? This is Rome, isn't it?"

"You haven't been arrested for drinking," Del Monte reminds me.

"Not yet, I haven't. Just you wait, that's next. They'll use any excuse to clap irons on me."

"Just try to control your temper. That's all I ask. No throwing hot plates of food into servants' faces, no flinging stones, no fistfights, no swordplay. At least until you finish the paintings for the chapel. Understood?"

With the *Calling* finished, I've turned back to the *Martyrdom*. This time I don't think about d'Arpino at all or what Contarelli expected. I paint what I want. The space is dark and bare, like the prison. There's the hint of a window, slashes of light picking out the broad steps, the suggestion of a spiral staircase in the back. That's it. The people are what matters, much bigger now, twisting and turning in the darkness, like a whirlpool. Facing the much calmer *Calling*, *The Martyrdom* is loud and frantic. I throw Matthew down on the stairs so that the murderer stands over him, his sword – my sword – poised to kill. But Matthew doesn't reach out to defend himself. Instead he holds his hand high for the palm of martyrdom that Giovanni, my angel again, offers from his heavenly cloud. The spectators Contarelli asked for become Onorio and Prosperino recoiling in horror while a young boy runs screaming from the nightmare. I give Mario a corner to watch from and I'm the small sad face furthest back, grieving for Matthew the way I mourned Beatrice Cenci. She taught me what martyrdom means and I pour that into the picture.

Del Monte comes to watch me paint. He'd seen the earlier feeble attempt and knows this picture hasn't been easy for me. I hold my breath, waiting to hear what he thinks of this new, bolder composition. With the deep darks and the bright gashes of light, the scene has an intensity that's far from traditional pictures of martyrdom as grisly, moralistic fairy tales.

Del Monte strokes his beard, paces back and forth in front of the canvas.

"Well?" I ask when I can bear it no more.

"It's magnificent. I've never seen the light of God, the glory of martyrdom, so powerfully portrayed." He turns to me. "I knew you could do it. And now all the world will know as well."

Del Monte's words prove prophetic. Once the paintings are hung in the chapel, they quickly become the talk of Rome, not all of it good. Some predictably condemn them as vulgar, too commonplace, not idealistic enough. The voice that's loudest in his disapproval is Baglione, the artist I was trying to play a trick on my last day at d'Arpino's studio. Hearing his idiocies, I can understand why the master detested him and I actually regret that I didn't succeed in tying the paintbrush to his horse's tail. He calls my art "low-brow, pandering to the public's brutish tastes." He says my scene of the *Calling* isn't sacred at all, but reeks of the smoky taverns frequented by cheats, whores, and drunkards. I might be insulted, except I've seen his insipid paintings, weak frothy pastiches. If he could actually paint, I might care about his opinion. But he can't, so I don't.

XXVII
Pietro Antonio de Madiis
Deposition, The Affair of the Artichokes,
18 November 1599

It was around five in the afternoon and the aforesaid Caravaggio, along with some others, was eating in the Moor of the Magdalene where I work as a waiter. I brought him eight cooked artichokes, that is four in butter and four in oil and he asked me which were cooked in oil and which in butter. I told him that he should smell them and easily know which were cooked in butter and which were cooked in oil, and he got up in a fury and without saying a word, he took the plate from me and threw it in my face where it hit my cheek. You can still see the wound. And then he reached for his sword and he would have hit me with it, but I ran away and came right to this office to present my complaint.

XXVIII
Mario Minniti
Personal Journal, January 1600

When Michele unveils his chapel, I stand there gaping like the rest of them.

"For a stubborn ass, he's good," Onorio whispers into my ear. "I'm relieved to be an architect, so I don't have to compete with his brush."

I gulp. I could never measure myself against Michele. Copying him has taught me a lot, but I'll never have his sense of color, of light, of how to twist and turn bodies into and out of the shadows.

For weeks, all anyone has talked about is Michele. Baglione makes a fool of himself with his pious platitudes, but everyone else is eager to praise the paintings as a forceful new direction, powerful energy injected into the soppy sweetness of art today.

Not just artists but ordinary people are moved by the expressive force of the altarpieces. I listen to a group of young nobleman who've made the pilgrimage to the most talked-about chapel in town.

"Usually pictures bore me stiff," one whispers. "But these are different."

"Why are you whispering?" his friend asks.

"I don't know." The youth smiles. "I suppose it's because for once a church feels holy."

I watch as an old woman and her daughter cross themselves and murmur prayers before the paintings, as old men hobble up to stare for long minutes at each scene. They seem drawn into the ancient drama as if it happened yesterday. That's Michele's gift, the life he brings to these familiar stories.

The powers-that-be in the art world, who of course don't include Baglione, are so impressed, they elect Michele to the Academy of Saint Luke, the traditionalist guild he despises as the home of d'Arpino and his like. For the moment his name is so golden, even the sbirri leave him in peace. I know he's thinking about St. Peter's, that his fame is so big now that a commission there is inevitable. Is he so successful now that there's no longer room for someone of my meager talents? Maybe it's time to go home to Sicily.

XXIX

With the chapel commission finished, I feel drained, my days suddenly empty after so much time living with the two large canvases. I don't know what to do with myself and wander the streets of Rome, followed by Giovanni and Raven. The dog is good silent company while Giovanni likes to tell me the city gossip. I let his words pour over me until he gets so vulgar I snap at him to stop. Then he gives me a triumphant grin, as if he's hit his mark, found the level I won't sink to. I suppose it's comforting to know there are limits, even for me.

When Mario isn't busy with his own painting – which is improving with each work he finishes – he and I play tennis at the courts near the mound over Emperor Augustus' mausoleum. It's the most popular game these days, ever since Henry VIII of England made it a royal favorite. Any young man with thoughts of nobility must now be as skilled with the racket as the sword. I wield the one as well as the other, but Mario is too clumsy to be much of an opponent. His brush will grow masterful before his tennis playing.

We follow the course of the Tiber, take long walks along the Appia Antica where there are more Roman ruins to explore. And nights we join our usual group of friends for the usual evening of messing around.

But what I'm really doing is waiting, waiting for my next great commission. I try to talk to Del Monte about it one afternoon when I catch him alone in the Music Room.

"My reputation seems made now by the Contarelli chapel, but what comes next?" I ask.

"Don't worry," Del Monte says, setting up the chessboard. "You'll have a new commission soon. Your name is on everyone's lips. Everyone wants a painting by Rome's greatest new discovery."

"Even the pope? Does he want something by me?" I press.

"Stop worrying about Pope Clement and play chess with me." Del Monte grips me with his eyes. "I promise you, by this time next year, you'll be the most famous painter in Rome."

I search the cardinal's face. Will I truly be the most-sought-after artist? I'm too preoccupied to play well and Del Monte captures my king in eight moves, a shaming defeat.

"Good thing you paint better than you play!" Del Monte chuckles.

A servant interrupts us with the news that a visitor is waiting in the salon.

"Who is it?" Del Monte asks.

"A gentleman, an artist, signore, but he's not here for you," the boy answers. "He's come to see Michelangelo."

"You see? It starts already, the spreading of your fame." Del Monte stands up and turns to the door. "I'll leave you to your guest then. Tonino, bring some refreshments for Michelangelo and his visitor."

The servant bows and leaves. I'm alone with the chessboard and the silent musical instruments scattered around the room. Who can the visitor be? I try to think of an artist I want to meet, but though the city is full of them, none particularly interest me. Annibale Carracci and Cesare d'Arpino are the best known, but that doesn't make them the most talented. I like Orazio Gentilleschi's work, but I have to admit it's because he imitates my style. And then there are the usual hacks, like Baglione and Zuccari. I hope it isn't one of them! I'm too blunt to be polite and I'm bound to say exactly what I think of their sloppy work and stuffy airs.

I open the door to the salon, ready to roar at whoever's waiting there. I see the tray with the carafe of wine, platter of cheeses, bowls of olives, and soft rolls first. Then I see the man sitting behind them, his eyes as intelligent and alert as ever, his skin as pale and fine, his eyes as coldly blue.

It's Cesare d'Arpino, the man who set me up to be kicked by a horse and left me in a hospital to rot away. I haven't set eyes on him since that night, but seeing him now brings the memory back in a rush. How stupid he must have thought me!

"Signore," I spit out the word. "What can I do for you?" I pour myself a generous portion of wine, knock back a healthy swallow and remain standing, waiting for the brute to answer.

"Come, Michele, we're old friends!" D'Arpino leans forward and pours himself some wine. "Sit down, I promise not to take up too much of your valuable time."

"Too late for that," I grumble, thinking of the years I wasted painting flowers and fruit for this tyrant.

"I just want to congratulate you on your success!" He gives me an oily smile. "I always knew you were destined for greatness. Didn't I say so?"

I don't remember any such praise from him. All I can recall is criticism of my brutal realism, my disgusting use of living models instead of relying on elegant drawings of ideal images. D'Arpino cuts off a hunk of cheese and nibbles at it. I have a decision to make. I can either coldly stomp off or sit down and see what the man wants. For once, curiosity wins out over anger.

I sit down across from my former master, carve myself a large slice of cheese and grab a flaky, soft roll, the kind the cook knows are my special favorite. I chomp loudly, rudely, and wait for d'Arpino to say something.

"You know, Michele, I'm the one who nominated you to the Academy of Saint Luke. Someone like you belongs in the painter's guild. Perhaps you could give a talk there, speak about how you see religious painting."

"Ah!" I bark, my mouth full of bread. "Thank you so much, Cavaliere, you can't imagine what it means to me to be included in such august company."

"But of course!" D'Arpino demurs, blushing. He thinks I really mean it, the fool. That I want to be part of that mummified cadre of talentless hacks!

"And naturally, as your former teacher, I'd be honored to introduce you on such an auspicious occasion," he goes on, sipping his wine like a little old lady at communion. God's blood, but the man gets to me with his dainty manners, his blasted arrogance, as if I learned anything from him!

"I'm sure you would. And I appreciate the thought, I really do." I pause to take a generous swallow of wine, show the man how it should be done. "But I don't think I'll be giving a talk. The kind of things I'd say wouldn't be welcome."

"What do you mean?" he stammers. Is it finally dawning on him that I'm not his cozy protégé?

"I'd have to say how relying on classical models and imagined drawings saps your art of any real power. The real world, real people are the only possible models for honest painting."

"But surely for religious art, you need to turn to ideals. You can't use sinners to paint saints." D'Arpino's already pale skin grows even more waxen and sweat beads his brow in a sudden panic.

"Oh, but I can, and I do!" I feel a surge of triumph. I think of Beatrice Cenci, the painting of *Judith and Holofernes*, of *Saint Catherine*. "I show the divine in all of us, how it comes from here." I pound my chest. "Not up there somewhere in a puff-pastry heaven with clotted cream clouds!"

D'Arpino dabs meekly at his mouth with a fine damask napkin. "Perhaps I've made a mistake in nominating you," he squeaks. "I've been proud to tell everyone that I trained you, but. . ."

"You trained me?!" I leap up and grab his collar, the tray of wine clattering between us. "You did nothing of the sort! You fettered me to stupid still lifes, tied me down to fruits and flowers. You never thought I'd amount to anything – and now you're taking the credit for my genius!" I can feel the heat in my face, the black anger surging through me. If I had my sword, I'd thrash him with it. Instead I squeeze his collar tighter, watch as my spit flecks his face.

"Michele, there you are!" Mario strides into the room, surprising us both. I drop the limp fool, try to calm my breathing, cool my hot blood.

"Ah, the Cavaliere d'Arpino," Mario says to the trembling figure reaching for his hat and cloak. "So nice to see you again, but I imagine you're a busy man and are just leaving."

"Yes, yes," d'Arpino stammers. "I was on my way out. Good to see you, too. Good bye to you both." And away he scuttles, like a terrified spider, running from a maid's broom.

Mario bursts out laughing. "What did you do to him? Did you see how frightened he was?"

"I should hope so. If you hadn't come in, I might have beaten him to death."

"Come now, you're not a violent man." Mario pauses. I wager he's remembering how I threw him to the ground the morning I was first released from Tor di Nona. "Well, not a murderer."

"The puffed-up blowhard is taking credit for my success, telling everyone I learned from him when the only lesson he gave me was NOT to tie anything to a strange horse's tail."

"Well, that was a valuable lesson," admits Mario.

"The jackass is just trying to climb on top of my shoulders, to hoist himself to greatness on my back."

"No one would believe him anyway." Mario sits down and pours a fresh glass of wine. "No sense wasting all this."

He has a point, my reasonable friend. I sit back down and we finish off the carafe, sharing old stories from our days at d'Arpino's. If I gave a talk at the Academy, maybe that's what I should discuss, the petty rule of one Cesare d'Arpino based on his senseless philosophy of depriving the senses. He's far too dainty for Rome. What did he think he'd get from me?

Then it dawns on me – the miserable creature is scared stiff. He must see how his painting on the ceiling of the Contarelli chapel has vanished from the public eye, plunged into shadow by the dramatic light of my pictures. It's a pathetic comparison, one he's eager to shake off by owning me instead. Then his art can be seen as the precursor to mine rather than a limp, ineffective loser to it. Well, I'm not his student, never was his student, and I'll make sure the whole world knows the truth of it.

Mario listens to my theory, nodding his head. "You're probably right," he says. "Let Del Monte know. He'll make sure everyone hears the real story."

"He'll tell the cardinals, the bankers, the patrons of the arts. We'll tell the artists. Every gossip, every tavern keeper will know exactly what I got from d'Arpino – a kick in the gut!"

Mario laughs. "It's not hard to start rumors in this city. All you have to do is whisper in one ear."

"And I know just whose ear! Tonight we're going to Fillide's!"

Mario smiles. "A well-chosen ear indeed."

It's certainly a beautiful ear, like a delicate shell, leading to the elegant line of her neck and the handsome curve of her shoulders. How could I have forgotten how beautiful Fillide is? That night when I see her again, it's like drinking cool water after a long, dry thirst.

"Michele," she coos. "It's been far too long. But I understand you've been busy. Everyone's talking about your chapel. There's a sudden interest in church-going, thanks to you."

"Have you seen it?" I ask, suddenly caring very much that she has.

"Of course." She lowers her dark lashes modestly. "I especially liked the naked back of that one figure, the one in the lower right corner of *The Martyrdom of Saint Matthew*. It reminded me of yours."

"Really?" Obviously I haven't painted my own back, I'm not a contortionist, and for a moment I can't remember whose back it is. Ah, yes, it's Prosperino's, but I won't tell her that.

"You have a gift for painting flesh, for making it breathe, you know. I almost thought I could touch it and feel its warmth."

I smile, basking in her praise. She's not an artist, but still, I care about her opinion. "And how does it compare to the painting on the ceiling?" I ask.

"The ceiling?" Fillide's nose wrinkles, as if she smells something slightly off, a bit of rancid cheese perhaps. "Is there something on the ceiling? I don't remember anything. The chapel vibrates with your painting. Everything else is in dusty shadows."

That's exactly the answer I want to hear, what everyone is probably thinking. Poor d'Arpino, lost and forgotten already and he's barely past thirty.

I'm about to tell her about the arrogant painter and his ridiculous boast when the door opens and three men push into the room. They're dressed like soldiers or guardsmen and carry themselves like thugs.

"Welcome, gentlemen, sit down," purrs Fillide. I'm surprised she knows such low-lifes, but I suppose a courtesan entertains all kinds, so long as their money is good. And fighting pays good money.

"Michele, this is Ranuccio Tomassoni, his brother Giovan Francesco, and his brother-in-law Ignazio Giugoli. You might already know each other since the Tomassoni family patrols and controls a large section of Rome, the area near the tennis courts. And this is Michelangelo Merisi da Caravaggio, the painter who's made his mark with the pictures in San Luigi dei Francesi."

We nod stiffly to one another. Ranuccio carries himself like a gang boss, an ugly sneer pasted on his face, his nose bent from having been broken, his arms knotted with muscles. His brother is a slimmer, younger version of the same brutishness while his brother-in-law is an older, paunchier one. What a trio!

The conversation immediately descends to the level of the sewers beneath the city streets. There's belching, grunting, lewd jokes, rough barroom stories, not the kind of thing I expect at Fillide's, and I decide to take my leave. I drop my hint about d'Arpino, watch Fillide's eyes light up as they do whenever they spy a juicy tidbit of gossip, and say my good byes. Fillide's clearly moved on, with new lovers, new interests. Power has its own naked appeal and I can understand the allure, though I don't share it. At least she's not sleeping with that milksop d'Arpino.

The evening is still young but I've lost my taste for cheap entertainment. I meet Mario at the tavern on the corner and we share a few rounds while I try to wash out the taste of the Tomassoni brothers and their goatish brother-in-law.

"Fillide's changed," I complain. "As beautiful as ever, but not as selective in the company she keeps."

"Hah!" barks Mario. "She saw you when you were a

poor painter wearing his clothes to rags, which actually you still do even now that you have money. She's never been choosy."

"But I'm brilliant, talented, charismatic! And I know how to carry on a conversation. You can't be comparing me to the Tomassoni louts!"

"I'm just saying that Fillide has a certain reputation. I've heard Ranuccio is her pimp."

"Pimp!" I squawk. "She needs a pimp? And such a nasty one?"

Mario shrugs. "She's a smart woman. She knows how useful muscle can be. And Ranuccio's not a bad choice since he controls most of the prostitution in this neighborhood, most of the gambling as well."

I can't help but grimace at the thought of such a vile man being close to Fillide. "What you're saying is that he's a crook, pure and simple, making money off people's vices."

"You indulge in those vices yourself! Anyway, Ranuccio is a good protector. He can commit all the crime he wants. He'll never be jailed for it because of his family."

"Don't tell me that thug comes from a noble line!"

"Not exactly, but they're all mercenaries who've fought in the pope's armies and for the Farnese. They have powerful patrons. I heard that Ranuccio even killed a man and got nothing more than a light fine for it. After all, his father was the castellan, the head jailer, of Castel Sant'Angelo until he died a few years ago."

I rest my chin in my hands, suddenly exhausted. "So I can't blame Ranuccio for being a toad, he was born that way. I can only blame Fillide for being a fake."

"She's not a fake. She was truly fond of you, but she's a

courtesan. She's always been honest about that. You've never been her only lover."

"I know," I sigh. "I just wanted the illusion that I was." I swallow the last drops of wine in my glass. "I won't see her again, but at least I know the little seed has been sown. By the end of the week all Rome will know the truth about d'Arpino."

"And you'll never see the Tommasoni brothers again."

"I'd drink to that but the wine is gone. Time to go home."

I lurch off my stool, grab my hat and cloak from the hook by the door. "Besides," I say, getting in one last word about Fillide. "She didn't even notice my beautiful sword."

"Ah," Mario says, understanding. "That is truly unforgivable."

XXX
Fillide Melandroni
Personal Journal, February 1600

He doesn't come by for months – months! – and then he acts surprised that I have other visitors! He used to call me his treasure, his muse, his inspiration. Then he disappears into those paintings, the ones for the church, and suddenly I'm so much bean soup, not worth a second thought.

When I went to see them, those altarpieces everyone was talking about, it was a strange experience. I felt proud to know the artist but also like I didn't know him at all. The man I'd held in bed – that man had nothing to do with these visions. The pictures are so much bigger than he is. It made me wonder if I really knew him at all.

Seeing him again tonight, I felt both drawn to him as on that first day and completely cowed. I'm not in the habit of feeling beneath my admirers. I suppose some women would clamor to be close to a genius, to bathe in his aura of greatness, but I want more than that. The day will come when my looks will wilt, my charms will fade. It's time to find some naïve young nobleman or some old dotard, someone who will keep me for the rest of my days.

As for Michele, he can come again if he wants, but I won't encourage him. Now I need someone more dependable than a brilliant painter. I need a simple man, a simply wealthy man, someone I can direct as I please. Maybe that foolish Pietro Strozzi?

XXXI

Captain Barolomeo Iannini

Police Report, City of Rome, 19 February 1600

Last night while on patrol, I found in Campo Marzo Michelangelo Merisi da Caravaggio who carried a sword without a license, although he insisted that he was in the household of Signore Cardinal Del Monte, which gave him the right to carry an arm. But since he didn't have the proper papers and I didn't know if what he said was true, I brought him to prison in Tor di Nona.

XXXII

I search for the right time to talk to Del Monte about d'Arpino, but the house is full of clerics and scholars, the French ambassador, Florentines from the Medici court. I walk into a room and the intense discussions immediately stop, all eyes glaring at me for interrupting.

"What is going on?" I ask Mario.

He shrugs. "Something big, but I don't know what. Maybe Prosperino knows. He has connections with the papal court because of his brother."

When we arrive at our favorite tavern that night, Lionello, Prosperino, and Onorio are already there.

"Who's heard the gossip?" I ask. "Why is everyone huddled together at Del Monte's as if they're planning for Christ's second coming?"

"Maybe the pope is dying, the old weasel, and they're plotting who should wear St. Peter's ring next," Onorio suggests.

"Or maybe the French king has decided to convert back from being a Catholic into a Protestant again. That would explain the French ambassador," says Lionello.

"It's none of those things," Prosperino says. "It's Bruno, Giordano Bruno, the Dominican friar."

"Who?" I ask.

"Haven't you met him during your stays in Tor di Nona? He's been imprisoned there for the past seven years."

"For what?" I can't imagine seven years rotting in that dank, fetid darkness.

"For heresy. The Medici and your patron, Del Monte, have worked for years to get him to recant. He's a brilliant philosopher, teacher, and religious thinker and they don't want him punished, but he's written things that the Church can't ignore."

"Like what?" Onorio asks.

"He writes about the plurality of worlds, that there are other planets where people live. Moreover, he argues that the earth revolves around the sun. Some of the same kind of nonsense that Galileo suggests – another friend of Del Monte, I might add. He chooses some strange causes."

"They aren't strange at all!" I protest. "He supports Galileo because he observes the natural world. There's nothing wrong with using a telescope to study the heavens. It sounds like this Bruno fellow is philosophizing on the sorts of things Galileo notices. That's what Del Monte appreciates – careful looking and understanding of the world we live in. It's why he likes my art. I paint what I see, not some idealized, invented image."

"No need to take this personally, Michele," Prosperino

says. "Bruno is nothing like you. He also denies the Virgin birth."

"Well, I have to admit, that's always been hard for me to swallow."

"Hush!" Prosperino looks around as if there were spies everywhere. "Best not to talk about this. Bruno's been wasting away for years in prison, but now the Inquisition is torturing him. Which means he'll soon be found guilty and condemned to death. That's why there's such a hubbub about him after all this time."

"Any chance he'll recant?" Mario asks.

"If he's smart, he will," Prosperino says. "And if we're smart, we'll talk about something else."

Mario and I exchange a look. Our friend is actually scared. And perhaps he has good reason to be.

We spend the rest of the night playing cards and drinking, finishing up with footraces along the Tiber. No more talk of politics or heresy, just the sound of boots pounding the cobblestones. Prosperino wheezes to a stop, giving up after only a few seconds.

"I'm done for, boys. It's time to go home."

The moon is a cold sliver overhead, the night chill seeps into my bones. He's right. The games are over.

On the way home, we speculate on what Del Monte's role is in all this.

"He doesn't have much sway over Pope Clement or he would have had the Cenci family pardoned," Mario observes.

I shiver, thinking that Del Monte's protection clearly goes only so far. Yes, he's gotten me out of prison every time so far, but will the day come when his influence isn't enough? I'm not a heretic, like Bruno. I have no tempting riches for the pope to appropriate, like the Cenci family. I should be safe, no matter how many tavern brawls I get into, no matter how many plates of artichokes I throw in waiters' faces.

Still, the next time I find Del Monte alone I don't talk about d'Arpino. Instead, I ask about Giordano Bruno. It's late at night and Del Monte looks exhausted, but I beg him to stay up a little longer.

"I've heard the rumors about Bruno and I need to ask you, are they true?" We're in the Music Room, the chessboard between us, but neither of us can focus on a game.

"How should I know what the rumors are?" Del Monte snaps. "Ah, forgive my short temper." He rubs his eyes, the bridge of his nose. "This has been years coming, but that doesn't make it easier to take. Bruno was such a promising scholar, such a quick thinker. I loved his writing. Some of his Dialogues. . ." Del Monte sighs, toys with a pawn on the board. "But he went too far. He said God's love forgives all sinners. Which suggests there's no need for confession or indulgences, that sins are a matter between the sinner and God, with no Church intermediary. He says that God is love and is in every one of us. It all sounds too much like Martin Luther for the Church to let it stand."

I don't know this man, Bruno, I've never read anything he's written, yet his beliefs sound familiar to me. I've felt that too, that every one of us is divine. It's how I've painted people, what I've tried to reveal when I had Anna pose as the Virgin Mary, Fillide as Saint Catherine.

"It doesn't sound like an evil belief," I venture. "It sounds kind."

"Yes, Bruno is kind. He has faith in humanity, in its essential goodness, and in God as a loving presence, not a harsh, judgmental one."

"Do you agree?" I whisper even though we're all alone, the walls are thick, and there are no enemies hiding in this palazzo.

Del Monte slumps forward in sadness. "I don't know, I really don't. When Bruno said it, it sounded right, but now, the way the Church describes it, it all sounds wrong."

"So he's been tried and found guilty?"

"He's defending himself right now, with his usual logic and eloquence, when what he needs is humility and submission."

"Then he won't recant?"

Del Monte shakes his head. "Sadly, no. He's not that kind of a man. He'll die for what he believes in."

I'm struck by his words. "Isn't that the definition of a martyr, someone who dies for his beliefs?"

The cardinal pales. He leans toward me, staring intensely with those eyes of his. "Be careful what you say, Michelangelo. It's easy to be branded a heretic. A martyr dies for the True Church. Bruno, much as I admire him, is no martyr."

"But if Bruno is a heretic, what about Galileo?" I persist. I know I've been warned, but I feel I can say what I like to Del Monte. It's everyone else I need to worry about.

Tears cloud Del Monte's eyes. He blinks them away, straightens his shoulders, holds himself firm. "Nothing will happen to Galileo. He's much more prudent. And this pope is old. Who knows what the future will bring? And now to bed. There'll be news about Bruno soon, but I don't expect it to be happy. You have better things to look forward to, a new commission, I think. We'll talk more tomorrow when I'm not so weary."

He heaves himself out of his chair, suddenly looking much older. The late meetings have taken their toll, and all for nothing, it seems. Bruno will die no matter what. I promise myself I'll be there. Despite what Del Monte says, it's a martyr who will die and that's something I want to witness.

XXXIII

As Del Monte fears, Bruno is sentenced to burn at the stake as a heretic. Like Beatrice Cenci, he's defiant in the face of his condemnation. It's whispered that when he heard his death sentence, he answered, "You pronounce this sentence against me with greater fear than I receive it."

The pope wants to do more than get rid of Bruno, the man. The man's entire life is to be erased. His writing is put on the banned list. Anyone owning his works is ordered to burn them. Del Monte removes Bruno's books from his shelves, but I don't see him toss them into the flames. I suspect he hides them, desperate to keep some portion of the man alive.

I haven't talked to anyone about what Del Monte told me. No one wants to know the details of why Bruno has been branded a heretic, so no one asks. Not even Mario, but he's always up on the latest gossip, so he may have his own sources of information.

Pasquino, the statue for public posting of all complaints, is the only one who isn't silent. There are signs pleading for Bruno and others condemning him. One says, "Since when is calling God full of love and forgiveness heretical? What kind of pope hates Christian compassion?" Another one blares in bold letters "Those who say the Virgin Mary wasn't a virgin are evil sinners who deserve to die – Shame on Bruno!"

There are more postings against Bruno than for him, which isn't a surprise. You would have to be a nuanced philosopher to follow his arguments, to understand the depth of his writings. That's what Del Monte says. When he hears of the death sentence, he tells me, "These are difficult times for complicated philosophies based on observing the natural world. Man grows up, knows more about the universe than ever, but still has blinders on that keep him from seeing the truth."

"Is what Bruno says true then?" I ask.

"Parts of it certainly are. He examined the stars like our friend Galileo and defended the theories of Copernicus. He studied ancient Hebrew and Arabic traditions and mined them for useful insights into mathematics. He wrote on so many subjects, was so broad in his knowledge, some of it has to be true. I'm just not sure what, and now without him to continue his work, I probably never will be. A great mind will be snuffed out. It's a loss to all humanity."

The morning of the execution, the usual crowd forms. This one will be held in the Campo dei Fiori, early, before the fruit sellers, fishmongers, and vegetable vendors set up their stalls. A platform holding a pyre with a stake in the middle has been built in the southwest corner of the piazza. Mario and I, along with our friends, find a good spot to view the proceedings, right in front of the hole-in-the-wall bakery that makes the best bread in the city. Onorio jokes that if we get hungry, we can nip into the shop for a quick bite.

"I think the smell of roasting flesh will take away your appetite," Lionello says, disgusted at the thought.

"Mmmm, it might smell delicious, like pork or lamb." Onorio can't resist goading. No wonder he gets into so many fights.

I strain my eyes, searching for the procession of religious figures that inevitably precedes the condemned. I want to see Giordano Bruno, not to gawk at his death with gruesome glee, but because he sounds like a great man, someone who says what he thinks, who stands up to the pope, despite the risks.

I admire him, both for his philosophies and for his grit. I thought it was a miracle to witness Beatrice Cenci become a martyr, but here I'm about to see the making of another one. This makes me wonder: are so many truly good people, fearless in their beliefs, living in Rome now or is this pope more ruthless than others? Are these times of greatness or of great oppression?

A murmur runs through the crowd. The priests and confessors appear first, one holding high a crucifix, followed by a mule carrying a grizzled middle-aged man wearing a monk's habit – Bruno – and then a group of sbirri and executioners. Bruno sits proudly, his head high, though a cruel leather gag has been thrust into his mouth. The Inquisition is taking no chances. There will be no last minute speeches calling on God to witness the pope's depravity. Bruno will go to his death silent, and with his books burned, he'll stay silent.

There are no last rites for heretics. The priests don't

ask Bruno to recant. His chances are over. He's stripped naked and prodded onto the platform, tied to the stake, and the wood at his feet is set on fire. Bruno has no words, but the mob has plenty, booing, hissing, jeering at the former monk. There's no admiration or pity here. It's the standard entertainment. Death is always amusing until it's your own, or that of someone you love.

Onorio, Lionello, Prosperino, and Giovanni share the crowd's merry mood, but Mario is strangely quiet. Myself, I'm not sure what I feel, but my mouth tastes of ashes. As the flames start licking his flesh, Bruno writhes, but any screams are stopped in his throat. I swear that his eyes catch mine, just for a second, and in that flash, his rage and pride sear into me. I blink and the moment is gone.

I can't watch any more. I can't be part of it. I squeeze through the packed spectators, duck down a narrow side street and hurry off, stopping up my ears to snuff out the ugly laughter and curses. It's only when I'm so far away that I can no longer hear the crowd that I notice Mario is beside me.

"Why didn't you stay?" I ask.

"Probably for the same reason you didn't," he answers. "It was sickening. I should have stayed away like Del Monte and his friends."

"I thought it was important to be there, and it was," I say. "But I'd seen and heard enough."

"I'm still not sure how he was a heretic except for that virgin birth stuff, which wasn't even in his writings, just an off-hand comment someone reported he'd said. Which means he might not have even said it."

I stare at Mario. "How do you know all this?

His cheeks turn pink with embarrassment. "I listened

while Del Monte and his friends had their discussions. I'm not important enough to notice. I blend into the walls in a way. I did no harm! I was just curious."

"And what did you learn?" I ask.

"Bruno sounded like an intelligent man, a scientist like Lionello, trying to figure out how things work, lots of things, like memory or mathematical concepts. Most of it was beyond my understanding, but none of it sounded like it was talk against God." Mario shrugged. "I don't understand these things, but Del Monte does and he didn't think Bruno deserved to die. That's enough for me."

"Me too," I agree. "But as Del Monte says, there's a difference between speaking against God and speaking against the Church. You may feel you're saying nothing that offends God but the Church may certainly feel wronged. That was Bruno's problem. That and he thought he could reason with the Inquisition. There's no logical discussion there."

"Michele." Mario hesitates.

"Yes?"

"What if your painting is like that, not something that offends God, but that offends the Church? Could it be considered heresy when you use prostitutes as models for the Virgin Mary?"

"Don't be ridiculous!" I scoff. "You may not like it. You might consider it bad taste. But it's not heretical! Don't worry, Mario, the Inquisition won't bother with me. I may spend time in prison, but it won't be for my art. Artichokes, maybe. Art, never."

XXXIV

Tomasso Salini, painter

Deposition, 19 February 1600

I was going home in the company of Iacomo Segliani, who had come to see me about a vest I had borrowed that belonged to his patron, when I was in the street of the Pig, on my way to Campo Marzo, and encountered the aforesaid Michelangelo along with two or three others. They let me pass, but after a while, came behind me, and Michelangelo came closer with his sword and hit me with the flat part of it on my arm. I turned around, defending myself with my sword, and Michelangelo hit me so many times that if the noise hadn't brought people running, I could have been killed. Michelangelo, having injured me and cursed me with many ugly words, fled when the barber, the woodcutter and others nearby came quickly and put an end to the quarrel.

XXXV

Once again I'm waiting for Del Monte to tell me about my next commission, for St. Peter's this time. But days pass and not a word is said. I work on paintings that are simpler, smaller than what I really want to do, pictures for private collectors rather than major churches. Since the Contarelli chapel, I have a line of people waiting for something from my brush, all willing to pay handsomely. Still, despite the weight of gold in my purse, I'm edgy and prickly, picking fights constantly. I spend another few nights in Tor di Nona, but as I promised Mario, it's never for long.

"What are you doing with all your wealth?" Onorio asks me. "You could buy a horse, two horses, a carriage. You could live like nobility. Are you just using it to bribe sbirri instead?"

"If I were, I wouldn't be arrested!" I know Onorio thinks I should live like he does – in a grand house with a small army of servants, a retinue of apprentices. But why bother? I'm fine in my rooms with Del Monte. I'd rather buy a round of drinks for all my friends, spend lavishly on clothes, lend money to those who need it than think about running a household. I don't want to turn into d'Arpino.

Anyway, money doesn't interest me. What I want is fame.

When I can stand it no longer, I decide it's time to ask directly. No, demand! I find Del Monte in the courtyard, enjoying the thin spring sunshine after the winter chill.

"Ah, Michelangelo, I know what you want," Del Monte says before I can insist on anything.

"If I don't paint something important soon," I growl, "I'll get into such a big brawl, I'll spend a week in prison."

"No such thing will happen," Del Monte assures me. "You'll have your great commission, but it's not me you need to talk to this time. It's Giustiniani. Go see him this afternoon. He's expecting you."

Since that first meeting, two years ago now, Vincenzo and his brother have bought more paintings from me than anyone else besides Del Monte himself. I've spent many evenings in their palazzo across from San Luigi dei Francesi, listening to music or enjoying conversations with artists and writers. The two of them, Vincenzo and Benedetto, are immensely wealthy, bankers to the pope himself. Benedetto is a cardinal like Del Monte, but more importantly, he's the papal grand treasurer, in charge of the apostolic wealth. With such ties to the Vatican and talk of an important commission, do I dare hope that I'll finally get my chance to hang something in Saint Peter's?

It's not until I collect my hat, cloak, and sword, eager

to look like a gentleman, that Del Monte reveals he's sending me to Vincenzo, not Benedetto. I try to parse the meaning of that. Am I less likely to get a papal commission from one brother than the other?

I knock on the heavy door and in the time it takes for a servant to open it, I've already imagined the great painting I'll make, something truly grand like a Descent from the Cross or a Death of the Virgin, a complicated, passionate scene showing the divine right here in our lives today. I think of Giordano Bruno, of how he wrote about God in each of us, present in our daily routines. Is that such a heretical position? It seems natural to me.

The servant shows me into the library where Vincenzo sits at an enormous oak desk. My painting *Love Conquers All* – a naked, grinning Cupid – hangs on one wall. My version of *The Supper at Emmaus,* where the resurrected Christ miraculously reveals himself to two disciples over a simple meal, graces the other wall. It is an interesting contrast that speaks volumes about the man who chose them.

The banker looks up from his papers. "Michelangelo, welcome. Sit down, please!"

"You're satisfied with the paintings?" I ask.

"Of course! You know you're my favorite artist and I've been singing your praises all over the city. So loudly that you have a new commission that will bring you yet greater fame!"

I lean forward in my chair, waiting tensely. St. Peter's, I pray silently. St. Peter's!

"It's another dark chapel, but I have no doubt that you'll bring your powerful light into it. Annibale Carraci, who just finished the paintings in Palazzo Farnese, will paint the main altarpiece, *The Assumption of the Virgin,* while you'll paint the two side paintings, just like in the Contarelli chapel."

"And where is this chapel?" I lean on one elbow, stroke my beard in a way I imagine to be casual, nothing desperate about me, not at all.

"It's the Cerasi chapel, paid for by Monsignor Tiberio Cerasi, treasurer general for the pope."

"The papal treasurer?" My voice squeaks in excitement. I swallow and force myself to speak calmly. "Then I suppose the chapel is in St. Peter's."

"St. Peter's?" Vincenzo shakes his head. Blast it all! Another major commission that's not the right one!

"No," Vincenzo confirms my dreaded fear. "It's in Santa Maria del Popolo."

Despite my best efforts, my face crumples. The disappointment is searing.

"This is an important commission, don't doubt that for a second." Vincenzo tries to console me. "And you'll be highly paid, I assure you."

I grit my teeth. I don't care how high the pile of gold is. I have more than I need already. I want to have something in Saint Peter's, down the nave from my namesake's famous *Pietà*. What I really want, I realize, is to paint my own *Pieta* and place it right behind Michelangelo Buonarotti's. Then we'll see who is the better Michelangelo!

A servant enters with some wine. Good timing, too, since I need a healthy swig. Vincenzo waits for me to drink, then takes a sip.

"Do you want to know the subjects?"

I nod numbly. May as well.

"One is to be the Conversion of St. Paul, when the Jew Saul has a vision on the road to Damascus and becomes the Christian Paul. The other is the Crucifixion of St. Peter. Humbly choosing not to die like Christ, he insists on being crucified upside-down."

"I know the story," I mutter. "Every child does."

"I'm simply making sure you know which moment Cerasi wants depicted. You'll meet with him tomorrow afternoon at the chapel so you can see the site and he can clarify what he wants."

"Haven't you been specific enough?" I bark.

"There's one more thing." Vincenzo hesitates. "I'm sure you're aware that Pope Clement has new rules for artists. You must submit sketches for approval before you paint. I assume you have the necessary license."

"Those rules are idiotic!" I burst out. Reminding me of the pope's petty repressions is like lancing a throbbing boil. I explode, leaping up and pounding my fist on the desk. "A license to paint or you'll be put in prison? Where's the danger in art? Why is the pope so afraid of my brush! And I never make sketches! You know that! I work directly on the panel or canvas."

"Calm down, Michelangelo. For an artist of your stature, I'm sure something can be arranged."

"God's blood, but that pope is a pig's fart! Why doesn't the old goat hurry up and die and free us from his stupidity? He's choking the life out of the city, he is!"

Vincenzo sighs. He knows I'm right, but he can't say anything, he's far too diplomatic. He'd ask the pope for permission before picking his teeth!

"How's this – you paint your sketch directly on the canvas, as you normally do, blocking in the composition in darks and lights, and I'll have someone from the Academy sign off on it. Clement simply wants to be sure religious subjects are treated with the dignity and respect they deserve."

"I don't even know what that means," I slump down in the chair, exhausted by my outburst. "Dignity! That means putting fig leafs on all the nude sculptures, painting swaths of cloth strategically over anything that might possibly be arousing. It's enough to make you despair for the future of art in Rome."

"You're exaggerating. No one's complained about nudity in your painting."

"That's because there isn't any, not in anything that hangs in a church. But maybe this is my chance for a little flesh." I wink. I'm just teasing, of course. I'm not going to ruin my chances for St. Peter's. And anyway, who wants to see Peter or Paul naked? Not me!

"Michelangelo!" Vincenzo pleads. "Just accept this commission graciously, paint like the genius you are, and I promise all will be well. You'll get your chance for St. Peter's, I'm sure of it."

I finish off my wine. "I pray it's so. And don't worry, tomorrow I'll meet Cerasi and give him exactly what he wants – brilliant pictures so that his name is remembered forever."

"Thank you." Vincenzo sighs with relief. I like the banker, I really do, and I'm sorry to torment him, but who can be polite in the face of the pope's idiocy? The man is making sure every single person in Rome hates him before he kicks the bucket.

I take my leave, promising Vincenzo a small painting of his own before I do. The man deserves some kind of payment for how much he's helped me despite my ill-humor.

I don't want to go home yet, so I walk around Piazza

Navona, head over to the Tiber, and without meaning to, find myself in front of Castel Sant'Angelo, looking over to St. Peter's great dome. The nave and façade are still unfinished, but the central part designed by Michelangelo, the dome flanked by chapels, stands magnificent in itself.

I walk closer, imagining that my painting already hangs inside, that crowds admire it, sing my praises. I just have to be patient. Vincenzo is right – that day will come. I can taste the certainty of it.

Skirting the work crews, I enter the cavernous interior. In a side chapel, the marble *Pieta* glows with an unearthly light. Michelangelo has carved the Virgin Mary cradling her dead son with so much tenderness, your heart aches to see it. You would swear the stone breathes. And there, in the band across Mary's chest, are the words "Michelangelo Buonarroti the Florentine made this." It's the only sculpture he signed. Everyone knows the story – how he overheard someone claiming the statue was the work of another artist and that very night, Michelangelo came back to secretly inscribe his name. He was criticized for making the Virgin so young, but Michelangelo was proud of his work. And rightly so. He knew that in twenty years, no one would remember the storm of insults. Instead they would see only pure genius.

"You're the better Michelangelo," I whisper. "For now."

XXXVI

Onorio Longhi
Personal Journal, March 1600

I can see from Michele's face the moment he enters the tavern that something's wrong. He has what Mario calls his "black look." When he's like that, it's better to say as little as possible since there's no predicting what will set him off.

Lionello elbows me. He sees it, too. "Not a word about Fillide and her new lover," he whispers.

I snort. Does the man take me for a complete idiot? Even on a good day, that's not something to mention to Michele.

"Buona sera, Michele!" we call out in a chorus. Mario offers a tankard of wine and we rearrange ourselves to make room for our moody friend.

"Maybe yes, maybe no," he says. He gulps the wine quickly. "Maybe good, maybe bad."

There's a nervous silence. No one dares to ask. Even silence isn't safe. Michele slams his tankard onto the table and glares at us.

"So?" he roars. "Don't you want to know what's good, what's bad? Don't you care why I'm in such a foul temper?"

"Of course we care," Mario soothes. "But when you're like this, there's no right thing to say — or not say. No matter what, you'll be furious with us."

"I'm sorry, Mario." We watch as the rage seeps out of Michele. Only Mario can talk to him that way. Only he knows how to calm Michele's furies.

"So what is it then?" Mario asks. "Another commission that isn't for St. Peter's?"

He's hit the mark. Michele's face sags with despair. "Yes!" he howls. "Yet another chapel that's supposed to make my name. I thought my name was already made!"

"Which church?" I ask.

"Does it matter?" he snaps. "It isn't St. Peter's!"

"Of course it does," I insist. "There are other important churches in Rome."

"Santa Maria del Popolo," Michele grumbles.

"That's a major church! In a major piazza!" I say. Lionello and Mario nod their agreement. "Not some backwater chapel in Trastevere."

It takes a lot of wine but we manage to convince Michele that the commission is a good thing, that he's being richly paid, and that d'Arpino will eat his heart out in envy. We even get through the night without any fights, but we're all exhausted. Tomorrow night, I'm staying home.

XXXVII

Girolamo Spampani

Deposition, 28 March 1600

It was Friday evening around eight o'clock and I was coming from the Academy where I study. I got to the street of the Pig and while I was knocking at the candle-seller's door to buy some candles, the aforesaid Caravaggio hit me with a stick and said various things to me. I defended myself as best I could, yelling, "Traitor, is this what you do?" Some people heard my screams and came with torches and then Caravaggio took his sword and slashed at my cloak and tore it as you can see here, and then he ran away.

XXXVIII

I paint like a fiend that spring, but before I can finish the two large pictures, Del Monte asks me to go back to the Contarelli chapel. We walk down the dim nave together and turn toward the dark corner where my altarpieces glow. Usually once a picture is done, after all the intense time breathing its colors and forms, it no longer feels a part of me. But these two are different. I still feel connected to them, like a mother with her newborn babe.

"Fine work," Del Monte murmurs. "Divine even."

"Yes," I smile proudly. "These are pictures I could have put my name on." Like everything I've painted, there's no signature. I've always felt my art comes from something bigger and deeper than myself, that I'm a servant to it rather than its master. A signature seems an act of empty hubris. But I admit to that vanity now. These paintings made my reputation for good reason.

"So fine in fact that the committee has decided that the sculpture originally intended for the central altarpiece would look weak next to your work. Only you can compete with yourself. They want you to paint it now, the Inspiration of St. Matthew. They'll pay even better than before, if you're willing."

"But I'm working on the Cerasi chapel. That's a big commission," I say, though I'm flattered by the request. And the committee is right. Nothing can stand up to my dramatic altarpieces except another Caravaggio.

"You're almost finished. Take a break and do this one painting. I ask you as a personal favor." Del Monte turns and faces the nave. "Remember this is my church, where I'll be buried. I want as many of your pictures here as possible."

How can I refuse the man who has given me so much? "But I'll finish the Cerasi work first. It won't be long."

And in fact it isn't, but before I can deliver the altarpieces, Cerasi up and dies. Which shouldn't be a problem, he approved the work as it was progressing, but Cardinal Giacomo Sannessio is now in charge of the project. He comes to see me in my studio, all pockmarked cheeks and double chins.

When he sees the large paintings, he practically drools. He tries to appear impassive, but the look of naked greed is so strong, he can't disguise it.

"Interesting work," he drawls in a nasal tone, stroking his thinning beard. "But not quite what the chapel committee expected."

"What do you mean?" I roar. "It's exactly what's expected! The Academy approved the sketches, Cerasi saw the earlier stages. Everything is just as it should be!"

Sannessio's eyes dart nervously around, avoiding my glare.

There's a knock on the door and Mario enters. He must have heard me bellowing.

"Is there a problem?" he asks.

"According to this fool, my altarpieces aren't fit for Santa Maria del Popolo!"

"Now, now, I never said that," Sannessio says, twisting his hands nervously. "I don't mean to offend, and there is a simple solution to this, one I'm sure you'll be happy with."

"I'm listening," I say through gritted teeth. If I don't calm myself down, I'll choke his fat, wobbly neck. It's one thing to brawl with other artists, another to touch a man of the cloth. Even in my rage, I recognize that.

"I myself would be happy to personally pay you for these two paintings, so there would be no loss to you. And then you could paint new ones for the chapel."

"Why would I do that when these meet the terms of the commission precisely?" I bark. What is this bastard's game?

Sannessio clears his throat. "I'll pay you more than the original commission, so there's no loss for you at all. And you'll still be paid the handsome price promised you when you paint the new altarpieces. It's a good solution for everyone. You end up making even more money. And the committee will be satisfied."

I narrow my eyes, studying the cardinal's expression. I know lust when I see it. The fat pig wants my altarpieces for himself! So much so, he'll snatch them from the committee he himself heads. It's not a question of the paintings not being good enough for the chapel. He thinks they're too good – and belong in his own private collection.

I look at Mario and see that he understands exactly the same thing. A smile hovers over his lips.

"That could work," Mario says. "But the inconvenience to Signore Caravaggio is great. He has other pressing commissions. I would think the payment would have to be substantially more than the original price."

Sannessio gulps. His fingers twitch greedily. He's like a fish, gulping at the bait.

"Would twenty-five percent more do?" he asks.

"I should think not! More like seventy-five percent." Mario is firm.

It's a ridiculously high price and Sannessio blanches. "Fifty percent?" he offers.

Mario looks at me. I give a slight nod.

"Done!" Mario says. To be paid in full upon delivery. Tomorrow."

"Yes, yes, of course," the cardinal stammers, wiping beads of sweat from his brow with a lacy kerchief.

After he leaves we break into fits of laughter.

"Did you see how terrified he was that you wouldn't agree to his price?" Mario howls.

"You tortured the beast! And all for sport! You know I don't care about gold," I gasp.

"The money was more to punish him than to please you. The arrogant beast stole a commission – from a holy church! And the man's a cardinal! Think of it as a sin tax, a price for greed and corruption."

"But now I have to paint new altarpieces." I shake my head. "There's only one thing to do."

"Yes?" asks Mario.

"The next two must be even more magnificent, so

powerful that the cardinal is devoured with envy." I love a challenge and this is one I'll definitely rise to. The new compositions will be simpler, more forceful, with strong diagonals reaching into and out of the pictures. I can already see them. I owe the cardinal a debt of gratitude. These replacement altarpieces may finally be the works that make me the better Michelangelo.

I'm itching to get started, but I promised Del Monte *The Inspiration of Saint Matthew* once I finished the Cerasi chapel. I'm a man of my word and that's what I'll work on next. The incident with Sannessio has emboldened me, given me permission to paint exactly what I want without worrying about the Academy's approval – or anyone else's for that matter.

"You've made a good profit for the day!" Mario interrupts my thoughts. "Let's celebrate! It's been a while since we wandered the streets and drank ourselves into a stupor."

"Fine," I agree. It's a soft spring day, too beautiful not to be outside in any case. We head for Lionello's house, over by the mausoleum of Augustus.

Mario throws some pebbles at his window and yells, "Come out and play, Lionello! It's spring and a young man's thoughts should turn to love!"

Lionello pokes his head out of the window. "Don't throw stones! My landlady yelled at me for a week last time you did that. Just give me a moment."

The door opens, but instead of Lionello, it's the signora.

"Are you the brutes who almost broke a window the other day?" She shakes a gnarled finger at us. "I'll call the sbirri on you if it happens again, I will!"

"Sorry, ma'am, it won't happen again." Mario puts on his most remorseful face. He looks like a young, dark-haired angel. The old hag can't resist him. Her scowl softens.

"That's all right, then," she says. "So long as we understand each other. A nice boy like you, making such mischief! Your mother should be taking better care of you. It looks like she barely feeds you."

Before she can invite us in and offer us a big bowl of stew – as she looks like she intends to do – Lionello leaps out from behind her.

"Let's go!" he says. And we're off, weaving back through the narrow streets to find Andrea and Nico.

"It's such a beautiful day, why don't we play tennis?" Lionello suggests.

"Or take a dip in the Tiber. It's probably not too cold now," offers Mario.

"Let's see what Andrea and Nico want to do."

We pause to drink at the fountain on the corner when a voice calls out, "Is that Caravaggio I see? The man with the small paintbrush? Or is it small talent? With him, it's hard to tell."

Mario grips my shoulder as I reach for my sword. "It's probably some idiot you brawled with in a tavern one night. Let it go," he says. "He's baiting you."

A rangy figure flanked by two thuggish men emerges from a shadowy doorway into the sunlit street. It's Ranuccio Tommassoni, his brother, and brother-in-law, the ugly trio I met at Fillide's.

"Do I know you?" I demand. What grudge could he have against me, except that we slept with the same courtesan, a common enough occurrence in Rome.

"You know Fillide and that's the same as knowing me," he growls.

"Funny, you don't look anything like her. None of her charms, that's for sure."

"You hurt her feelings, you know. She cared for you and you just dropped her." Ranuccio's jaw juts out angrily and I can see a vein throbbing in his throat.

"She cared for my money, you mean. I was a customer, nothing more or less." The sight of Ranuccio's rage calms me, strangely enough. I feel icy cold and firm. The man doesn't scare me, and for once I'm in control of my temper.

"You painted her. That's something more. She said it was!" Ranuccio clearly has it bad for Fillide. Lucky her, to have so loyal and devoted a pimp.

"And now I'm painting others. Surely she doesn't hold that against me?" I keep my tone light and even. No point in challenging a love-crazed fiend like Ranuccio. We all try to appear calm, no weapons drawn, no fists clenched. Ranuccio stands there gawking a moment, then slumps a bit, the fight drained out of him.

But he can't quite let us go like that. He has his pride to consider. "Don't try to see her, that's all. You're not welcome in her home anymore," he orders, like the big boss he wants to be.

"I understand," I say coolly. "I will miss her beauty. She is truly a gem."

And that bit of flattery does it. Ranuccio nods stiffly, gratified that his woman has been properly appreciated. He crosses back over the street, into his dark doorway, followed by his silent shadows.

"We need some wine!" Mario says cheerily. "Something

to get the bad taste of those goons out of our mouths."

"And women, too," adds Lionello. "Not Fillide, of course, but Rome is full of beauties."

And just as he says it, a slim girl crosses in front of us, carrying a bucket of water from the fountain. Her glossy black hair is pulled into a loose knot, her eyes wide and dark. She looks nothing like Anna, not a jot like Fillide, but my heart leaps at the sight of her.

"May I help you, signorina?" I ask, taking the heavy pail from her.

She lowers her eyes shyly. "Thank you," she murmurs.

"I'm Michelangelo Merisi da Caravaggio. And you are?"

"Maddalena Antogretti," she says, her cheeks turning pink.

"Maddalena. A lovely name for a lovely girl." I look back and see Mario rolling his eyes. I wave him away and he gets the hint. They can carouse without me. I have other plans now, plans that last for days.

I call her Lena, caressing her soft cheeks, the tender nape of her neck, the secret places of her body. She's shy, this naive country girl, still dazed by the hustle-bustle of Rome, and I'm touched by her innocence. She moves me as no woman ever has, though she's not as elegant or witty as Fillide, not as hungry for love as Anna. I can't say why I feel the way I do, but perhaps that's the essence of love, the mystery of it all.

Lena lives with her mother and her infant son in a cramped house near the mausoleum of Augustus where we first met. The signora works hard cleaning churches for pennies, but when she's home, she dotes on her daughter and grandson, and now on me as well, welcoming me into the family. It's a strange feeling, having dinner at their simple table, feasting on peasant dishes like beans and sausage while the signora fusses over us, making sure that everyone has enough to eat and drink. It's an odd sort of comfort, one that keeps me in those dark, small rooms instead of carousing in the streets as usual.

In this poor neighborhood I find the model I need for Matthew in *The Inspiration of Matthew*, the altarpiece for the Contarelli chapel. The butcher across the street has just the simplicity I want. I pose him with Giovanni, my usual angel model. My Matthew is a hardy peasant type, with dirty bare feet, the pen awkward in his hand as he writes down the Gospel whispered to him by the angel. I think of Bruno's philosophy as I paint, of the divine being in every man, of the blessedness of the ordinary.

Sometimes Lena watches as I paint, her eyes wide in wonder. "This is Saint Matthew?" she asks. "He's writing the Gospels?"

"Yes," I say. "Does it look like Saint Matthew?"

Lena squints at the canvas. "It looks like Fernando, the butcher. Shouldn't Matthew be more. . . in other pictures he's more. . .he looks like. . ." She can't finish the sentence, but I have a suspicion she means my Matthew is too much like the man next door, too much like a common peasant.

"The men who wrote the Gospels were just that – men. I'm showing Matthew as he may really have been, with filthy feet, work-roughened hands, coarse skin. Saints are ordinary people who do extraordinary things." I think of Beatrice Cenci, of Bruno, two martyrs from our time who looked like their countrymen, neither better nor worse.

"But that's not how they look in churches," Lena

protests. She starts to say something, then bites her lip.

"Go on, say it," I demand. "Don't coddle me."

"What if," she pauses, gathers up her courage and continues. "What if people don't want saints to look like them? What if they want their saints to be purer, better, more spiritual somehow?" She lowers her eyes, fearful of my reaction.

The anger surges up in me so suddenly I have to clench my fists to keep myself from hitting her.

"Are you saying I should pander to people's stupidities?" I roar. "I'm showing them how they can be better, that godliness is all around us if they'd only open their eyes! You want me to pretend like all those feeble artists who daub ceilings with fluffy pink clouds and sugar-paste angels?" I throw down the old painting I use as a palette, hurl my brushes after it, and stomp off.

When I return to the studio hours later, she's gone home, probably crying into her pillow. I have a bloody nose, a black eye and a big bruise on my shin from a well-placed kick. Raven whimpers beside me as Giovanni silently offers me a basin of water and a cloth to wash away the grime and blood of the evening.

"A waste of a night, eh Giovanni," I say as he pulls off my boots.

"Not so bad, sir," he grins up at me. "No arrests, at least. And that last brute in the tavern looks a lot worse than you. All in all, I'd call it a fine evening."

"A success, then," I agree. I fall back on the bed and let sleep take me.

I wake up with Lena's reproach still scorching my ears. What if people don't want their saints to be real? No, I refuse to cater to poor taste, to insipid choices. I'll show the people how they should think and feel and they'll follow me, convinced by the power of my brush.

I finish the painting and step back, trying to see it afresh, as if someone else had painted it. True, Matthew looks a bit clumsy, as if he's never held a book before. There's not much wisdom in his face, though he listens intently to the angel, concentrating on the Gospel he writes. He's more the recipient of the divine than its spark. I find it compelling, a vision of the mystery of how God speaks to us.

I present the altarpiece to the Cerasi committee, proud of what I've accomplished.

"This will go perfectly between the two pictures already in the chapel, *The Calling* and *The Martyrdom*. It's Matthew at his most human moment, his most vulnerable."

There's a silence. Too long, too awkward to be appreciation. Instead there's the tension of something unpleasant in the room that no one wants to notice, yet no one can ignore either.

The senior member of the committee, the oldest Cerasi cousin, clears his throat finally and says. "It's not what we had in mind. Matthew needs more dignity."

"And we can't have bare dirty feet right over the altar – it would be sacrilege!" another Cerasi relative objects.

"We're sorry, but we refuse this picture. We will be patient and wait for you to do another one. Something showing Matthew's intelligence and spirituality, if you please." The elder Cerasi snaps his turtle lips shut. There's no please about it at all.

"You don't really mean it," I insist. "Other collectors would love to own this painting!"

"Then sell it to them!" Old turtle-face scowls. "Either you paint us something that can be seen in a church or your future work will be hung only in private homes. I think we've made our meaning clear."

The three men take their leave, eager to get as far away from me as possible. Have I gone from being coveted to cursed in one painting? Have I ruined my chance for St. Peter's?

They're fools, all of them. I'll give them what they want, but this painting isn't a piece of smelly garbage. I'll find someone who will pay handsomely for it – maybe I'll sell it to Sannessio, that worm. No, he doesn't deserve it. This Matthew is brilliant and should have a worthy patron.

And I know exactly who.

XXXIX

Now I have three paintings to redo – the two for the Cerasi chapel and the one for the Contarelli. It seems like a bad omen that all the projects I'm working on now are replacements for altarpieces I've already done, but I refuse to think that I'm moving backward. The new paintings will be more daring, even more naturalistic than the earlier versions. I will not be censored and I will not be tamed!

But before I can face the blank canvases, I want to be paid for *The Inspiration of Saint Matthew*. I send Giovanni out early with a message for Vincenzo Giustiniani. Then I pace the length of my studio, thinking of how to recast the subject. What kind of saint will this new Matthew be? More dignified? If I make him older, that will pass for dignity. And this time I'll cloak him in a deep red cloth, give him a wiser face. But the bare feet are staying, and the room will be plain, poor even.

By the time Giovanni comes back with Giustiniani's

reply, I've blocked out the composition. Just in time too, since I need the boy to model for the angel, as usual. Raven dozes at my feet and the room is quiet except for the occasional bored sigh that escapes Giovanni's lips. I'm so intent that the hours fly by and the knock at the door startles me.

"Signore Giustiniani to see you, sir," a servant announces. He bows himself out, letting in the banker.

"Sorry to disturb you," Giustiniani says. "This is the appointed time, is it not?"

"Yes, yes, of course." I set down my brushes and palette, wave Giovanni away, and pull up two chairs. "I have a painting to offer you," I say.

"So your note said, and I'm naturally eager to see it."

I unveil the large *Inspiration of Saint Matthew* set on an easel in a corner of the studio, explaining the Contarelli committee's reaction and rejection. "I fear the painting is too daring for them," I finish. "But not for you."

Giustiniani smiles. "You flatter me, Michelangelo. I didn't think you had it in you."

"I'm only speaking the truth," I sputter. You know I lack the courtier's silver tongue."

"I'm not so sure about that. You're rough and crude when you want to be, elegant and clever when it serves you." He walks toward the painting, examining it. I try to read his expression, but I can't tell if he likes it or agrees with everyone else who's seen it so far.

"You know, all Rome is talking about this picture." He turns to face me, a smile hovering on his lips.

"How could that be? It isn't in the church."

"According to Baglione, the public knows enough to pronounce it terrible. He says it pleases nobody."

"The dog!" I bellow. "He's spinning rumor out of malice! The man is devoured by jealousy! How can no one like it when no one apart from the committee has seen it?"

"Perhaps he's assuming everyone will share the committee's displeasure." Giustiniani is clearly enjoying this. Why is he baiting me? He can't agree with Baglione, that sad excuse for an artist. He paints men as if they have no muscles. Instead eels writhe under their skin, directing their movement. Probably because Baglione is all hot air himself, no sinew or bone, gristle or guts.

"I'll smash his head in! I'll slit his throat! I'll tear his guts out and throw them to the dogs!"

Raven whimpers and cowers in a corner.

"Why bother?" Giustiniani asks mildly. "He's not worth thinking about twice. You're right – the man has no talent and he's certainly jealous. You know he tried to copy the painting you did for me, the Cupid, *Love Conquers All*. It's a disaster, of course."

"He what?" I don't know if I should be even angrier or burst out laughing. "He copied me?" Laughter wins out. I clutch my sides to catch my breath.

"Badly, at that." Giustiniani sighs. "You really should have some compassion for the poor man. He's a talentless hack with a big mouth. Let him talk. Who listens?"

"You heard him." I gesture toward the rejected *Matthew*. "Forget Baglione. What do you think of this painting?"

"You know I want it. And I'll pay you whatever the committee promised you. It will be the star of my collection. Until you paint me something else." Giustiniani looks at the canvas I've just started, the angel floating in the air over Matthew's shoulder. "This one is even more brilliant. It's inspiring to watch your genius grow, an honor to own any part of it."

"You're wondering why I'm not working on the commission you got for me, the Cerasi chapel." I realize too late that I should have explained about Sannessio. Now Giustiniani will think I don't value him as a patron.

"Oh, that." He shakes his head. "Everyone knows about that, too. Sannessio is too pleased about his 'confiscations' not to brag about them. The official story is that he had to take them into his own collection for the sake of the Church, but everyone knows better. You're the painter everyone wants. No one is more in demand than you. If the committee for the Contarelli chapel doesn't recognize that, they must live secluded lives indeed."

"Does that mean a commission for Saint Peter's will be coming soon?"

"Finish my chapel first! Then we'll discuss Saint Peter's. You're rich, famous, sought after, fought over. What more can you want?"

"Something in Saint Peter's! Something that carries my fame beyond Rome, beyond Italy, down through the generations. Something that proves I am more than the other Michelangelo."

Giustiniani leans down to pet Raven on his way out the door. "You are that already – you're Caravaggio."

XL

Del Monte's tailor is posing for the new *Saint Matthew*, but he can't hold the pose for long. Giovanni is a statue compared to him. I paint with a desperate urgency, and not just because of the old man's fidgetiness. I want to finish this piece and get on to the next one, and the one after that. I can feel my fame growing and I yearn to watch it burst through the dome of St. Peter's for all the world to see.

This time Lena approves of the picture. I don't know whether to take that as a good sign or not. Perhaps she's simply learned to compliment me, no matter what.

"It's beautiful, Michele, but won't you stop for supper now? It's late and you've worked so much today."

"In a bit," I promise. "As soon as I get the face down."

"This face is down already, sagging with exhaustion," the tailor snaps. "Enough for today, I beg you!"

"If you're going to grimace like that, I may as well

stop!"

Lena smiles, satisfied that I can finally pay some attention to her. When the tailor and Giovanni have gone, she pulls me down to the bed. "Perhaps not supper just yet," she whispers.

A knock interrupts us. The door opens and Mario rushes in, followed by Fillide.

Her elegant dress is dirty and torn. Is that blood on it? Her hair is disheveled, her eyes wild, her hands shaking.

"What the devil is going on?" I ask.

"I beg you, Michele, let me stay the night here. I'll leave in the morning." Fillide's voice is raspy, as worn as everything else about her.

"Mario, get her some wine so she can calm down and explain herself," I say.

"I'll go," Lena offers, eager to escape the awkward situation.

"Sit, Fillide, and tell me what happened." I urge her stiff, frightened body into a chair. Mario's face is almost as pale as hers. "Do you know what's going on?" I ask him.

He shakes his head. "Just that Fillide pounded on Del Monte's door, clutching a bloody knife."

"So that is blood on your clothes! Whose?" I demand.

Fillide bursts into sobs, holding her face in her hands. This isn't the pretty weeping she did when she was my lover. She's forgotten her arts.

"Fillide, you must calm down." I stroke her back, try to be tender, to keep my voice soothing. "Who did you stab? Was it that beast, Ranuccio? Did he try to harm you?"

At Ranuccio's name, her sobs get louder, more wrenching.

"It's that toad! I knew it!" I'm ready to knife him myself.

"No, Michele, no! You don't understand!" Fillide swallows her tears enough to say something. "I love Ranuccio. And he loves me."

"Of course he does. You, and all his other whores." Fillide glares at me, some of her old pride gleaming through her misery.

"Excuse me," I correct myself. "I mean courtesans."

With perfect timing Lena comes in with the wine and discretely leaves. After a healthy swallow, Fillide steadies her breathing.

"I went to Ranuccio's house to surprise him with a lover's tryst, only what did I find in his bed already? Prudenzia, that strumpet! He was making love to that fat cow!"

"What a pretty picture!" I can't help laughing. "A toad and a cow!"

"Stop it, Michele! Ranuccio's not a toad!"

"Why are you defending him? He betrayed you," I observe.

"It wasn't his fault! That pig threw herself at him."

"Oh ho, so now she's a pig! Choose your animal and settle on it, Fillide."

"Do you want to know what happened or not?"

I nod.

"Then listen! When I saw that pig, that cow, that witch with her arms around my Ranuccio, I grabbed his knife and stabbed her."

"Is she dead?" I can imagine Ranuccio being violent, but not a woman like Fillide. Maybe she's more like Judith than I suspected when I painted her beheading Holofernes.

"I don't know. She was moaning and Ranuccio was

trying to stop the bleeding when I ran away."

Mario's been silently absorbed this whole time. Now he says, "Will Ranuccio try to kill you?"

Fillide looks startled. "Why? He loves me!"

"You've damaged some valuable merchandise, maybe even destroyed it. Prudenzia is popular with her clients."

"She's filth!" Fillide smoothes her wild hair, sits up straight with some of her old dignity. "Ranuccio knows I'm worth a thousand Prudenzias. I've done him a favor really, cleaned out his stable."

"Let's hope he sees it that way or you're in big trouble." Mario says.

"For tonight you stay here," I offer. "Mario and I will go out and see what the people in the taverns are saying. If Ranuccio is out to get you, we'll find out. Then we can figure out what you should do in the morning."

"But Ranuccio loves me." Fillide's lower lip trembles and the tears threaten to gush all over again.

"Are you so sure of Ranuccio's love? You should know men better than that."

"You're right," she wails. "Why should he be different than anyone else? Than you, for example?" Her face crumples and her body shakes with sobs again.

"Let's go, Mario. We'll find out what's happening." The best way to fall out of love with a woman is to see her swollen-eyed and hysterical. I feel compassion for my old lover, but not an ounce of desire.

We start at the Tavern of the Moor, a favorite hole of Ranuccio and his friends. The smoke-clouded room is full when we enter, the buzz of dozens of conversations melting into a steady hum. I look for the pimp or any of his buddies, but don't see anyone.

"Let's at least have a drink before we go," Mario says. "I need one after listening to Fillide."

We squeeze through the crowds and find a free corner of a table. Ranuccio may not be here, but gossip about him certainly is. A man in the group next to us is describing Fillide as a jealous, crazed wretch who carved her rival's face into a hideous mask.

"Is she dead?" his friend asks.

"Not yet, but if she lives, she'll never work again, not unless the customer is blind!" There's laughter after that, lewd winks and gestures.

Mario knocks back his wine and gets up. "Come on, Michele. Let's try somewhere else."

"Why not stay awhile? We're hearing about it, aren't we? Maybe they'll say something about Ranuccio."

Mario glares but sits back down.

"Where is she now, that wench Fillide?" The gossip continues.

"No one knows, but when Ranuccio finds her, she may end up worse off than Prudenzia!"

Mario and I exchange a look. We were right. He's furious and bent on revenge.

"That's it! Let's go!" Mario jumps up. This time I follow him back through the crowd and out the door.

"Maybe we can change Ranuccio's mind, convince him there's no point in losing another whore."

"As if Ranuccio would listen to you!" Mario says. "He hates you! He might even think you put Fillide up to it."

"Why would I do that?"

"To get back at him. Everyone knows you detest

each other. We'd best stay clear of all this. All we can do is warn Fillide. She'll have to find a safe hiding place, and that's definitely not with us."

"We're not going home," I insist. "Back to Fillide? No, thank you! Besides we haven't drunk nearly enough yet."

That's something Mario agrees with. We walk past the Pantheon, head north to the Stuffed Pig. We're in Ranuccio's neighborhood so it's no surprise to see him coming out of the Bread and Circuses Tavern.

He sees us, too, plants his feet firmly, sets his fists on his hips, and bellows, "Ho, there, Michelangelo Merisi da Caravaggio! What news of your fair lover, Fillide?"

"We've heard the story everyone's talking about. Is Prudenzia dead?"

"Prudenzia lives, for now at least. I've left her in the hospital. As for Fillide, I should have known that any courtesan who would welcome your attentions wasn't the woman for me. I'm done with her."

"What does that mean?" I ask.

"Do you care? Are you still in love with her?" Ranuccio narrows his eyes, scouring my face for proof of my devotion. "If you are, that's double the reason for me to kill her."

"Michele's long done with Fillide," Mario interrupts. "He has a new lover. Why would he care about an old one?"

"Does he really? I haven't heard that from any of my whores."

"Because she isn't a prostitute!" I say. "She's no one you know, no one you've touched."

"If she's sleeping with you, that makes her a slut, even if she isn't one of mine."

The rage rises like a furious wave, ringing in my ears. I

pull out my sword and lunge forward. I'll finish the job Fillide started, stab the toad so he can join his bloody cow.

"No, Michele!" Mario grabs my arm, tries to pull me back. Ranuccio has his own sword in one hand, his dagger in the other.

"Let me go!" I yell. "I'll kill him!" I wrench myself free and swing the sword, aiming for the toad's ugly head.

Ranuccio ducks to the side. He's slow with drink but powerful and his sword strikes mine with such force my shoulder aches.

Metal clangs on metal as we parry back and forth. A crowd has gathered around us, but all I see is the glint of Ranuccio's sword, the blade of his dagger, and his jeering face.

"Stop in the name of the law!" a voice roars. Blasted sbirri! There are six of them, drawn by the cheering mob. Three pin back my arms and the other three set on Ranuccio.

"I'll get Del Monte's help!" Mario promises. But not until morning as usual, I bet.

Dragged by the sbirri to Tor di Nona with Ranuccio pulled along behind me, I swear every oath I know. Another night in prison, right when I have so much work to do. And I didn't even touch Ranuccio. If I'm going to jail, there should be more satisfaction in committing the crime.

The old wrinkled jailor welcomes me, grinning. "Been a while, Michele, a few weeks at least. Had me worried there."

"Very funny," I grumble. "Just lock me up and let me sleep."

"As you wish," he says, pushing open the thick door to my regular cell. "We keep this one empty just for you."

I lay down on the familiar wooden bench in the corner. I wish I'd had more to drink. Then sleeping would be easier.

As it is, the drafty chill seeps into my bones and the howling from some miserable wretch in a nearby cell keeps me awake most of the night.

In the cold, gray light of dawn, I'm led out into the street where Mario, Giovanni, and Raven wait for me.

"Where's Fillide?" I ask as we head home.

"Gone," says Mario. "She has some powerful noble who'll protect her. Strozzi, I think. She can stay with him until things simmer down. Or maybe even forever. The fool wants to marry her, even knowing she's a courtesan."

"Good for her. She deserves better than Ranuccio. Who's been freed as well, I'm guessing."

"Yes, he was let out last night. He has friends in high places, too, including the head jailor at Castel Sant'Angelo, his father's old position. There's no point fighting with him, Michele. You can't win."

"A sword isn't swayed by influence," I growl. "And mine is as sharp as his."

"I'm not saying he's a better man, just that he has patrons who protect him. As do you, of course."

"Are you painting today?" Giovanni pipes up. "Do you need me to model for you?"

"Yes, let's finish it up today if we can. Then I can start on the Cerasi altarpieces. I shouldn't be wasting nights in jail! If I'm the most-sought-after artist in Rome, what am I doing in Tor di Nona?"

Mario shrugs. "If you'd control your temper. . ."

"That beast was asking for it!" I bellow so loudly, my throat burns. I want to hit somebody, stab somebody, pound my fists into someone's chest. Mario and Giovanni hurry away, their eyes big with fear. Raven whimpers, his tail between his legs, cowed by my anger.

I stick my head under the jet of a fountain, letting the cool water drain the rage out of me. Raven licks my fingers, trying to calm me in his doggish way. I shake the water from my hair like a dog myself. It's not over between Ranuccio and me. Next time, I'll prove to him who's the better the man, and no one will stop me.

XLI

Ranuccio Tomassoni

Private Journal, 8 October 1600

No one makes a fool of a Tomassoni. We've fought for kings, princes, popes, dukes – and for ourselves. That pug-nosed painter with his stupid airs won't get the better of me. One day I'll find him alone on the street and I'll stab him in the blink of eye, leave him to die in the dirt like the dog he is.

XLII

Captain Pino, Officer of the Law

Deposition, 12 January 1601

Last night around 2:30, I was with my
officers doing the watch at Santo Ambrosio
al Corso when along came by the aforesaid
Michelangelo, carrying a sword and a dagger,
and I stopped him and asked if he had a permit
to carry weapons and he told me no, that he
had verbal authorization from the Governor of
Rome in place of the normal written permit,
so I arrested him and took him to prison, and
gave a description of what had happened.

XLIII

The new *St. Matthew* is a great success. Even Baglione can't say anything bad about it without looking like the ignorant, envy-ridden clown he is. Everybody who's anybody is after me now to paint their portrait. Which I do, in between working on *The Crucifixion of Saint Peter* and *The Conversion of Saint Paul*. For the Giustiniani brothers alone I do eight portraits. Suddenly my naturalism, my careful way of looking at my models, is a good thing, not in poor taste at all. Which gives me the courage to paint exactly what I want for the Cerasi chapel.

The composition for *The Crucifixion of Saint Peter* is very tight. The bare, dirty feet of the man pushing up the cross with his back are closest to the viewer. His rump and muscular legs drive the cross up at a diagonal, while two other men pull it up from above. Peter, nailed on the cross, twists and turns, his brow furrowed in pain and sorrow. Yet the picture isn't one of agony, but of purpose. Peter's faith sustains him, even in the cruelty of death. The light shines full on him, cloaking the executioners, and it's the light that infuses him with the meaning of his martyrdom. If people complain again about bare feet, I'll tell them they aren't looking where they should, at Peter, his acceptance of suffering, his sense of God's plan and his part in it.

Across from it, *The Conversion of Saint Paul* shows Paul accepting God. He lies flat on the ground, stunned by the divine light, his arms open and welcoming. Here too it's the light that tells the whole story. It gilds his face, penetrates his breast, is held in his flung-open hands. It's so bright, Paul closes his eyes – he remains blinded for three days after the miracle of his conversion. Behind him stands the horse he's fallen from, his servant holding the bridle, both oblivious to the presence of God. I'm particularly proud of the horse. Like the executioner in the facing painting of the crucifixion, he's turned so his powerful hindquarters fill the upper left half of the altarpiece. I think of when I was hurled to the ground, not by God, but by a kick from Baglione's horse. All I learned then was the truth about d'Arpino, his petty maliciousness. Paul sees God, the error of his ways, and the true path forward.

Michelangelo Buonarotti painted both of these scenes in the Sistine Chapel, but I don't fear the comparison. Let all Rome judge whose compositions are more powerful, whose light more blazing, whose darks more encompassing. Who is closer to the truth.

When Giustiniani sees how I've finished his commission, he's so pleased he sends over a dozen bottles of his best wine in thanks. "You've done it, Michelangelo," he says. "You've made Sanessio green with envy – how he wishes he could get his hands on these magnificent paintings, so much more forceful than your first versions! You'll have all Rome at your feet now."

"And a commission for Saint Peter's?" Mario asks. He knows my mind well.

"Just wait. It's coming, any day now, I'm sure." Giustiniani pours us each a glass of his fine wine and lifts his goblet high. "A toast! To Michelangelo Merisi da Caravaggio, the finest artist in Rome, whose fame spreads far and wide even as we speak."

Mario and I clink glasses with the banker. I've been in Rome now nearly nine years and my reputation is made. I've painted the same subjects as Michelangelo, shown myself his equal, if not better, but Saint Peter's still gnaws at me. I'll toast once I have a painting there. For now the wine, good though it is, tastes bitter.

We're in the studio, admiring the paintings I've started since finishing the altarpieces, when a servant knocks at my door. "Yes?" I ask, praying it's the pope who's already heard of the pictures' magnificence and wants something of his own.

"Someone to see you, signore," the boy says.

"Who is it?" I ask, still hopeful.

"He says he's your brother, a Jesuit priest, Giovan Battista Merisi."

"Your brother?" Mario asks.

"He's not my brother," I snap. "Tell him to go away. I don't know him."

"Why would he say he's your brother if he isn't?" Mario wonders.

"He's a fool, that's why. We share the same mother, that's all. I wasn't raised with him. He has the blood of that commoner, Merisi, my mother's husband. My father was Francesco Sforza, Duke of Milan." I walk to the window and watch as a short, stout man dressed in Jesuit black leaves the palazzo. He turns and looks up. For a moment our eyes lock, but there's no sign of recognition. Not from him and certainly not from me.

Giustiniani sets his glass down carefully. "You're Sforza's son? You've never said anything about this before."

"I have no proof. He died when I was twelve, before he could officially recognize me." The priest crosses the cobbled street and disappears into San Luigi dei Francesi. I wonder if he'll look at my paintings in the chapel there. But it's not him I want to see them – it's Sforza! I turn away from the window, trying to control the rage surging in my chest.

"I know Sforza would have welcomed me as his son if he'd lived longer! My weak-willed mother was too ashamed of birthing a bastard to admit anything to me. My grandmother knew the truth of the matter, though. She told me I was born eight months after my parents' hasty marriage. Besides, why else was I raised in the palazzo in Milan and not back in Caravaggio with my younger half-brother and half-sister?"

"Whatever your grandmother suspected, there's no way for your nobility to be recognized now. It will have to be enough that you know the truth – and we do, as well." Giustiniani finishes his wine and sets down his glass. "Let me think about this, see if there's anything your many admirers can do for you."

"They can get me a commission at Saint Peter's!" I growl.

"That will happen." Giustiniani smiles. "As for this other issue, we'll see."

In Del Monte's music room that night, the talk is all about the Cerasi chapel. Painters, musicians, philosophers, and several cardinals, along with the Giustiniani brothers are there.

"I agree it's brilliant," Cordier, the French sculptor says. He's never liked me or my work, so I take it as a measure of my new status that now even my enemies don't dare criticize my work. "But what about that horse? The most prominent thing in the painting is the rear end of a horse. Seems a bit crude, no? A little like sticking your thumb in the Church's eye."

"It's a horse, not a thumb," I retort. So I'm not above reproach after all, at least not to Cordier.

"But why so central, so beautifully painted? Are you saying the horse is divine, that it's God?" He's like a terrier with a bone, that man.

"No," I snap. "It's a horse. Standing in God's light."

"Standing in God's light! Well said, Michelangelo!" Del Monte cheers. "That's exactly what your art shows, how all of us are bathed in God's light, in His blessing, if we just open our eyes to it."

Toasts are made, praises heaped on my head, but it all rings hollow. I told Giustiniani about my true parentage, but it hasn't made an iota of difference. How can I be recognized for the nobleman I am? My brush is the only way to make my name.

It flits through my mind that once I'm rich and famous enough, I can marry into nobility, buy myself a title as so many bankers have. But that's not the kind of recognition I want. I want people to see me as I am, a genius of the highest rank, well-born and well-educated, not a brawling, crude but talented thug who's thrown into prison constantly. I refuse to be anything like Ranuccio and his friends.

Later that night, Onorio, Mario, and I are making the usual tavern rounds when who should we run into at the Green Mermaid but Baglione.

"What do you have to say about my art now, you bilious fool?" I demand. "Or has envy eaten away your tongue?"

Baglione puffs himself up like a rooster showing off for his hens. "Why would I be envious of such a meager talent as yours? Your altarpieces desecrate the churches they hang in! The Academy should condemn you with your giant horse's rear shoved in the public's face."

"Better to paint one than be one!"

Baglione sputters but he's too much of a coward to fight. He stomps out of the tavern, followed by his equally timid friends. I want to follow, to force him to fight, but Mario holds me back.

"You've done enough damage with your tongue," he says. "Besides, it's time to grow up, to stop brawling and spending nights in jail. You're the most famous painter in Rome!"

"Does that mean I can't have fun anymore? And I only fight when provoked."

"Except that everything provokes you," Mario observes.

"Oh, leave him be," says Onorio. "There's nothing wrong with the occasional tussle. And a night in Tor di Nona never harmed anyone."

"You would say that! You get away with fighting because you're noble."

"I've been arrested, too. I just get released sooner than Michele thanks to my good name." It's true, Onorio's temper is as bad as mine, but he's more clever at avoiding the sbirri and getting out of their clutches when they do catch him.

"Well, I for one am ready to settle down. You're thirty years old now, Michele. I'm twenty-seven. I'm going home to Sicily to marry the girl my father's chosen for me. Maybe there, I can make a name for myself as an artist."

"You're leaving Rome, Mario!" I can't believe it. To me, he's still a young dewy youth, not a husband, father, small-town painter of madonnas. "I can't believe you'd leave me."

"I can't make a name for myself here. The competition is far too good. I'm far too mediocre. You're the most famous painter in Rome. I'm the most obscure. And I'm almost thirty. I want a family, a wife to cook for me and bear my children."

'You'd leave Anna?" He's been far more loyal than I have, staying with her these past years.

"She's sick now, Michele. I fear she's dying. I've promised her I'll stay until her funeral. But I fear that won't be long." Now Mario really does look older, drawn and tired. When did he grow up? When did I?

"This talk is to sober for my taste! I thought we were going to have fun tonight." Onorio complains. At least he's not ready to grow up yet.

"It's late, I'm tired." Mario gets up from the table. "You stay if you want. I'm going home."

"I'll go with you," I offer. He's been loyal to me for so long I feel I owe him at least that.

"Well, I'm staying until they have to roll me out the door. Waiter, bring me another!" Onorio holds his glass high and gestures to the innkeeper across the crowded room.

We squeeze our way through sweaty, wine-ripened bodies into the cool night air.

"Do you really have to go, Mario?" I ask.

"I can't live in your shadow forever."

"Is that what you're doing?"

"Listen, Michele, I'll always be your friend, and if you're ever in Syracuse, you must come see me. But I need to do this. Please understand."

I put my arm around him and we walk like that in silence for a while. "I do understand," I say finally. "I'll miss you."

We're walking through the empty dark streets, just like we did in those early days, so long ago. I know the city so much better now than I did then. And the city knows me. I'm no longer a nobody.

We walk south toward the Forum. It's a route we've taken many times before, past the bakery, the cobbler, the fountain where water spouts from the keg held by a sculpted man. To the east, an ancient Roman victory column pierces the sky, to the west the Tiber River flows before looping around in a slow southeastern bend.

The streets are still and quiet, the stars bright overhead. So it's jolting to suddenly run into a dark figure walking towards us. For a second I think it's Ranuccio, and my hand flies to the hilt of my sword. But as the shadow comes closer, I realize the man is too tall and slender to be the toadish pimp. As he comes closer still, I recognize the thin-lipped face of Cesare d'Arpino. Rome, for all its crowds of people, really is a small town.

"Michele." He nods stiffly.

"Cavaliere." I nod back. "How nice to run into you. I haven't seen you since you tried to pass me off as one of your students."

"You did work in my studio!" d'Arpino sputters.

"I slaved away in your studio." I keep my hand on my sword and narrow my eyes. I couldn't fight Baglione, but I may get my chance with d'Arpino – even better! "I have an old score to settle with you."

"What are you talking about?'

"Don't you remember the trick you asked me to play on Baglione, the one that sent me to the hospital with cracked ribs? Where you left me to rot."

"Don't be ridiculous! I'm hardly responsible for every childish prank you chose to play."

"Even the ones you suggest to your gullible and faithful assistants?"

"You're hardly gullible or faithful, though I'm gratified you finally admit to being my assistant," d'Arpino sneers.

"That's it!" I yell, drawing my sword. "Fight like a man, you miserable cur!"

D'Arpino holds himself stern and tall, mustering as much dignity as he can. "I'm a Papal Knight. I won't deign to fight with someone of lower rank." He turns and walks away, slowly and ponderously, as if daring me to run my sword through his back. My fingers itch to do exactly that, but Mario is gripping my other arm.

"Let it go, Michele. He's not worth your spit."

"He's a knight, he's nobility, and I'm not!" The injustice eats at me. "I'll have my title if I have to marry it!"

"You know the truth of your birth. You've proven the nobility of your brush. Leave it at that," Mario advises.

"What's a Papal Knight anyway? How can I be named one?" My heart pounds wildly and I can feel the blood pulsing in my ears. I wave my sword, slashing the air since I can't stab my enemies.

"Get your commission for St. Peter's, do a magnificent job, and you'll be awarded your knighthood. Come, Michele, let's go home now. Nothing can dim your star."

I look up into the night sky, at the stars twinkling above us. Is that true, I wonder. Will my fame grow until nothing, nobody can touch me? I think of how the evening started, with all the praise for the Cerasi chapel. Maybe Mario is right. I just have to keep painting and let it all come to me.

XLIV

Michelangelo Merisi da Caravaggio

Deposition, 20 May 1602

I was taken the other night in the street della Ternita which leads to Piazza del Popolo. It was around ten at night and along with me were also taken Spaventa, Ottavian, and another whom I don't know, and they arrested me because they said that a stone had been thrown and I had heard it being thrown and I should tell them who had thrown it, but I didn't know.

When I heard the stones, I was talking with Menicuccia who was in the same street and the stones were thrown in front of us, and I believed they were being thrown at me and my companions. When I was arrested, the police asked me who had thrown the stones and I told them to look for themselves and I don't remember saying anything else to them. I didn't say the insults that the police now claim, and when they told me I was insolent, I didn't tell them to stick it in their ass, nor to lick my butt, nor any other such thing.

XLV

I paint *The Sacrifice of Isaac, The Kiss of Judas, Saint John the Baptist, Christ's Entombment, The Crowning of Thorns,* portrait after portrait, all for private commissions. I'm now making so much money, I move out of Del Monte's palazzo into my own rooms, closer to Lena. Mario is right – it's time to grow up, to live on my own, to be my own man.

But still, nothing from the pope.

Rumor has it that the Jesuits are looking for a painter to adorn the main chapel of their enormous church, Il Gesu. They want an impressive Resurrection of Christ. I haven't had a church commission in over a year, but I'm so sure I'll get this one that I start thinking about compositions, looking for models. Mario hasn't left Rome yet, as Anna languishes in her illness, so I ask him to find out what's going on.

He joins me for dinner at my new place, looking haggard and miserable.

"You look terrible. Has Anna taken a turn for the worse?"

"She's taken a turn alright. She thought she was ill with swamp fever, but she's not sick at all!"

"That's good news, Mario! She doesn't have to die to give you permission to leave the city. You can go whenever you want."

Mario clutches his face in his hands. "Good for her, she's not sick. Bad for me – she's pregnant!"

"She's pregnant?" I stare at my friend. "I'll admit that's not great, but why the desperation? Plenty of women, prostitutes or not, bear bastards." Look at me, I think. Look at Lena and her baby.

"And she insists I'm the father!" Mario wails.

I roll my eyes. "With all the men she's slept with, how could she possibly know?"

"She insists whatever herbs she uses protect her from her clients, but she doesn't always bother with them when she's with me."

"Then it's her fault. She knows how to protect herself and doesn't. How are you to blame for that?"

"It's my fault, too," Mario insists. "So now I have to marry her and give the baby a name. I'm Sicilian, remember – honor is everything."

"Well, you wanted to get married anyway, didn't you?"

"Not to a prostitute! My father will kill me, if my mother doesn't do it first."

"Lie to them. Say she's a tavern maid, a cook, a servant. She could be anything."

"I'm talking about my honor, and you tell me to lie!"

Nothing I say is right. I may as well keep my mouth

shut.

Mario sighs, lays his head on his arms, and looks utterly dejected. "There's nothing I can do. Nothing anyone can do."

Raven hears the misery in Mario's voice and licks his fingers, doing his doggy best to cheer up our friend. Mario strokes the dog's head absently, lost in his misery.

"I'm sorry about Anna, but did you hear about Il Gesu?" I ask, trying to change the subject without inflaming Mario more.

"Oh, that's more bad news," Mario lifts his head up wearily, shaking off Raven. "They've already chosen someone."

"Who could it be? I haven't heard a word!"

"You will," says Mario. "It'll be all over Rome tomorrow. It's Baglione."

"Not him!" I howl, banging the table in fury. "He's never had such a prestigious commission!"

"He does now," Mario says dryly. "And he's telling everyone."

Those penny-pinching Jesuits chose Baglione because they could get him cheap. Well, they'll get exactly what they've paid for – a worthless smear of color with no backbone, no power, nothing but simpering sentimentality. I'd like to track Baglione down right now and throttle him, but I can't leave Mario to his gloom. Tomorrow, I promise myself, I'll beat him up.

"Michele, I know what you're thinking," Mario says. "No more fights. No more prison. You promised me."

"But Mario, surely this time you can't blame me! I have to do something!"

"Just paint better than him. Isn't that enough?"

No, it isn't, but I have an idea. "What does Baglione's name sound like?" I ask.

"Baloney?" suggests Mario.

"That's good, yes, I can use that."

"Use it for what?"

"I'm not going to beat up Baglione but a few verses in his honor, or in the honor of Mr. Baloney, seem appropriate. Now what rhymes with Baloney?"

"Big phony!" Mario laughs.

This is working. I can cheer up Mario and get revenge on Baglione at the same time. It takes the rest of the evening but when we're done, we have a lovely poem to put up on Pasquino for all Rome to read. It goes like this:

"What ugly stink has escaped that ass, the painter Baloney?
What he calls art, I call phony.
He thinks he can paint when he only farts.
I call it rancid. He calls it art.
His masterpiece belongs in a ditch, not a church.
He brings no honor, but can only besmirch
The world with his vision of muddy crap.
We want art, he offers us pap.
His figures have muscles like macaroni.
And that's why he's called the painter Baloney."

I admit it's not a work of literary genius, but it gets the point across. I tell Giovanni to post it on Pasquino and give copies to Onorio, Lionello, Nico, and Andrea. By the end of the week people will be chanting it in taverns throughout the city.

It doesn't take that long. Three days later, I walk into an inn and what do I hear but my own verses sung back to me. They're even better coming from someone else. It cheers me so much I almost don't bother to go to Il Gesu, but I can't help myself. I have to see Baglione, needle him with a line or two to see if he's heard it as often as I have.

The church appears empty, but there are curtains sectioning off where Baglione must be working on his pathetic altarpiece. I poke my head in and am disappointed to find no one. Just messy blots of color, an attempt at Christ rising to heaven. To think I could have painted something great here and instead the idiots wanted this mediocrity!

I draw out my sword, tempted to slash the canvas, but I can hear Mario's voice urging me to behave. Instead I stab the curtains, pulling my sword through with a satisfying rip. Again and again, until there are only shreds of cloth hanging around the altar. That will have to be enough, at least until all Rome sings my verses.

Onorio loves them so much, he declaims them loudly in the middle of Piazza Navona, like a wandering preacher calling on passers-by to repent. He's added some lines himself about Baloney's face looking like a donkey's snout and his paintings looking like the other end of the donkey. Lionello added a couplet about how Baloney makes paintings the way a butcher makes sausage, by grinding scraps together and presenting them like a tasty dish. Even Giovanni has added a line or two about the rank stench coming out of Baloney's mouth and his paintbrush. I'm hoping others will follow suit and there will be an endless round of Baglione insults.

Mario comes to dinner again, in better spirits this time. He's almost his old cheerful self.

"So how are things with Anna? Better, it seems."

"She still pale and tired. Can't keep anything down, but her mother says she was the same way when she was big with Anna."

"And how are you? You look happier."

Mario shrugs. "This isn't how I planned my life, but it's not so bad. I do care for Anna. I'm not sure about love, but that doesn't really matter in a marriage."

"I'm not one to say. I can't imagine marrying anyone. My art comes first. Anyone else is a distant second."

"Even me?" Mario teases. "I thought your friends were important to you, much more important than your women."

"Of course! I can talk to you. Who can talk to a woman? Fillide was the most intelligent one I've known and look what happened to her."

"Are you saying Lena's not smart?"

"I shrug. "She may be, but I love her for her devotion, her kindness, the way she cares for me. It doesn't hurt that she's beautiful as well."

A knock at the door interrupts us and Giovanni comes in, looking pale and upset.

"What is it?" I ask.

"The sbirri," he says. "They're here to arrest you."

"What for? For once I haven't done anything!"

"Michele, you promised me," Mario pleads.

"And I kept my promise. This must be a mistake."

Four tough Roman police shove past Giovanni. "Which one of you is Michelangelo Merisi da Caravaggio?"

I stand up. "I am. What's the charge?"

"Libel," says the shortest man. "Against Giovanni Baglione."

"Libel?" I echo, disbelieving.

"He says you're responsible for the insulting poem that's all over the city, claims you're ruining his reputation."

"What reputation?" I snort.

Mario glares at me. "Don't say anything. I'll talk to Del Monte. We'll straighten this out."

Usually I'm freed after a night in my cell, but ten days later I'm still in Tor di Nona. Not alone, at least. Onorio and Lionello are keeping me company, also charged with libel.

"You shouldn't have shouted those verses so loudly in front of everyone," I complain to Onorio. "You have only yourself to blame for this."

"How did they know you were involved? You've been quiet and you're still here with us."

"That's because Baglione hates me and suspects me of every pebble that falls in his shoe."

The case actually goes to trial. Among the three of us, we've been arrested seventeen times: for brawls, fistfights, throwing stones at windows, carrying swords without a license (that's me and Lionello), public disturbances. But this is the first time any of us has gone to trial.

The judge questions me like this:

"Who do you consider a good painter?"

"Someone who paints well," I answer.

"I mean, give me the name of someone whose painting you admire."

That's a hard one for me, but I have to name someone. "Annibale Carracci is a fine artist. So is Mario Minitti." I add a few other names of men I like, whether or not they're skillful artists. I don't include Baglione.

"What is your opinion of Giovanni Baglione as an artist?"

"He has tried to imitate my style and has only managed to corrupt it. I don't consider him a successful artist." I keep my tone even and calm. But I'm not going to praise a hack like Baglione. After all, I'm under oath.

"Did you write these verses?" the judge persists.

"I may not admire Baglione's work. I may think him an inferior artist, but it's hardly worth my time to write poetry about him. Besides, I'm an artist, not a writer." I think I've managed to answer honestly without incriminating myself.

The judge tries several times to get me to admit to the verses, but I can truthfully say that no, the handwriting on the paper posted on Pasquino is not my own. No, I did not distribute them all over town. No, I never recited them in public.

I'm taken back to my cell while Onorio and Lionello are questioned. That night we compare notes. We've all said the same careful phrases, though Onorio had to admit to public declamations since there are witnesses to attest to that.

"So what?" Onorio snorts. "I'm not the only one singing those verses! Anyone who goes to a tavern has sung along. They can't arrest a third of the city. When did it become a crime to repeat a catchy tune you've heard?"

"It's Clement VIII. He knows he'll die soon and he's trying to clamp down on any hint of sin, the quicker to send himself to heaven," Lionello says.

"Insulting Baglione is hardly a sin! It's practically the duty of any right-minded citizen. We're protecting the honor of painting from his clumsy, insincere tripe." I lean back against the cold, dank wall. "The worst part of all this is knowing that Baglione's laughing at us. I bet he's saying plenty of poisonous things about me. He's the one committing libel!"

"I believe if it's spoken, it's slander." Onorio comments dryly. "It's only libel if it's written."

"Slander, libel, either way, he spouts nonsense as much as he paints it." I pace across our narrow cage. "We've got to get out of here! Onorio, I thought you had powerful protectors."

Onorio shrugs. "I thought you did."

"Jailor!" I roar at the door, hoping some sound will reach the old man's ears. "Jailor!"

"Why bother?" Lionello asks. "No one can hear you. No one cares." He slumps down on the floor. We're a pathetic lot. We've been here eleven days and already, we've reached our limit.

The door creaks open and the toothless old jailor pokes in his balding head. "You called for me?"

"What news?"

"When do we get out of here?"

"Is the trial over?" We all speak at once.

"Just a minute, now!" The jailor holds up his bony hands as if to press back our words. "The judge is still hearing testimony. I believe Signore Baglione himself speaks today."

"What if we're found guilty?" Onorio asks.

"The penalty for libel?" The old man strokes his chicken neck. "Could be the galleys. Could be exile. Could be ten years in here. Depends on the judge's mood."

"All that for words on a piece of paper?" I can't believe such harsh punishment for a silly poem. It seems completely disproportionate, especially when the poem is simply an honest portrait. Honest? That gives me an idea. "Doesn't libel mean spreading lies?" I ask.

"Yes, exactly." The old man's head bobs on his neck like a child's toy.

"Mind you, I'm not saying we wrote those verses – we

didn't. But that's hard to prove. It might be easier to prove that they're not libel."

"What do you mean?" Onorio asks.

"All we have to do is prove they're true! And since they are, that shouldn't be hard. We ask as many people as we know to testify that yes, Baglione is a horse's ass. We can start with d'Arpino!"

"Oho, Michele, that's good!" Onorio chortles.

"It's brilliant!" Lionello grins.

"Tell the judge we want to call our own witnesses!" I order the jailor.

"Hummmph," he grunts. "We'll see about that."

"Just tell him," I insist.

"I'll do that. Good day, gentleman." The door thuds shut behind him, but at least now the atmosphere in the cell isn't so bleak. There's a thin sliver of hope like a dash of color in the dull grayness of the prison. We spend the next couple of days compiling our list of who to call to testify to Baglione's incompetence and despicable nature.

On day fourteen of our imprisonment, when I'm ready to wring the jailor's neck for his evident failure to tell the judge our request, the door opens again at last.

"Did you talk to the judge?" I ask.

"Doesn't matter anymore," the jailor says. "You're all free to go."

"How? We haven't presented our evidence yet."

"The judge agrees with you, not about Baglione, but that there isn't enough proof to convict you. More important, Signore Philippe de Bethune has interceded on your behalf and pressed for your release."

"Bethune?" Onorio asks. "Do you know him, Michele?

I certainly don't."

"Yes, he's the French ambassador. I've met him at Del Monte's palazzo, but I've only painted something minor for him, a Danae receiving the shower of gold from Zeus. Hardly a reason for such a favor."

"Maybe he interceded on behalf of France, not for himself personally. Think about the Contarelli chapel. That's in San Luigi dei Francesi, the French church in Rome. Reason enough to help you, I should think."

"Are we going to stand around discussing this or get out of here?" Lionello grumbles.

"But you have to steer clear of Baglione," the jailor warns. "Not a peep out of any of you!"

"Don't worry about that," I say. "None of us has any desire to go near Baloney or his art."

"Don't you be calling him Baloney!" The jailor shakes his finger at me.

"Sorry, I meant Baglione. You can't arrest me for a slip of the tongue."

"Get out of here. I'm sick of the pack of you." The jailor shoos us out, down the familiar corridor, up the winding staircase, down another dank hallway, and finally, finally out into the light of a hot, summer Roman day.

XLVI

Mario Minniti
Personal Journal, August 1603

It seems like Michele is in prison for an eternity. I beg the cardinal to help him. I ask the Giustiniani brothers. I plead with everyone I can think of. They all say Michele will be released soon, no need to worry, yet another day passes and another and another.

Anna tries to comfort me. She calls me her prince, her darling, her sweet, kind husband. But I don't feel like any of those things. I'm a useless hack painter who can't help the man who matters most to him. So I spatter Baglione's windows with rotten vegetables, piss on his doorstep. And I do what Michele couldn't – I tie an old, moldering paintbrush to his horse's tail. Not that I'm braver than Michele, just wiser. I have Giovanni help me with this, distracting the brute with a palmful of oats. It's some satisfaction, but not enough. I can't rest easy until my friend is out of jail, back in the studio where he belongs.

XLVII

Ainolfo Bardi

Acts of the Prison, 25 September, 1603

I, brother Ainolfo Bardi Conti di Vernio promise and give my word to the illustrious Monsignor Governor of Rome that Michelangelo da Caravaggio, painter, will not offend nor make others offend either the life or the honor of Giovanni Baglioni, painter, or of Tomaso also known as Mau, painter, and if he does the opposite, I promise to punish the aforesaid Michelangelo as is done with those who break their word, and as a token of my faith I have signed this document with my own hand.

XLVIII

The night after I get out of prison, Mario comes pounding on my door, wild-eyed and frantic.

"Come quickly, Michele, Anna's had a seizure! I don't know what to do!"

I rush out behind him, Raven at my heels. "Have you called a midwife?"

"She's there already. She says this often happens. A woman's blood beats wildly, there's vomiting, and then seizures."

"And then?" I dread the answer.

"Then Anna could die!" Mario wails.

I haven't seen Anna since her belly started to swell, but seeing her now is like looking at a corpse. Her body is bloated, her skin pale, blue shadows sink under her eyes. Her mother wipes the beads of sweat off Anna's forehead, while an older woman who must be the midwife puts an ear to her belly.

She looks up and shakes her head.

"Save her!" Mario pleads. The anguish in his voice is wrenching.

"There's nothing to be done," the midwife pronounces.

"My dear one!" Mario kisses Anna's cheeks, strokes her hand. "Come back to me, we'll get married tomorrow, I promise."

Anna's mother locks eyes with me. "Take him away. This is woman's work."

I nod and put my arm around Mario, lift his grieving body up, away from his lover.

"Is she dead?" he asks me, tears streaming down his face.

I look back at the midwife, at the signora.

"Any minute now," the midwife says.

"Then I can't leave her!" Mario wails.

"Hush, Mario," I soothe. "There's nothing we can do here. Anna can't hear you."

"Yes, she can, she knows I'm here." He tears himself from me and throws himself on the still body.

"I'm sorry," I mumble to the signora. "He loves her."

"Enough to kill her," she snaps.

"Noooo!" Mario howls. "I would never kill her! I love her!"

I stand there awkwardly, feeling the midwife's eyes drill into my chest. I'm the enemy simply by virtue of being a man. Mario's loud sobs echo in the small bedroom until he cries himself out. Then a leaden quiet fills the air.

"She's gone now." The midwife straightens up and makes the sign of the cross.

"Mario, we should go. Come with me." I try to heave him up while Raven licks the salty tears off his face. "I'll take care of the funeral arrangements," I say to the signora, unable to meet her eyes. "No expense will be spared." It's a feeble offering, I know, but all I have to give.

I half-carry Mario home and put him to bed, but I can't sleep. I think of how much he loved her and how he has nothing of her now, just his memories. I can't get the image of her swollen, pale body out of my mind, how innocent she looked, alone in her suffering.

So I go to my studio and start to paint, all of it, every detail I remember of Anna on her deathbed. I don't stop until the thin morning light flows in through the tall windows. Then I collapse in a chair and allow my heavy eyes to close.

When Mario shakes me awake, the room is awash in the bright light of afternoon.

"Mario, how are you?" I ask.

He shakes his head sadly. "All I can think of is Anna."

I take both of Mario's hands into my own. "She was a truly good soul. She'll have a decent burial. In a church, as she deserves."

"Then I want her in Santa Maria del Popolo, as close to your paintings as possible. You know, she loved them, Michele, especially the *Saint Paul*. She felt you understood ordinary people and welcomed them into sacred scenes." Mario sighs. "Your painting her was the best thing that ever happened to her. She felt beautiful – and important."

"She was both of those things. And blessed as well. I'll put her in one more painting, I'm just not sure what."

"But she can't model for you anymore."

I gesture to the canvas on the other side of the room.

"She already has."

Mario stares at the picture. Tears pour down his face, but he looks happy.

"She would be honored. Thank you, Michele."

We spend the rest of the day arranging the burial. The signora agrees to Santa Maria del Popolo. She doesn't care, so long as her daughter lies in holy ground. I talk to Giustiniani and make sure there are no problems. I even arrange for a funeral Mass.

Onorio left town after being released from prison, determined to get far away from Baglione for a while, but Lionello, Nico, Andrea, and our old friend Prosperino, all help me get Mario into a new set of clothes, his hair neatly trimmed by a barber, prepared for his role as mourner. When there is nothing else to do, the grief sets in, swallowing us all in Mario's misery.

"We should go out drinking," Lionello suggests.

"No," says Mario. "You go without me."

"But Mario, you're the one who needs cheering up," Nico says.

"I can't, not yet." He looks up with red-rimmed eyes. "Just leave me alone."

"You all go," I offer. "I'll stay with Mario. No sense in all of us moping."

After they've gone, I take out a deck of cards, hoping to interest Mario in a game. But all he wants to do is sit and stare at the floor.

"What will you do now?" I ask gently. "Will you go back to Sicily?"

He nods.

"I'll miss you, Mario, more than you can know."

He nods again. "I do know. And I'll miss you, too. But I have to go. My father wants me to marry the woman he chose. And now there's no reason not to."

"I understand."

We sit like that together, not saying much. It's nothing really, but it feels like everything, just being there with him.

After the burial, he packs his bag and leaves, getting a ride with one of Giustiniani's couriers. I think of how young and sweet he looked when I first met him, a boy of fifteen. I thought he wasn't very bright then, but I've learned how wrong I was. Now he's in his twenties, a young man with a face molded by suffering, as loyal and big a heart as I'll ever meet.

I walk around the streets with Raven, feeling how empty the crowded city feels with just one less person in it.

XLIX

In the midst of that emptiness, I get a Church commission, a big altarpiece for Santa Maria della Scala in the Trastevere neighborhood on the other side of the Tiber. They want a Death of the Virgin and I know who I want to pose for the Virgin – Anna. I take the painting I did of her the night she died and use it as the basis of my composition. I pour all of our grief into the faces of the saints around her.

It feels like a second funeral, doing this painting. And a kind of blessing. I wish Mario could see it, could know how I've captured his Anna. She'll live forever in this picture, her face calm in death while the mourners' are furrowed in anguished sorrow. The light touches her face and hands with a gentle radiance. She is bathed in its holiness. And she is at peace.

I write to Mario, tell him next time he comes to Rome, he must go to Santa Maria della Scala and see his Anna again.

The picture is attracting a lot of attention. Del Monte tells me that some famous Flemish painter, Peter Paul Rubens, has seen it and wants to buy it for his patron, the Duke of Mantua. I tell him it already has an owner, one who paid well for it.

Not all the voices are complimentary. Baglione spreads his usual poison, telling everyone that I committed sacrilege by using a prostitute as a model for the Virgin. I wish I could have him arrested for slander. Worse yet, I have to face the growing storm of criticism alone. No Mario, no Onorio. True, there's still Prosperino, Lionello, Nico, and Andrea, but they aren't my closest friends. They're little more than drinking buddies.

I do have Lena, but she's hurt that I painted Anna again when I haven't used her yet as a model. The only one who doesn't criticize, nag, or borrow money is Raven. His favorite place is by my feet. Sometimes I stumble on him as I paint, but that doesn't deter him from staying as close as he can, like a second shadow.

Now, he licks my fingers and looks up at me, eager to please. Across the room, lying on my bed, Lena looks nowhere near as grateful.

"I thought you loved me, Michele. You say I'm beautiful, but you don't paint me."

"Lena, cara, you have no reason to be jealous of Anna. And I will paint you, I promise."

There's a knock on my studio door, and Giovanni pokes his head in.

"Vincenzo Giustiniani has sent for you, signore."

I settle my hat on my head and fling my cloak over my shoulder. "I have to go, Lena."

She grabs my arm. "If he asks for an altarpiece, you

will paint me, right?"

"Didn't I already promise you?" I keep my voice gentle, control my temper. Maybe Mario's right, I'm growing up, calming down. Or Raven is keeping me steady. I snap my fingers and he heaves himself up from the floor, ready to follow me.

At Giustiniani's, I'm shown into the study where my paintings hang and am offered the usual wine.

"Thank you for coming." Giustiniani gestures for me to take a sip.

"Of course, always a pleasure to see you." I savor the wine, wait to hear what the banker has to say.

"This is a bit awkward and I want you to hear me out before you get angry."

"Get angry? Why should that happen?" I drink more wine. Now I worry I may need it.

"It's about *The Death of the Virgin*. It's an impressive painting, an undisputed masterpiece, a work of absolute genius." There's a pause and I'm sure I won't like what comes next.

"But the priests feel that it has to be taken down. There are too many rumors that the Virgin was modeled on an actual dead prostitute. Which the Church, of course, would consider sacrilege."

I seethe silently. Now is not the time to rant. I need to wait and see what comes next out of his mouth before I explode. Raven, lying at my feet, senses something's wrong. He snuffles my heels, licks my boots, tells me I'm loved, at least by him.

"I've already found several buyers. There's no shortage of people willing to pay a generous price for it. So your honor is saved. And the priests actually make a profit on selling it. I just wanted to tell you before you heard it on the streets. Or from that vile Baglione."

I nod, teeth clamped shut. So now I have to paint a replacement. That will make the fourth altarpiece that's been rejected – or confiscated in the case of the first two Cerasi pictures – and had to be redone. This isn't the kind of reputation I want.

"I suppose you might be worried about doing another altarpiece for the church." Giustiniani searches my face. "Are you? You're very quiet. What are you thinking?"

"It's a brilliant painting, but I'm sure the second one will be even better. I seem to work that way." I pet Raven, trying to calm myself with his good-natured loyalty.

"Well, that's the thing." His tone is off, weaselly almost, not the forthright man I know. "They don't want you to paint a replacement." Before I can bellow like a bull, he rushes on, the words tumbling out in a desperate torrent to calm me. "They aren't asking you to take the picture back. They bought it; they'll sell it. But they want someone less controversial to take on the commission."

"What!" I can't contain myself any longer. "They're turning me away? Me, the most sought-after painter in Rome?"

"It doesn't matter, Michele, really. It's a provincial little church in Trastevere. Who bothers to go there? I've found you something much better, a commission for a church in the heart of Rome, close to here in fact, right between Piazza Navona and the Pantheon. Sant'Agostino."

It's not Saint Peter's, so what do I care. "How do I know what I paint won't be rejected again? I won't have that happen to me again – never!"

"No, it won't, I assure you. This committee chose you because they want your style of honest painting. They want your dramatic darks and lights, your forceful compositions, your powerful sense of ordinary people."

I want to reject the commission as I've been rejected. I want to say no to everything until Saint Peter's begs me for something. I clench my fists, trembling with rage.

"Please consider it. As a favor to me."

I nod stiffly and get up. Raven scrambles to his feet, sticking his wet nose in my palm. If I open my mouth, I'll spew curses everywhere, so I take my leave without a word, seething until I'm out on the street and can pound my fists on the stone wall of the palazzo. Raven whines at my heels, scared by my outburst. Giovanni looks just as terrified, though both of them should be used to my temper by now.

"Let's go!" I roar at Giovanni. "To Lionello's!" I need someone to drink with, someone to fight with me, someone to help clear the rising blackness away.

I wake up the next afternoon with no memory of what happened the previous night, but my knuckles are scraped and my entire body aches. I wish Mario were with me, to help me see myself more clearly. The only time I feel truly myself is when I'm painting. So whether I like it or not, whether it hurts my pride or doesn't, I take the commission Giustiniani offers. And I keep my promise to Lena. I paint her and her son as the Virgin and Christ child welcoming pilgrims to the shrine of the Virgin's house.

This time there are no ugly rumors, no sniping. Except the usual garbage from Baglione who sniffs that the praying peasants on their knees before the holy couple stick their dirty bare feet into the viewer's face.

Despite Baglione, maybe because of Baglione, the altarpiece is an immediate success, especially among the poor. The city has been flooded by pilgrims and in response, Pope Clement has ordered them to be declared vagabonds and chased away. Any poor person who stays in the city without a home for more than ten days can be sentenced to three years in the galleys. The papal ships need a constant source of manpower and the poor are favorites, so much more docile than convicted criminals.

For the pilgrims, my painting is a welcome contrast to the pope's iron fist. They see an ordinary old man and woman, people like themselves, kneeling before the Virgin and Child, part of the same world, close to divinity, blessed by it.

Lena is especially touched by the painting, not just because she's in it, but because of the old peasants.

"You've made them holy, too, Michele. Devotion glows from their worn, wrinkled faces, like an inner blessing."

"So you don't see them as undesirables, to be shooed out of the city?"

"Of course not! That's what happened to my fiancé. Before we could go to the church for our vows, he was sentenced to the galleys for poverty. Being poor is terrible, but it shouldn't be a crime!"

"You'd told me your intended had died," I say.

"Aren't the galleys the same as a death sentence?" Lena's eyes spark with anger. "He'd done nothing wrong except sleep on the street one night too many."

"Clement has a lot of crimes on his soul and as he gets closer to death, he seems to sink even deeper into sin."

"Hush!" Lena looks around the room as if the walls are listening to us.

"I can't criticize a bad pope?"

"No! You have to be careful! Spies for the Inquisition are everywhere and even if what you say isn't heresy, it could mean the end of Church commissions."

She's right. Now that someone from the Church has to "license" every altarpiece, artists must pass a censorship test before setting brush to canvas. I still don't do sketches, so I submit my underpainting, the early stages where I block out the composition.

"Don't worry – the cardinal who approved the altarpiece loves my work. He was practically drooling over the *St. Jerome* in the corner there. If it weren't already sold, he would have paid twice the original offer. We had a nice chat about painting and the role art can play in people's spiritual lives. He struck me as a thoroughly sensible fellow."

"Which cardinal is that?"

"Camillo Borghese. If he were pope, I'd have something in Saint Peter's tomorrow."

"Well, Clement can't live forever. Maybe your Borghese will be the next pope."

I shake my head. "There are a lot of contenders for that position. The French and Spanish factions are already lining up candidates. I'd stake money it'll be a Medici, someone favoring the French."

Lena knows nothing about the French or the Spanish. Papal politics are a mystery to her – or a complete bore – but she sweetly tries to take an interest since she knows these are the kinds of things that make or break an artist's career. The papal court creates fame and erases it with an arbitrary judgment that can drive a true man of talent crazy.

Better to make your name the way I've done – purely

through the work I've created. There are always men of discernment who will recognize that kind of worth, the Del Montes, Giustinianis, Borgheses of the city.

L

Lionello

Personal Letter, May 1605

First Onorio leaves, then Mario. It's not the same with just me, Prosperino, and Michele. Andrea and Nico have always been mostly silent, a few jokes now and then, but you can't depend on them to make an evening lively, so I don't count them at all. And now that Mario's gone, there's no one to calm Michele's temper. He's always at a boil, that one.

To be honest, I'm thinking maybe it's time for me to go as well. Onorio says he can find me work in Genoa or Milan, up north where the Church doesn't hound you. If he's not coming back to Rome, maybe that's a sign that I should go, too. Then I wouldn't have to hear Michele whine any more about his blasted Saint Peter's commission, the one he doesn't have. That would be a blessing right there.

LI

Salvatore Gualante, Officer of the Law Deposition, Arrest for Injury to Police, 28 May 1605

It was ten o'clock at night and my men and I were in the Piazza del Popolo when we saw Michelangelo da Caravaggio carrying a sword and dagger. I asked him if he had a permit and he said yes and showed it to me, so I let him go on his way and said to him, "Good night, sir," and he responded, "In your ass." I told him that was no way to speak to an officer and I tied his hands and brought him to the prison, Tor di Nona.

LII

Lena's mother comes into my rooms, flustered and gasping for breath as if she's run the whole way.

"What is it, signora? Is something the matter with Lena?"

"No, nothing like that," she says, wringing her hands. "It's the notary, Mariano Pasqualone. He's been sweet on Lena for months and keeps badgering her to marry him, but she wants none of him. You know she's faithful to you, signore."

"Of course," I say, ushering the round little woman into a chair and pouring some wine to calm her. "Lena's mentioned this fellow and his unwanted attentions. She even pointed him out to me one evening when we were walking along the Tiber. He seemed a harmless enough sort, spineless and pinched like a priest."

"But he's saying worrisome things now," blusters the signora. "He's insists that posing for you is ruining Lena's reputation, that no one will want to marry her." She looks at me with her bleary eyes moist with anxiety. "Is this true? Is being a painter's model the same as being a prostitute?"

"Pasqualone is an ignorant fool and a manipulative brute who's trying to push Lena into his bed." I pick up my sword and slide it into the sheath on my belt. "Don't worry about him. I'll teach him to take art seriously."

I slam the door behind me and head toward Lena's small house. The notary lives on the same street so he shouldn't be hard to find. It's a soft spring night, the breeze light and gentle on my face. Smells of meat roasting, garlic simmering, and tomatoes braising fill the streets. The whole city is cooking supper. It's the quiet hour before drinking and brawling usually start. I should be home myself with Giovanni and Raven, enjoying a superb meal whipped up by the cook I hired several months ago. Instead, I stride through the streets, stomach growling from the rich aromas of other people's kitchens. I find the notary's house – at least there's a notary's insignia in the window advertising his services – and pound on the door.

A rabbit-faced woman opens the door. "Yes?" she squeaks.

"Is Signore Pasqualone in?" I ask, my right hand gripping the hilt of my sword.

"I'm afraid not. Do you want to come back later or wait for the master?" The woman's nose twitches nervously. She obviously doesn't welcome the idea of me staying.

"Can you tell me where he is?"

"He went out for supper, to the Spotted Cow in Piazza Navona. I'm sure you can find him there." Before I can say anything else, she closes the door. I can hear it latch on the other side. Do I look that threatening? I hope so! I want to terrify Pasqualone just with the sight of me.

I hurry off to Piazza Navona and start across the big, open oval towards the Spotted Cow. A man walks in front of me, hunched over and narrow-shouldered like a bookkeeper. Or a notary! Yes, it's him. Even from the back, I recognize the man Lena pointed out to me that day along the Tiber.

I sneak up behind him, take out my sword and hit him on the back of the head with the flat of the blade. The blow is so forceful, he falls down, an "oof!" of surprise and pain escaping his lips. The sword trembles in my hand, the tip of it drawn to the prone man's back. I could end the matter right now, run him through with the sharp blade. I breathe loudly, savoring the rage surging through me, the strength of my arm, the force of my intention.

If Pasqualone had moved, if he'd tried to fight, I'd have killed him for sure. But he lies there, stunned, maybe even unconscious. I can hear Mario's voice whispering in my ear, "Leave, Michele, before you're caught. Get out while you can."

I look around, but no one is watching. There's been no noise to alarm anyone, nothing unusual about the night.

Mario's right. The notary's been punished. That's enough. I put away my sword and leave him there in the dirt. Maybe someone else will rob him, strangle him, toss him in the Tiber. That's not my concern. Now it's time to go home to a hot meal.

The next day Lena comes running to me in tears, terrified that Pasqualone will accuse me of assault. "He says he knows you're the one who attacked him. He's pressing charges and he has friends in the Inquisition. You have to get out of Rome for a while, Michele, please!"

LIII

Mariano Pasqualone di Accumoli,
Notary to the Governor, Denunciation,
Acts of the Police, 29 May, 1605

I am here at the office because I was attacked by Michelangelo da Caravaggio, painter, in the manner which I will describe to your honor. The Signor Galeazzo and I were strolling in Piazza Navona around two hours after sunset, in front of the Spanish Embassy when I felt a blow to my head from behind, and I fell to the ground, wounded, I believe, by the flat of a sword. As your honor can see I am wounded in my head. Although I couldn't see who had attacked me, it could only be Michelangelo, because that evening we had exchanged words on via del Corso because of a woman named Lena, who is Michelangelo's woman.

LIV

I'm not the type to run from trouble, but I've been meaning to visit Onorio, hiding out himself in Genoa. Why not visit an old friend now? I tell Lena that's what I'm doing, but before I go, I send notes to Del Monte and Giustiniani stating the truth of the matter. If I'm facing charges, I want them to tell me about it.

Giovanni and Raven come with me in the carriage I hire. I walked into Rome twelve years ago in weathered boots and worn-out clothes. I leave in rich silks and velvets, with gold in my purse, an elegant sword at my side, driven in style like a lord. I may not have a title, but I can live like a wealthy man. And no one will treat me like a common criminal.

Onorio is thrilled to see me when we get to Genoa and we spend the next few days swapping stories, getting drunk, and playing cards.

"Are you coming back to Rome?" I ask over a savory

fish supper. "What keeps you away?"

"I'm still worried about trouble over the libel case. When I'm sure I won't be arrested again, then I'll go back."

"Weren't we cleared?" I reach for a bowl of ripe berries and help myself to a handful.

"You were, thanks to the French ambassador. I'm not so sure about me. I've been writing to men with influence on the papal court, and something will be worked out. I'm just waiting to hear."

While Onorio waits for some kind of assurance, Del Monte writes me that with the help of Cardinal Camillo Borghese, the notary's charges have all been dropped. I'm free to come back to Rome whenever I want. And he mentions in a postscript that Onorio has also been cleared.

Onorio claps his hands when I tell him the news. "Bravo, Michele! It takes you getting in trouble for me to get out of it! I suppose I was too much of a small fry to bother interceding for, but you are another matter entirely!"

"Oh, is that how you see it?" I arch a skeptical eyebrow.

"Obviously. You're a big fish, someone they all want back in Rome to paint for them. I'm a minnow, not worth their bother at all. But while they're fixing things up for you, oh by the way, let's pardon another man, a friend of Michele's. I'm sure that's exactly what they thought!"

"We'll have to ask Del Monte when we next see him. In a couple of days?"

"Yes!" Onorio jumps up from the chair he's been sitting in. "I'll start packing at once. Tomorrow we leave for Rome!"

The time in Genoa has been short, but long enough that while we're on the road between one place and another, everything shifts. We get the news as we enter the city gates and hear all the church bells in the city tolling.

Pope Clement VIII is dead and a new pope must be chosen.

Onorio and I exchange a look. You'd think all Rome would be celebrating. By the time he died, everyone hated the old buzzard. Instead the city is tense and edgy, waiting to erupt into fights between Spanish and French factions.

"Stay at home for a few days," Onorio warns me. "Don't get into trouble now."

"This isn't my fight," I say. "I'll leave it to those who care who wears Saint Peter's ring. It's all the same to me." I get out of the carriage, followed by Giovanni and Raven. The dog is so happy to be on this familiar street in front of his favorite house that he scratches at the door in excitement.

"That's right, Raven. We're home now." I try to open the door but the lock is jammed and my key won't turn. A head pokes out of an upper window, my landlady.

"You!" she shrieks. "You haven't paid rent for the past month and no one's answered for days! That's why I've locked you out!"

"You old witch! A few weeks late and you treat me like this? If you wanted your filthy money, all you had to do is ask!"

"All you had to do was pay!" she spits back.

I grab some stones on the ground and start pelting them at her ugly face.

"I'll call the sbirri!" she screams as she ducks back in and slams the window shut. I keep throwing stones until Onorio grabs my arm.

"I told you this isn't the time to get into trouble. Come

stay with me until this is settled."

So back we go into the carriage. I'm once more Onorio's guest, this time in his family's Roman palazzo. The place is full of people, his mother, sisters, aunts, uncles, cousins, friends, business associates all gossiping about who the new pope will be. There's no corner free of the constant chatter.

"Maybe I should stay with Lena," I suggest.

"Definitely not! She may have married that notary while you were gone. Send Giovanni to speak to her first, see what's happening. In the meanwhile you're welcome here for as long as you want."

"But I don't want to be here!" I pound my fist on the table. "I want to be home!"

"It's here or Del Monte's. Or maybe Giustiniani's, at least until things get sorted out. If you had your own palazzo, you wouldn't have these problems. You're the highest-paid artist in Rome, you could live as grandly as d'Arpino, but you choose to rent cramped, fetid rooms like a beggar."

"I don't need froufrou fa-la-la stuff all around me. And the last thing I want is the noisy buzz of dozens of assistants. All I need is a room to paint in, a place to sleep, and a decent cook."

"If I had your money, I'd want much more than that! If you can put up with that hole you call home, why is my place so terrible?" Onorio puts on an exaggerated pout.

"It's not exactly peaceful with all the people here now. And where can I paint?"

"It's no more quiet at Del Monte's. The place must be jammed with Medici cousins and nephews and followers and toadies, all pushing for a Medici pope."

"You're probably right." I slump down in my chair.

"Let's hope a new pope is chosen soon. Rome won't be normal until then."

"Some things will stay the same – there are plenty of inns and taverns eager for customers. Come on, I haven't been in the city for months! Let's round up the usual crowd and go drinking."

I'd rather paint, but since there's no chance of that in the packed palazzo. I grab my hat and cloak and we head for Lionello's, but not until I've first sent Giovanni to talk to Lena. With any luck I'll be in her bed tonight, far from any political discussions.

Walking north toward the Piazza del Popolo, I can't help looking westward toward the Vatican. A thin plume of black smoke hovers over the Sistine Chapel signaling that a new pope hasn't been chosen yet. Even the vendors on the street, the beggars, the pilgrims hobbling from church to church, all turn their eyes to the sky above Saint Peter's. Everyone is watching and waiting for the smoke to turn white. I've never been in Rome before while a pope was being elected and I'm struck by the strange atmosphere that cloaks the city, as if the stones themselves are holding their breath.

The taverns are as crowded as ever, but the mood is far from the usual drunken exuberance. There's a tension even in the dark rooms where pleasure is supposed to be the only thought.

Lionello, Andrea, and Nico are full of the latest gossip. They only want to talk about which horse to back in the papal race. They didn't give a fig about Clement, but the thought of a new Vicar of Christ fills them with an odd excitement.

"Think about it – we might know the next pope! Michele, you've met a lot of cardinals in your work. Del Monte of course, but then there are also the ones who've approved your altarpieces. Who was the last fellow you submitted something to?" Lionello's eyes glow with the kind of fever usually reserved for gambling.

"Cardinal Camillo Borghese," I answer. "But I doubt he'll be elected, though the Borghese family is certainly powerful. If he were a cardinal, I'd bet on Scipione Borghese, Camillo's nephew. He has the manipulative skills of a pope."

"You know who everyone's saying will get it?" asks Lionello. "Cardinal Bellarmine, the Inquisitor, the man who had the Cenci family tortured!"

"Didn't he also condemn the monk, Giordano Bruno, to be burned at the stake for heresy? In fact, doesn't that sniveling notary, Pasqualone, work for his office?" I shake my head. Just what I need, a new pope who will consider me an instant enemy.

"We thought Clement was bad! If it's Bellarmine, things will get much, much worse," Onorio declares. "I might go back to Genoa where I can breathe more freely."

"Don't say that!" Lionello objects. "You just got here. And I'm betting on Cardinal Baronius, the scholar. The Inquisition disgusts too many people to put Bellarmine in such a holy position. But who can argue with a great Church historian?"

"What a boring choice! It won't be him," Andrea insists. "Besides, you've forgotten this election is really about who has more power – the French or the Spanish. If the French win, the new pope will be someone from the Medici family. They're longtime backers of the French crown. Now, who would the Spanish pick?" He strokes his chin as if searching inside the Spanish king's mind.

"I came to a tavern to escape this kind of talk!" I bellow. "Tell me something I care about — what the most important commissions are now, what great works are being painted as we speak?" No one says a word. "What? Can you at least tell me who was last arrested? Who fought with whom?"

"That we can do," Nico says. "It was Lionello. He punched some sot in the eye and spent two days in Tor di Nona for it."

Lionello shrugs. "I don't even remember why I hit the fool, but I'm sure I had a good reason."

I laugh and slap him on the back. "Now that's the kind of thing I want to know!"

"What kind of thing?" a familiar hoarse voice asks.

"Ranuccio?" I try to remember the last time our paths crossed. Was it when Fillide slashed his lover? "How's pimping going? How's Fillide?"

"I don't see her anymore. She got herself set up with some rich young fool willing to pay well for her practiced charms."

"Sounds like you miss her — and her charms."

"She's easily replaced." Ranuccio pulls up a stool and settles himself next to me, gesturing to the boy to bring him some wine.

"You're by yourself tonight? Where's your brother and brother-in-law, your usual chums?" What does he want, I wonder, why is he cozying up to me?

"They're busy. Thought you could keep me company."

"Are we friends?" I ask. "I always thought you hated me."

"Hate? No. Despise? Maybe. I thought you were some guy with a small paintbrush who turned Fillide's head for a while. But that's history now. I don't care who she sleeps with. And anyway. . ." Here he talks a large gulp of wine. "She's not with you, that's certain."

He's trying to insult me and I should be furious, but it all strikes me as pathetic. The idiot is still clearly besotted by Fillide and being close to me is as close as he can get to her. It's sad, really, that he's trying to pick a fight over an old, dead grievance.

"Yes," I agree. "She's not with me." I push back my stool and stand up. "And neither are you. I'm sure you can find someone willing to be your drinking companion, but it won't be me."

Lionello, Onorio, Andrea, and Nico all get up with me and we shoulder our way through the crowd and out the door.

"Who was that guy?" Nico asks.

Onorio starts to explain the whole, long, convoluted, boring history.

"Stop!" I say, holding up my hands. "He's a blowhard, a bully. That's all you need to know. The rest doesn't matter a bean."

We weave our drunken way home. I haven't thought of Fillide in months, but that night I dream of her, and I have to admit, despite Ranuccio's foulness, it's not a bad dream.

LV

Registration of Acts, Rome, 19 May, 1605

    Michelangelo Merisi guarantees that he will not cause further offense and pays the fine of one hundred scudi for having damaged the door and the face of the house of Laura and Isabella della Vecchia.

LVI

A clangor of church bells wakes me up the next morning. Every bell in the city is tolling, some deep, some brassy, all blended together in a chorus ringing out the news that a pope has been chosen. A thin sinuous line of white smoke drifts out from the Sistine Chapel, confirming the bells' announcement – there is a pope once again to rule over the Church and the city.

I stumble downstairs and ask the first person I see, "Who? Who is it?"

The servant looks startled. "Ask the master, signore. I don't know anything."

I shove past the boy and find my way to the great salon. Though it's early, the room is full of Onorio's friends and architect colleagues. Onorio is there, too, though I'm sure he's nursing a worse hangover than I am.

"Who is it?" I ask again. "Do you know?"

Onorio nods. "It's a Medici, like we thought, Alessandro. But he's so old, sixty-nine years already, the same age as the pope we just buried. How long can he last?"

The hum of voices is loud as people dissect what the choice means.

"Thank the Lord it's not the Inquisitor!" I say. I don't know anything about Alessandro de' Medici, but anyone is better than Bellarmine. "So it's a vote for the French then."

"Looks that way and the Spanish aren't happy about it. There'll be fights in the streets today. Best stay home."

"And miss the celebrations? Won't there be dancing in the streets as well as brawls? Come on, let's head toward Saint Peter's. That's where the action will be."

Onorio shakes his head. "I don't think that's a good idea."

"Since when did you become so cautious? You always tease me for saying Baglione's out to get me and here you are fearing the entire city."

"I'm not afraid of anyone! I just don't want to be imprudent."

"I thought Imprudent was your middle name!" If Onorio wants to turn monkish, that's his choice. Me, I'm going out. I shake Giovanni awake, find my cloak and hat, call Raven, and the three of us head out the door.

"Did you talk to Lena?" I ask Giovanni as we make our way to Saint Peter's.

"I couldn't find her, signore. I talked to her mother. She said Lena was arrested by the sbirri for being out past curfew dressed as a man."

"What? Why would she do that?"

"She was trying to get to her lover's house and it's not

safe for a woman on the streets after dark."

"She was trying to get to my place?" I feel terrible. Lena's in Tor di Nona all because of me.

"Not your house, signore." Giovanni studies the cobblestones.

I grab his arm and force him to meet my eyes. "You said her lover's house."

He nods, miserable. "The other notary, Gaspare Albertini. He got Lena out of prison and she's there now. She wants to marry him."

"The blazes!"

"Her mother told me to tell you that Lena loves you, truly loves you. But she knows you'll never marry her and she wants to be an honest woman. Albertini will wed her."

I have to admit she's right. I'd never marry Lena. But I think I made her an honest woman by portraying her as the Virgin – that's as honest, as pure, as blessed as you can get.

Bursts of firecrackers jolt me from my thoughts. A cluster of young men run by yelling, "France won! Blessed be the French!" A group of men and women dance in the piazza, whooping and hollering. It's hard to stay angry surrounded by such joy. The cream, ochre, and burnt orange walls of the buildings seem to vibrate with excitement.

The Spanish have controlled Rome and the papacy for the past forty years. Now their power has disappeared in a puff of smoke over the Vatican. We pass French soldiers drinking in the streets, pouring wine and beer for everyone they see. The whole city is lifting a glass to the French, to being free from Spanish rule, to new beginnings and the hope they bring. It's an intoxicating atmosphere and I want to be part of the festivities.

We walk toward my neighborhood where people lean out of windows throwing down old furniture as if it's the New Year. Glass and pottery smash on the cobblestones in festive explosions, like downward-spiraling fireworks. We dodge the debris, laughing and yelling our own cheers for the French, for the new pope. Raven yelps beside us, confused by the whirl of noise and movement. I reach down to pat him, to reassure him this is a good kind of chaos, the wild joy of celebration.

When we get near Lena's house, I hear scuffling, angry shouts, heavy thuds as objects are hurled and land on the ground – or on people. The street opens onto a piazza where French and Spanish soldiers battle each other, slashing and stabbing with their swords. Some pry cobblestones from the ground and throw them both at people and windows. Others swing clubs into bodies, doors, even marble fountains in a rush of mindless destruction.

I back down the street. This is the kind of thing Onorio wanted to avoid. I don't care if the Spanish and French kill each other, so long as they leave Romans alone. Most of the screaming men in the piazza look like foreigners, each one eager for his bit of blood. But when I see a man run from the throng and grab the hair of a girl inching along the wall of a nearby building, trying to sidle her way home, I can't watch and do nothing. I pull out my own sword and rush at the man, now dragging the girl down a narrow lane.

"Let me go!" she shrieks, clawing and spitting. She's got fight in her, she does.

But she's a slight thing and he's a hulking brute. He pushes her down and yanks up her skirt just as I run up behind him and whack him in the back of the head full force, the way I struck Pasqualone. The same blow knocked the notary flat.

This man, bigger, heavier, stronger wavers a moment, then turns and faces me, eyes bulging in fury.

He roars, throwing himself on me, but I slice with my sword, gashing his arm, his chest, his cheek.

"Run! Get out of here!" I yell to the girl. She scrambles to her feet and dashes away.

Raven leaps on the man's back, biting at his hefty thighs. Giovanni lunges at him, trying to beat him with a stick. The brute is getting it from all sides now. I bellow with rage, stick my sword deep in the man's leg and pull it out, blood spurting everywhere. He stumbles, falls to his knees, then flat on his face.

I tell myself he's not dead, it's only his leg, hardly a mortal wound. Anyway, I'm not going to wait and find out. I run back out of the narrow alley, yelling at Giovanni to follow me.

Only when we're away from the fighting do I stop to catch my breath. Giovanni's face is pale with panic. Raven pants beside him.

"Good boy!" I say, fondling the dog's silky head. The dog licks at the gashes on my knuckles, the scrapes on my arm and shoulder where the brute tried to pin me down.

"Did you see that, Giovanni? Raven was a real hero back there! And you, too!"

The boy nods, his face still white. "You could have been killed," he whispers.

I shrug. "I promise you, when I die, it won't be like that."

We walk the rest of the way to Onorio's in silence, still dodging vases, crockery, and chairs thrown from windows with abandon. When we get back to the great salon, Onorio takes one look at my bruises and torn clothes and laughs.

"Thank you, Michele, for showing me all I missed by staying home." He leans back in his chair, annoyingly smug.

I slump down next to him. "Until that last bit, it was a wonderful celebration."

"And the last bit," prods Onorio. "The bit where you got beaten up?"

"Oh, that." I shrug. "The Romans are all out celebrating, but the Spanish and French are settling their differences the way they know best."

"Why'd you poke your nose in that? Let them slaughter each other!"

"My sentiments exactly!" I agree. Why say anything about the girl? I don't want to tarnish my reputation as a short-tempered brawler. Let Onorio think what everyone else does – that Michelangelo Merisi da Caravaggio is a wild, moody creature, quick to anger, even quicker to draw his sword. Better to be feared than loved, I always say, following Machiavelli's advice. Sometimes those Florentines actually know a thing or two.

It turns out, however, that they don't know how to live a long life. Only a few weeks after taking office, Alessandro de' Medici, or Pope Leo XI, dies. He's quickly dubbed "Papa Lampo" or "The Lightning Pope" for the brevity of his reign, like a flash in the sky. The tense waiting begins all over again.

I'm on my way to Lionello's with Giovanni and Raven when we hear worse fighting than the day of Leo IX's election. Like then, it's a pitched battle between Spaniards and French, but this time there are at least thirty sbirri trying to disperse the crowd and arrest the most violent men, those with pikes, daggers, swords, and pistols.

I flatten myself against a wall, trying to make out who's winning without getting in the way. Giovanni cowers next to me, Raven crouching between us, his muzzle pressed into my thigh.

Ranuccio Tomassoni and his brother Giovan Francesco face the sbirri, yelling at them to leave the Spanish alone.

"This is our fight!" Ranuccio roars, his face red with rage. He has a pistol in his belt and waves a sword and dagger in each hand. "We're in charge of this area, the head of the militia here, so clear out!"

The sbirri are clearly daunted. They cluster around their leader, swords drawn, but not advancing.

With Ranuccio and his men on their side, the better-armed Spanish are winning. I watch, fascinated, as they herd the defeated French supporters into a nearby house, slashing at them with swords and pikes, then saunter off, leaving the Tomassoni brothers in charge of the prisoners.

"You need to hand those men over to us," the police officer in charge orders. "We'll take them to Tor di Nona where they belong."

"I don't think so," Ranuccio mocks. "I'll do what I like with them."

"You must obey the law!"

"I am the law!" Ranuccio spits at the sbirri's feet. "You're miserable cowards who sweep the streets of beggars and leave the real work to men like me."

I don't like Ranuccio or the Spanish, but I like the sbirri even less and I'm enjoying seeing them put in their place.

"This isn't the end of the matter!" The cop makes one last pathetic attempt. "I will report this to Cardinal Aldobrandini."

"Go tell your papa, too while you're at it!" Ranuccio laughs. "And your mama as well!" He sneers broadly while the officer sputters, desperate to recapture some of his dignity.

Giovan Francesco turns slowly, lowers his breeches, and lets rip an enormous fetid fart. The two brothers link arms and go into the house holding their prisoners. The door shuts firmly and for a long minute all is quiet.

"Why are you standing around like blithering buffoons?" the head cop yells. "There are streets to patrol – get moving!"

When I describe this story to Lionello, he doesn't believe me.

"Are you saying the Tomassoni brothers have more power than the sbirri?"

"That's exactly what I'm saying. You've heard the story about Ranuccio killing a man. Did he spend one day in jail? Of course not! He literally gets away with murder!"

"You sound like you admire the brute."

"I almost do," I admit. "He's a thug, no question about that. But he can do what he wants with absolute impunity. Me, I've been arrested eleven times in the past year alone and spent two weeks in Tor di Nona for that stupid libel accusation. Would that ever happen to Ranuccio? Certainly not!"

"If the new pope is for the French, he'll lose his protection."

"Maybe, but cockroaches like Ranuccio have a way of thriving when everyone else struggles. French pope, Spanish pope, he'll do fine."

That evening I host a small supper and Del Monte, my old, faithful patron is one of the guests. Onorio, Lionello, and Prosperino round out the table.

I'm back in my own rooms after paying off my extortionist landlady. I had to add a generous tip before she'd return all my belongings, but it's worth it to be home, surrounded by my familiar things and now by familiar friends.

Lionello's heard the story of the fight, but I tell it again. "Those Spanish got away with it," I say. "Not just the Tomassoni brothers."

"Not for long." Del Monte gnaws on a chicken bone. "The new pope won't be a supporter of Spain. Those days are finally over."

"Another Medici?" Prosperino asks.

Del Monte shakes his head. "You'll see soon enough."

Del Monte knows more than he's telling, but I don't press. Instead, I avoid the streets, bristling with fights, and stay home and paint. When the streets are ruled by the likes of Ranuccio, it's time to stay inside.

Three days after the French-Spanish street battle, a plume of white smoke wafts up over the Sistine Chapel again, and the church bells resound loudly throughout Rome. Cardinal Camillo Borghese, the man who approved my altarpiece for Sant'Agostino, becomes Pope Paul V.

Someone I know, someone who admires me, is pope!

I'm not alone in my excitement. Borghese is politically neutral, neither for the French nor the Spanish, but wholly for the Romans. There couldn't be a more popular choice. This time the streets are full of clamorous celebrations and not a single fighting soldier. We're free of Clement and his oppressive legacy. Rome will be a great power once more.

And I am her best artist. With a pope who likes my work, my time for a commission at Saint Peter's has finally come.

LVII

Usually I throw on whatever's near me or wear the same clothes I've slept in, but this morning I dress with care. No stained or wrinkled shirt, no torn breeches. I've been summoned to the palazzo of Scipione Borghese, Pope Paul's nephew and now a cardinal himself. All Rome knows that this Borghese is determined to amass an impressive art collection. Already, he has bought up a treasure-load of ancient Roman sculpture, lined his palazzo floors with antique mosaics. And he's started building an enormous villa in the great open park northeast of Piazza del Popolo. It's a mere foundation now but soon it will be the Villa Borghese.

I assume Borghese wants a portrait or some religious subject for his personal collection and I plan on demanding an enormous sum. If he can't pay my price with gold, perhaps, just perhaps, he can offer me a title. Something like a papal knighthood. Once I get my title, the first thing I'll do is pick a fight with d'Arpino, get back at him finally for all his insults years ago.

A servant dressed in scarlet livery ushers us into a big room. Ancient Roman statues on pedestals stand in every corner. Two paintings have clear pride of place in the room, in the center of the main wall with nothing around them to distract from their impact. I stand gaping at them when the double door opens and the cardinal walks in.

"Michelangelo Merisi da Caravaggio! A true pleasure to meet you at last!" The voice is rich and thick, like melted butter.

I turn around and bow slightly, still astonished by the paintings.

"Ah, you're admiring my latest acquisitions, I see. Splendid, aren't they? Absolutely brilliant!"

"But how did you get them?" I'm trying furiously to figure out the mystery. "Did Cesare d'Arpino sell them to you?"

"Not exactly." Borghese gestures to a blue brocaded chair. "Sit down and I'll tell you the story."

I sink into the cushion, facing the pictures I painted so long ago when I first came to Rome. Hanging on the walls is my young self-portrait as Bacchus, the one d'Arpino criticized for the poor anatomy of my arm. Next to it is the painting of Mario with the basket of fruit. I thought d'Arpino had cut it up, burned it as he'd threatened to do. Here it is, as luscious as ever.

"Perhaps you thought these destroyed?" Borghese asks.

"D'Arpino made it clear how much he detested both of them."

"So much so that he kept them all these years? He had them hidden away, you know, only showed them to those he really wanted to impress. They were the prize of his private collection."

"Not so prized that he wasn't willing to sell them," I remark dryly. "Though I'm sure you offered a persuasive price."

"Actually no. I didn't pay a penny." The cardinal's full lips twitch in a sly smile.

"He gave them to you? For a favor of some kind?" I can't imagine the skinflint being generous, and he already has a title, so I wonder what he got for the pictures. My next thought is to wonder if I can make a similar trade.

"They were confiscated by my uncle, the pope, seized when the Cavaliere d'Arpino failed to pay his tax bill in full. The entire collection, one hundred and seven paintings in all, were graciously given to me, as my uncle knows what an avid collector I am. And these two are the best of them all."

"I'm honored to hear you say so." There goes my chance to swap art for a title, I think. All I'm getting is a reminder to make sure I pay my taxes.

"But of course I didn't bring you here just so you could admire your own pictures." Borghese pours some wine from a crystal decanter on a silver tray next to him and offers me a goblet. "I think you'll enjoy this. It's a little wine from my own vineyards near Frascati. I'm a bit of a connoisseur, like all Romans I suppose."

The wine is superb, like everything else in the room.

"You can see, Michelangelo, that I'm a great admirer of your work."

I nod, silent, waiting. What does he want? I'd wager a portrait or maybe something large, an impressive religious scene like a Deposition from the Cross, something to fill up a wall.

"I'm talking to you as a representative of sorts, on behalf of the papal grooms, the palafrenieri."

"The men who take care of the pope's horses and stables?"

"Yes, they have their own chapel and naturally they need an altarpiece for it. They want a picture of the Virgin, the Christ Child, and Saint Anne, the Virgin's mother. The Madonna and Child should be shown trampling on evil in the form of a serpent. And Saint Anne, who is the patron saint of the grooms, should have a prominent place watching as good defeats evil."

"An interesting subject, one I've never painted before." I'm already imagining the picture in my mind's eye, conjuring up the composition I want, how the lights and darks will play over the surface.

"So you'll take the commission?" Borghese leans forward, looking at me intently as if afraid I'll refuse.

"Well, there's the question of money of course. And where is this chapel?" I ask.

"Saint Peter's." Borghese leans back and laces his fingers together, the sly smile playing on his lips again.

Have I heard right? Does he mean the pope's own church, the Saint Peter's designed by Michelangelo, the other Michelangelo?

"It's truly shocking that such an important church has gone so long without an altarpiece by the famous Caravaggio. But I'm here to remedy that situation. If you'll agree."

"Yes, of course, I'm honored," I babble. After so long, so much yearning, can it really be happening just like that?

"Shall we talk about money now?"

"Later, later, we can discuss those details later." I take out a handkerchief and wipe my flustered face. My heart is pounding so loudly I'm surprised the cardinal doesn't comment on the noise.

"This is naturally an important commission, but there is another one that I ask you to complete before the altarpiece. One that is, dare I say, of even higher priority."

"Higher?" What could be more important than Saint Peter's?

"Yes." Borghese nods slowly. "You must understand, Michelangelo, I'm a great connoisseur of art and I know genius when I see it. I plan on showing you off to the world. Your art will be spread throughout Rome. This will become the city of Caravaggio, the place where your brilliance shines brightest."

I sit there, stunned. Del Monte has praised me and I know how Giustiniani values me but I've never heard such appreciation – not counting, of course, the false praises that courtesans like Fillide excel at. But Borghese isn't flattering me. Why would he, a man of such importance? He must believe what he says.

"I thank you, your grace," I murmur.

"No one but a man of your talent can paint the portrait of the new pope. He would like you to start tomorrow. He'll send for you when he's ready to sit for you, but I expect it will be in the afternoon. You can arrange that, can't you?'

"Certainly!" The pope! I'm to paint Pope Paul V's official portrait! And Saint Peter's, both at once! It's too much for me to grasp. I grin like an idiot, an enormous smile plastering my face.

"I see you're pleased and that pleases me." Borghese

takes a slip of paper that's been folded discretely on the tray with the wine. "This is what you'll be paid. I trust you'll find it to your liking."

I unfold the paper and read a vast sum, five times what I made for the Cerasi chapel. Borghese is not only making me the most famous artist in Rome, he's making me the richest. By far.

We probably exchange more pleasantries, talk about art, but I can't remember a word. I float back through the streets, all the way to Saint Peter's. This time I go into the church knowing I have earned my place there. I find the chapel of the papal grooms and already I can see it hanging there, my masterpiece, the work that will prove me a greater artist than the Michelangelo who carved the magnificent marble *Pieta* nearby.

Then I walk around the corner to the Vatican Palazzo. The Swiss Guards flank the entrance, protecting the home of the pope. It's blocked now. But tomorrow it will be open to me.

LVIII
Cardinal Scipione Borghese
Personal Journal, 4 August 1605

How fortunate Rome is that I have a vision for this city and the power to make it happen. People talk of Paris and its elegance, of Madrid and its charms, but nothing, nothing will come close to Rome once I've shaped it. Fountains by the best sculptors will grace every piazza, enormous paintings by the most talented artists will hang in every major church, thanks to me. All will be swirling forms, rich colors, blazing light. And Caravaggio is just the man for this new Rome. His drama, his deep shadows and golden beams of light, his vibrant compositions – that's my sensibility exactly. How blessed I am to live at this time, to make this moment happen. Thank the Lord, and his newest servant, my uncle, the pope.

LIX

Acts of Notary, Rome, 16 August 1605

The notary Domenico Marcone, called Paracinio, formalized the peace concluded between Michelangelo Merisi, painter, and Mariano Pasqualone di Accumoli: Caravaggio, in declaring the proper formula, admitted having wounded Pasqualone with the sword when the latter was unarmed and for this reason asks of him "pardon and peace," adding that Signor Marian, can demand an answer from Caravaggio whenever he likes once he is also armed with a sword.

LX

The pope isn't a stranger to me. We met when he approved my design for the Madonna in the church of Sant'Agostino, but Camillo Borghese is much more intimidating now as Pope Paul V. He tells me the composition he wants, he selects the pose, and then he sits, glaring at me, daring me to do his power justice.

I start with his shrewd, piercing eyes. The intelligence smoldering there is cutting, not kind. This isn't a compassionate man, nor a particularly spiritual one, but there's no question of his power and determination. He means to make the papacy greater than ever.

As I paint, I talk about Saint Peter's, the plans to finish it.

"My nephew is helping me with the grand architectural plans for Saint Peter's. We'll put our mark on this city, you may be sure of it. He has some ideas to make the piazzas in the city more sumptuous."

I cock my head. "Sumptuous is an interesting word to describe a piazza. They're just big open spaces."

"That's what they are now, but they're important public places and should be marked as such. With fountains and sculptures that will define Rome as the art capital of the world."

"Too bad I'm simply a painter," I say. "I won't be part of this big project."

"I wouldn't worry about that." The pope allows himself a sliver of a smile. "Scipione has plans for you as well. You're part of his vision of this new, lavish, opulent Rome. Your dramatic style suits our tastes perfectly."

I don't see myself as lavish or opulent. But I am painting Pope Paul's portrait and I'll prove my worth with that.

A bell chimes the hour and the pope stands up briskly. "That's all for today. I'll send for you tomorrow when I'm ready.'

"Yes, your Holiness." I bow my head, dismissed like a servant, not like the most famous painter in Rome. Nobody reminds you of your lowly station more than a pope.

Still, as I pack up my paints, palette, and brushes I savor being in the Vatican. Maybe by the time I finish the portrait, I'll be a papal knight.

That night I dine at Del Monte's. Naturally everyone wants to hear my impressions of Pope Paul V.

"He's imperial, like an ancient Caesar," I say. "There's a force to him that brooks no argument. He's actually impressive, and I don't say that lightly."

"I'm not surprised. He's already clamping down in big ways and small," Del Monte says. "He's out-Clemented Clement with new laws cracking down on courtesans, cheating innkeepers, and spreading false news. Be glad your libel trial is a thing of the past! And if you're caught with an unlicensed sword now, you'll face more stringent penalties than before, including a heavy fine."

"I thought he had a broader mind than the old pope." I frown. "I didn't expect him to be worse."

Del Monte shrugs. "He has a wider view, I'll grant you that. But he's more power-hungry and autocratic than Clement. He's whipping up the Inquisition to widen its reach. I've written to my old friend Galileo warning him to be careful. This pope is out to prove his word is law."

"And he's a good friend of the Jesuits," Giustiniani adds. "Have you heard the news from Venice?"

Del Monte nods. "Fighting with the Doge! Can you imagine?"

"What do you mean?" Without Mario, I don't hear the freshest gossip anymore.

"It started when two priests were accused of murder in Venice. The Doge should have handed them over to Rome to be tried, but Venetian tribunals judged them instead. The pope was furious and ordered Venice excommunicated," Giustiniani explains. "The whole city!"

"How do you excommunicate a city?"

"If you're pope, you can do anything." Del Monte say. "Or so you think. Anyway, the Doge retaliated by throwing all the Jesuits out of the city and confiscating their property."

"That's not all!" Giustiniani grins. "The best part is what the Doge said. He proclaimed the new papacy to be 'without natural reason and against divine scriptures and doctrine.' He practically called the pope a heretic! You've got to admire his nerve!"

"All of Europe is admiring it. If Paul V doesn't reconcile soon, others will follow the Doge's example. Think of all that prime Church property that would suddenly be freed up, like what happened in England under Henry VIII." Del Monte shakes his head. "Not a good way to start a new regime."

"But what will he do for the arts?" Prosperino asks.

"He has big plans," I say. "Or I should say his nephew does. He wants to remake Rome into a grander place, more sumptuous. That's the word he used – sumptuous."

"But what does it mean for ordinary people?" Onorio presses.

"You're not ordinary – what do you care? You're an architect. It probably means more work, more sumptuous work," Prosperino says.

"But will Rome be a freer city or more oppressive?" I wonder.

"It hasn't been long enough to judge," Giustiniani says. "We'll know in the fullness of time what kind of pope we have. But in the matter of Venice, he'll back down. He has to, and he's too intelligent not to understand that."

"And the kind of city this will be?" I persist.

"Don't worry, your altarpieces bring fame to Rome, especially your next one in Saint Peter's. A toast!" Del Monte lifts his goblet high. "To Michelangelo Merisi da Caravaggio and the light he brings into all our lives!"

I raise my glass with everyone else. Del Monte's right – I have the two most important commissions I could imagine and I'm a favorite of the pope's nephew. What more could I want?

The pope has time for only two more sessions with me. In the last one, he's so angry about an old man who wrote an unofficial biography of Clement VIII, comparing Clement to a decadent Roman emperor, that he spends the hour grumbling about ways to punish the writer.

I try to lighten the atmosphere, inspire a more spiritual expression for his face, but I'm left with a dour glare, so that's what I paint. I try to show sensitivity in his mouth, intelligence in his eyes and forehead, but there's no masking the frightening intensity of the man. And maybe that's for the best. He's a lion of a man and should be seen as such.

"You'll finish the rest in the studio," Pope Paul says as he examines what I've done.

"Yes, your grace. It won't take long." I try to read his expression, but I can't, so I'm forced to ask. "Are you pleased so far?"

He slides his eyes from the canvas to me. There's a moment's silence, then he nods curtly. "You've captured me, so how can I complain?"

I lower my eyes, dip my head in a bow. "I'm honored to hear you say so."

"Just finish it up and get to work on the chapel altarpiece. My grooms are waiting."

I nod again and pack up my things. The portrait is important, but will hang in the Vatican, hidden from the public. The altarpiece matters more, much more, and I'm eager to get started.

As soon as I deliver the portrait, I go to Lena's mother's house. I haven't seen her daughter for months. I know she's living with the notary, but I need to get a message to her.

"Michele, come in!" the signora says warmly. "And your servant and dog, too. You're all welcome. I've missed you!"

"And I've missed you, especially your cooking." I unload the gifts I've brought, bolts of cloth, silk ribbons, a new soup pot.

The signora's cheeks turn pink with pleasure. She sits me down at the big kitchen table and ladles me up a big bowl of bean soup, handing another one to Giovanni. Raven lies down at my feet, his tail wagging. He remembers this place.

"Here's your chance, then. Eat and we'll have a nice visit. Tell me what brings you here – and with such beautiful presents. Not my old face, I'm sure."

"It's a commission. For Saint Peter's." I dip a hunk of bread into the soup and take a bite. She's a good cook, the old woman, better than the one I have at home.

"Saint Peter's!" Her face glows watching me devour her food. She must be lonely with her daughter and grandson gone.

"And I'd like Lena to model for me, pose as the Virgin again."

"My Lena in a picture hanging in Saint Peter's!" Her jaw goes slack in wonder and tears run silently down her cheeks. "Oh, Michele, I'm so sorry she left you! She's a fool, she is. And here you are, willing to take her back! You're too kind, too good! She doesn't deserve you!"

"Please understand me, signora," I pause to finish up the soup, wiping the bowl with more bread. "I don't want Lena to leave the notary. I just want her to pose for me. Could she bring her son, too? He's a perfect Christ Child."

Now the old woman really bursts into tears. She flings her arms around me, hugging me tightly. "Michele, you're an angel! Such a generous spirit! Those people who call you a hot-head don't know you!"

I pull away. "So you'll bring Lena to my studio tomorrow morning? I want to start as soon as possible."

"Don't you worry, Michele. Just leave it to me." She gives me a broad toothless smile and starts fluttering around the kitchen, filling a basket with bread, cheese, a slice of egg pie and a leek tart. "Here, take this back with you, so you can put some meat on your bones."

"Thank you, signora, for everything." I pick up the basket but I'm not ready to leave yet. I study Lena's mother's face. I had thought her too old-looking for the part, but now I realize she would fit the role of Saint Anne well. Who could make a more natural mother for my Virgin than her actual mother?

"And signora," I say. "Would you come as well and pose for Saint Anne? It will really be a family portrait."

Now the old woman looks ready to faint, she's so overcome. She puts a hand to her chest, another to her head. I wish I could capture that expression! It's full of wonder and awe as if she's seen an angel.

When I see Lena the next day, I'm surprised how little I feel – no anger, no bitter sense of betrayal, no lust even, as if all that has died between us. She, for her part, seems nervous, as if prepared for a fight.

"Michele," she lowers her eyes. "So good to see you again. It's an honor that you've asked me to pose for you, one I thought I'd never have again."

"Come, Lena." I lift her chin up so she's looking at me. "I'm not upset with you. I just want you to be happy. Are you?"

She nods, her eyes dark with confusion. Does she want me to be jealous? I sigh and pick up my stained palette. "Then let's get started."

LXI
Maddalena Antogretti
Private Journal, 5 October 1605

When his eyes are on me it's as if God is looking deep into my soul. There's nothing I can hide from him. Is that why I care for him so?

I remind myself that he would never marry me. And if he did, what kind of life would I have? He's a man who gives all his money to his friends for drink, for rent, for their latest stupid schemes. I saw him give that Lionello fellow a big, fat purse so he could work on some silly device to travel underwater. He may as well have thrown the coins into the street!

He's a man who lives in ordinary rented rooms with not a single stick of good furniture and only one servant. He should have at least a dozen apprentices, yet he has none. He lives like a poor craftsman when he's the most famous artist in Rome.

That's not the life I want, not for me, not for my son.

As for love, I know better than to rely on it. Love doesn't put food in the cupboard or clothes on your back. That's what a husband is for.

LXII

Police Records, Rome, 18 October 1605

Lieutenant Sacripante encountered Michelangelo da Caravaggio, armed with a sword and dagger, around ten at night near the alley of Bufalo, and asked if he had a permit. He said he did and showed it, so the lieutenant wished him good night and said he could go. Caravaggio responded loudly "In your ass!" At which point, the officer told him not to behave this way or he would be arrested and he answered "Kiss my butt, you and everyone like you!" and the officer arrested him and brought him to prison at Tor di Nona.

LXIII

I stand before the white canvas, frozen. It feels like something is caught in my throat, as if I can't breathe. Lena, her boy, and her mother form a mute tableau, waiting for me to start. But I can't.

Silence fills the studio, heavy and thick. I stare at my brush, my hands, the colors on my palette. And still I can't move.

"Is something wrong, Michele?" Lena finally dares to murmur. "Should we change positions?"

"No, no," I say. "Stay just as you are." I tell myself all I need to do is look at her, to really see her, to capture her in paint. Then I stop thinking. My brush dips into the ochre and makes broad strokes on the canvas, setting down the forms and shadows, the guts of the painting.

I'm doing it, I'm making the altarpiece that will hang in Saint Peter's. And I'm doing it all by myself. There's no army of apprentices hovering around me, like others use. Only my hand will touch my picture, because not a single inch of the canvas is less important than another. How could I trust any of it to a painter-in-training, to any brush but my own? Even the parts other artists consider unimportant, mere "background." To me, they're essential, the dark shadows, the luminous light that reveals my holy family – especially the rich, thick darks, the golden light. I don't want a raking glare or a dead, flaccid area of nothingness. I want the secret suggestion of darkness swallowing form, the warm, spiritual light bathing my figures in a divine glow.

My only assistant is Giovanni and he's allowed to mix colors, nothing more. Even that he does under my sharp eye. No sugary pinks or watery blues for me. I leave those vapid colors to Baglione. Let him paint pastry. I'm creating art.

The signora stands with her hands clasped, looking down tenderly at her holy child and grandchild. It could be a domestic scene, except for the haloes. And of course the snake of sinfulness, coiled in treachery at their feet. Mary's foot crushes its head while the Christ Child's foot rests on top of hers, like they're playing a kind of game. Their faces are intent, but not distressed, fully expecting that evil will be conquered.

It's the most important altarpiece of my career and yet it's simple, with only three figures. That's what makes it especially challenging – how to make something so plain also powerful, how to show the divine in an everyday moment. It's the kind of subject I like best, where each face holds a world, each expression tells a story.

I give Saint Anne the weight of worries in her brow, a deep resignation in her interlaced hands, but there's pride too, and a quiet dignity, a noble acceptance of the suffering both Mary and Christ will embrace.

In Mary's curved shoulders, her hands clasping Jesus, I show her motherly devotion, her urge to protect her child. Yet she allows him to help strike at the snake. She knows he must face darkness without fear.

The Christ Child looks almost sorry for what he must do, trampling on the snake. There's no anxiety in his face, no terror, but a calm sense of purpose beyond his young years.

I don't know if it's my finest work, but when Lena's mother sees it she kneels down and kisses my hands.

"God bless you, Michele," she murmurs.

Lena doesn't say anything. She looks more embarrassed than anything else.

"What's wrong?" I ask. "I've painted you modestly. You don't look indecent."

"No, no, of course not." She shakes her head. "You've made me lovely."

"Is it the boy? You don't like him being naked? I painted him nude the first time for the Sant'Agostino altarpiece. It's to show his purity as Christ." She had no objection to that painting. True, in this one the boy isn't curled up in her arms, but stands facing the viewer so his babyish male organ is in plain view. But he's a child. And he's pure. I think of all the ancient Roman statuary with completely naked bodies. And of how Michelangelo painted Christ in the Last Judgment of the Sistine Chapel. There he's a man, facing forward in his magnificent nudity, as are all the saints, from Saint Bartholomew to Saint Peter to Saint Paul.

"No, it's all perfect, Michele, more than I deserve." She lowers her eyes and a flush creeps up her cheeks.

I smile. "Lena, you don't have to sleep with me for me to want to paint you. Thank you for posing, and for letting your son pose."

There's an awkward silence. I don't know what else to say. The signora takes the situation in hand, dressing her grandson, and ushering the family noisily out of the studio with kisses, hugs, blessings in a flurry of parting.

I'm left alone with the painting, and for once, I'm too exhausted for the usual round of drinking. I just want to sit staring at my picture until darkness fills the room and I can't make out the forms anymore.

LXIV

I deliver the altarpiece to Saint Peter's as soon as it's dry, savoring every step of the journey, every minute it takes for the large painting to be hung. But I can't draw the moment out forever. All too soon, it's done, my picture is there, filling the chapel wall.

It's even better in the church than it was in my studio, expanding in the space as if the picture itself were a living, breathing thing. I stand there, gaping at it, at my place in Saint Peter's, when I'm startled by a voice over my shoulder.

"Bravo, Michelangelo, bravo!"

It's Scipione Borghese. He's seen the picture early on, once the figures were blocked out, so he could approve it for the church, but this is his first time with the finished work. I swell with pride at his praise.

"I'm pleased if you're pleased, your grace." I give a slight bow, all decorum, not a trace of the hot-head now.

"It's a masterpiece, as I knew it would be." He clasps his hands behind his back and rocks on his heels as if he's admiring something in his own home, not standing in a chapel in the greatest church in the world. "There might be a bit of a fuss about the Christ Child, but nothing you need to worry about."

"What fuss? What do you mean?" I sputter.

"Well, you have painted him, ahem, in the raw, as they say."

"But you knew that before! You approved it!" I feel the anger rising up my stomach, filling my lungs. I will not have another piece rejected. This one has been approved by the pope's own nephew!

"Yes, of course I did. I think the symbolism is brilliant. But. . ." he coughs into his fist, clears his throat loudly.

"But what?" I seethe, trying to keep myself from yelling in a sacred place. "You told me Michelangelo Buonarotti himself had painted many nude figures in the Sistine Chapel. In the Last Judgment, remember? Majestic nudes, I think you said. Adult male nudes, not even cherubs or children, but men, naked men."

"Yes, yes, that's true," Scipione hastens to say. "But. . ." Once again his voice trails off.

"But what?" I say through clenched teeth.

"Well, I thought you knew the story. Everyone does."

"Evidently not me, so I beg you, enlighten me."

Scipione sighs. "I have to say first that I strongly feel there is nothing wrong with the Christ Child's nudity here – or with any of the nudity in the Sistine Chapel. That is my opinion. Unfortunately, Pope Pius V thought otherwise, and he had a painter, Daniele da Volterra, paint drapery on the backsides or exposed parts of all the nudes. Surely you've heard of him? His nickname was 'The Breeches-Painter.' You can understand why."

"Are you saying some dolt is going to paint breeches on my Christ?" I can practically feel myself snorting like an enraged bull.

"No! Not at all! That was in 1565, forty years ago and more. Times have changed. I just wanted to prepare you in case there's any criticism on that account."

"Why didn't you tell me this when you saw the underpainting?" I want to grab his throat, shake some sense into the conniving vulture, but after the pope, he's the most powerful man in Rome. I tell myself that he'll protect me if anyone – specifically that fool Baglione – lashes into me for the Christ Child's nudity. But then why the warning? Why didn't he say anything when he saw the composition blocked out?

"I shouldn't have said anything. Let's go back to my palazzo and I'll pay you what you're owed. We'll toast your great achievement with some fine wine. You should be celebrating, not worrying!"

I want to recapture that feeling of being at the peak of my career, on top of the world, but it's gone. Even the rich wine tastes dry as dust, and when I dine later that night with Del Monte and Giustiniani, all their praise and congratulation feels empty. The only voice that matters is the one I'm imagining. It's Baglione's telling me what an insult I've painted and how my indecent altarpiece isn't worthy of the greatest church in the land.

LXV

Vincenzo Giustiniani
Personal Journal, 23 May 1606

I wanted to be the one to help Michelangelo get his Saint Peter's commission. It was a secret competition between Francesco and me, who could pull the right strings first. Disappointing that in the end it wasn't either of us, but Borghese. Can't say I've ever liked the man. He's too oily for my taste, not trustworthy at all, but he has a discerning eye, no question about that. He recognizes genius when he sees it and he's been slavering over Michelangelo's painting for years now. Drooling, but too cheap to open his purse. He's a sly one, waiting for his uncle to become pope, then using his power to nab two wonderful early Caravaggios, those paintings d'Arpino had been hoarding, waiting for their value to increase. I 'd offered to buy them many times, but d'Arpino always turned me down, saying he was waiting for Michelangelo to get his Saint Peter's commission – then he could ask whatever he wanted. As it turned out, he should have sold them to me since Borghese didn't have to spend a cent. It was a brilliant plan, confiscating them for tax delinquency, a scheme worthy of Clement VIII himself.

I admit I'm a bit jealous, both that Borghese snagged those pictures and that he earned Michelangelo's gratitude for the Saint Peter's altarpiece. Knowing Michelangelo, he'll paint something marvelous as a thank you. That study he did of light, of reflections and refractions, is still one of the pieces Francesco prizes most. That was a thank-you painting. I wonder what Michele would have painted for me? I suppose I'll always wonder.

LXVI

Three days later it isn't Baglione I hear from, it's Scipione. He's sent for me, and although I'd like to think it's about another commission, it's more likely he'll order me to paint some floating drapery over my Christ Child in the manner of Daniele da Volterra and the other Michelangelo. I feel cursed by my name, more than ever.

Since the altarpiece has been unveiled I've heard high praise and scathing criticism. Naturally Baglione is foremost among the chorus of hecklers. My experience is that when there's both, it's the critics who win. I'm prepared to bow my head and accept a drape across baby Jesus, so long as I get to be the one to paint it.

The cardinal welcomes me into his salon and pours us both wine before he says a word. I arch an inquisitive eyebrow, but he refuses to say anything until he's taken a good, long draught from the goblet.

"Welcome, Michelangelo," he begins.

"Thank you for inviting me, your grace," I say, though this was a summons, not a request.

Scipione tents his fingers and rests his chin on them, trying to look sage and diplomatic. I assume he has something dreadful to tell me and is trying to soften the blow with soulful gravitas.

"Remember I told you that there might be a bit of controversy over your altarpiece?"

This is it, I think, it's coming, the order to paint clothing.

"In fact, it's turned out to be more serious than that," Scipione continues.

I say nothing. Just stare at him. I won't make this any easier for him. He'll have to spell out every nuance, every inch of flesh he wants covered.

"It seems that, well, I hate to say this. God's wounds, don't look at me like that. I warned you! You know I did!"

"You approved the painting!" I yell, unable to contain myself any longer.

"I did! I did! And I'm taking care of it."

"How?" I roar. "Are you going to daub a dainty cloth on Jesus for me?"

"Of course not!" The cardinal looks affronted as if I've asked him to pick up some kitchen trash. That's what he's asking me to do — hold my nose and in proper servile fashion add an insipid drape to my masterpiece.

"The painting won't be changed — it stays just the way it is. But it had to be moved. It's in the Church of the Palafrenieri, the church of the papal grooms, right near by."

"NOOOOOOOOOOO!!!" I throw my glass down,

shattering it and leap to my feet. There's no stopping the boiling rage this time. "You can't do this! You can't take my painting out of Saint Peter's!"

"Michelangelo." The cardinal's icy voice cuts a chill through my anger. "It's done. I'm sorry about this. I offered to buy the painting myself, and the grooms are considering my offer. But in the meanwhile, it does hang in a church, and one quite near Saint Peter's."

There's nothing more to say. Certainly nothing more I want to hear. I rush out of the room, grab my sword, hat, and cloak and thunder out of the broad doorway. Giovanni and Raven race to catch up with me.

"Master, what's wrong?" Giovanni pants beside me.

Who should I turn to? Onorio? Del Monte? Giustiniani? I can't decide, my mind is misted by fury. I just follow my boots as they stride in quick scissor steps, slicing the air as I walk.

My feet choose for me and I find myself at Onorio's door, pounding on it with all my anger.

"Michele, what happened?" he asks when he sees my face, purple with rage. "Lionello, Nico, come quick, it's Michele. Something's happened!"

All three of my friends surround me, peppering me with questions, but I'm too angry to speak.

"It was the cardinal, Scipione Borghese," Giovanni explains for me. "Something he said to the master."

"Is it about the pope's portrait?" Lionello asks. "I thought he was pleased with that."

I shake my head, clenching my teeth, holding in the unbearable truth.

"It's the Saint Peter's altarpiece!" Nico shouts. "The

naked Jesus! I knew it – they've refused it haven't they?"

"Is that it, Michele?" Onorio looks horrified.

"Yes!!!" I bellow. "It's already gone. Up in Saint Peter's for a mere three days – three blasted days!"

"Too bad for those fools if they don't recognize genius!" Onorio scoffs. "Michele, listen, you're at the top now. This story will only add to your reputation, will only make you more mysterious and desirable."

"Who gives a toss about that? I want my painting back in Saint Peter's!"

"And it will happen," Lionello soothes. "You'll get another commission and you won't have any naked bodies, right?"

"After all," Nico adds, "It's expecting a lot for a church to accept full, face-on nudity. No coy turn of the leg to cover crucial bits."

"It's a little boy! The Christ Child!"

"Nico, you're making things worse," Onorio scolds. "Come, Michele, we'll go to the Blackamoor and drink away your anger and sorrow. Tomorrow everything will seem much better."

"Through the haze of a hangover," Lionello adds.

"Come on," says Nico. "Enough wine makes everything better."

I snort. Nothing can make this disaster better. But at least if I'm drunk I'll forget it happened. That's some consolation.

It's early for drinking, mid-afternoon, with a clear spring light washing over the stone buildings. The heat of summer hasn't arrived yet so people are outside, sitting at tables set up in front of inns and taverns, enjoying the long rest after the midday meal before business starts up again in an hour or so. Walking past one inn with the rich smell of beef stew, my stomach starts rumbling. I realize I haven't eaten anything today and suddenly I'm ferociously hungry.

"Should we eat before we start on some serious drinking?" I suggest.

"Good idea," Onorio agrees. "Let's go to Bread and Salt, around the corner from the tennis courts."

We all know the place and head toward it, talking about which of the dishes there is the best: the fish, the chicken, the pig, or the rabbit. No one can agree and the topic is getting heated. For a brief moment I'm not even thinking of my rejected altarpiece. Then I remember and rage floods through me, churning my stomach with bile.

"Michele!" a familiar voice calls out. It's Ranuccio, that wart on the buttocks of Rome. "You're showing your face around town? I would think after being kicked out of Saint Peter's, you'd get the hint and leave the city." He's flanked as usual by his brother Giovan Francesco and both of his brothers-in-law, Ignazio and Giovan Federico Giugoli, all armed with swords and daggers and ugly arrogant sneers.

"Shut up, Ranuccio!" Onorio barks. "What do you know about art, with clay for brains in that thick head of yours!" Onorio has had his own run-ins with Ranuccio and they hate each other almost as much as he and I do.

"Oh, Onorio, I didn't see you at first. But I certainly should have smelled you!" Ranuccio holds his nose and gags. "Call the street cleaners and have this mess removed!"

Giovan Francesco laughs at his brother's sparkly wit. Ignazio and Giovan Federico grin like idiots showing off the wide gaps in their teeth. Most of them have probably been knocked out in fights.

Onorio draws his sword. "Say that again and you'll be eating steel!"

"Now, Onorio, you don't want to get in trouble again for fighting me. Have you forgotten what happened last time? Weren't you ordered to stay away from me or go to prison? Better be a good boy now."

"Onorio, put it away!" Lionello hisses. "This donkey isn't worth the effort. Just ignore him!"

Onorio is seething, but he sheathes his sword and spits on the ground. The glob lands at Ranuccio's feet.

"That's your kind of weapon, isn't it Onorio – spit! You're pathetic. But not as pathetic as your friend Michele here who paints worse than that fool he mocks, Baglione."

Now it's my turn to grab my sword and pull it out. "Onorio can't fight you, but I can, you ass!" I lunge forward, aiming for his arm, but he's fast and pulls his sword out to meet mine. Blade clanks against blade as we parry and thrust, all my anger focused on my sword.

All around us, there's the sound of metal clashing. Onorio, Nico, and Lionello are fighting the three brutish sidekicks as I slash madly at Ranuccio.

I'm trying to aim either for Ranuccio's arm or leg, like the soldier I hit attacking the girl. He's fast, and twice his blade slices dangerously close. Then I see my chance. Ranuccio steps backs and stumbles on a piece of firewood in the street. I reach forward, aiming my sword straight for the meaty part of his thigh, ready to skewer him. He falls and my sword hits high, missing his leg and running clean through his stomach. Ranuccio looks surprised, landing flat on his back, blood gushing out.

"You murdered him!" his brother roars, rushing towards me and slashing at my head, almost slicing off my ear. I turn to face him, my sword still red with Ranuccio's blood. Before I can attack, Lionello throws himself on Giovan Francesco and pierces him through the leg. Now the two brothers-in-law are on top of Lionello, stabbing his arms, his legs, his face.

Onorio grabs me. "He's dead, Michele. Run! Now!"

I stare at Lionello's battered, still body. Ignazio and Giovan Federico are bent over Ranuccio, but they'll be on us next.

"Nico!" I yell, pulling at my friend. He's throwing up on the street. "Let's go!" We all start running.

"We should split up," Onorio pants. "We'll be harder to catch. We need to get out of town, all of us." Nico nods, his face white. It's only now I notice that he's holding one arm, trying to hold in the spurting blood.

"Nico, get to a doctor first. Lie low, alright?" I can hear the sbirri's whistles. They've found the bodies by now and will be looking for us. "Where are Giovanni and Raven?"

"Giovanni ran off as soon as blood was drawn. He's probably safely home with your dog. Take care of yourself!" Onorio pulls up, breathing hard. "I'm going this way. Good luck to you both!" We hug each other quickly and part.

I run all the way to Giustiniani's palazzo, strangely numb. What have I done?

When Giustiniani sees me, he sends for his doctor right away and puts me to bed. I haven't realized how much blood I've lost until I lie down and am overwhelmed with dizziness. Maybe I fainted or maybe I slept. I don't remember anything until the next day when Giustiniani comes to my room and asks if I'm well enough to tell him what happened.

My throat is dry and raspy. My head throbs with thudding pain. I touch the bandages gingerly. At least I still have my ear. I take a deep breath and try to sort out exactly what happened.

I describe Ranuccio's insults, the fight, his tripping, my fatal blow, Lionello's murder, and our escape.

"At least I think Onorio and Nico got away. Have you any news of them?" I ask.

"Onorio's gone, to Milan or Genoa, I'm not sure. Nico's in Tor di Nona."

"He was trying to protect me! You've got to get him out!"

"I'm looking into it," Giustiniani assures me.

"And those thugs of Ranuccio's? What about them?"

"Ranuccio has powerful friends among the Spanish. They'll never be punished. You, on the other hand, will be."

"What do you mean? Won't the pope intercede on my behalf? Or Cardinal Borghese?"

"It's complicated."

"Don't tell me that! Ranuccio was vermin and deserved to die! He killed a man himself and was never punished for it. And look at all the artists who have killed and been pardoned. My old master, Cesare d'Arpino, stabbed someone in a duel years ago and was forgiven. Benvenuto Cellini, the sculptor, killed three men, raped several women, and was instantly pardoned by the pope each time. Aren't I the greatest artist in Rome? Don't I deserve the same?"

"Ranuccio was buried in the Pantheon this morning. The Pantheon. Where Raphael is buried. Does that give you an idea of his status?"

I sink back into the bed. That thug has more stature in Rome than I do. I thought my name meant something.

"I'm sure once things quiet down, Pope Paul will pardon you, but in the meanwhile you have to get out of Rome. Del Monte and I have friends in Naples and Sicily. You'll be safe there. But no matter where you go, you must be careful."

"Leave Rome? Can't I hide out here?" I ask.

"You've been sentenced to Banda Capitale – that means you're not only condemned to death, but there's a price on your head. Whoever kills you gets to collect it."

I shiver despite the blankets, despite the warm spring day. I'm not the greatest painter in Rome – I'm a condemned criminal.

LXVII

Del Monte arranges for me to be smuggled out of Rome under some straw in a farmer's cart, trundled like a bale of hay. He sends me to Naples where the Marchesa di Caravaggio now lives, the family patron of my earliest days. With any luck, a papal pardon will be waiting for me by the time I get there.

The Marchesa greets me warmly. "You've grown and so has your fame since you left our home. Did you know that now when people hear the name 'Caravaggio' they don't think of a town outside of Milan? They think of a great painter."

"You're too kind, Marchesa." I kiss her gloved hands, soothed by the elegant ritual of the courtly palazzo. Surrounded by such rich comforts, I can imagine I'm not a wanted criminal on the run.

"When word got out that you'd be staying here, people flocked to see if they could commission a painting from you.

You can name your price!"

I swallow the fear rising in my throat. "People know I'm here?"

"Silly boy, are you worried about the price on your head?" She taps my arm playfully with her folded fan. "The pope is sure to overturn it any day. No one would dare hurt you."

That evening the Marchesa entertains the cream of Neapolitan society, and every church, organization, and guild asks me to paint something for them. I accept the most prestigious commissions, but I feel no safer because of them. The Spanish control Naples. Four thousand soldiers are garrisoned in the city. It's practically Ranuccio territory.

I'm introduced to so many titles and names, I remember none of them. Until the Marchesa brings me a young man whose story she's sure will interest me.

"This is my second son, Fabrizio Sforza Colonna, and he was in a similar situation. He might be able to help you."

"A pleasure to meet you, signore." I'm tempted to mention that a Sforza was my real father, but that may not help my case. Instead I ask, "Is it possible you've also killed a man and had a price set on your head?"

Fabrizio takes my elbow and steers me to a corner where we can speak freely without being overheard. "Yes, I've killed a man. I was a prior in Venice at the time, and it was in a duel. I wasn't sentenced to death like you, but spent four years in prison. My rank protected me. Besides my family name, I'm a knight of Malta. After my release I was named Captain-General of the Galleys for the knights. And that is how I think I can help you."

"I don't understand."

"When I next take ship for Malta, come with me. If you apply to become a knight, the title will protect you."

A knight? A title? Is it possible that as a murderer I'll finally get the recognition of my nobility that I've craved all my life? I study Fabrizio's face. He has frank gray eyes and a kindness to the set of his mouth that makes me believe him. "Can I really become a Knight of Malta?" And why, I wonder, aren't I one already.

"It's a bit complicated, but it can be done. You can't join my order, the Order of St. John, but. . . ."

"Why not?" He's tempting me with a title, then yanking it away.

"The members of that order come from the noblest families and are warrior knights, like those who fight the Turks."

Once again, I'm not noble enough. At least not in a way I can prove.

"There are other orders," Fabrizio hastens to reassure me. "We all take monastic vows of poverty, chastity, and obedience, and dedicate our lives to protecting the Catholic faith against the infidel hordes."

"Maybe knighthood isn't possible for me," I growl. "I don't mind poverty, but chastity and obedience have never been easy for me."

"At least pretend to honor the vows! You can join the Knights of Grace. That order is for men like yourself, of ordinary birth, but distinguished character. Because of your fame as an artist, you're very likely to be accepted."

I bristle at being called of ordinary birth, but swallow my pride. This is my chance to get the title my Sforza father denied me and I can't let vanity get in my way. If what Fabrizio says is true, the title will clear me of the murder, though I'm not sure how.

"There's one small impediment, but from what my mother says, it shouldn't be too difficult to overcome." Fabrizio strokes his beard thoughtfully.

"What's the problem?" I ask. I wonder if I need letters of testimony or to pass some arduous test.

"The murder, of course. Criminals can't be knights."

"I thought the point of the knighthood was to win me pardon from Rome. From what you say now, I can't get the title without the pardon." The issue seems more than minor to me. It seems unsolvable.

"Here's what you do. Once you get to Malta, you'll make yourself invaluable. You'll paint pictures for the order and if you're smart, you'll paint the portrait of the Grand Master himself. Once you've curried his favor, he'll intercede with the pope, asking for special dispensation to make you a knight. The dispensation doesn't pardon you for the murder, but allows you to be knighted in spite of it. Once you're a knight, the pardon is sure to follow. And until it does, you'll be protected by the most accomplished warriors in the world, the Knights of Malta."

"Thank you, Fabrizio! I can't believe my good fortune in meeting you. I've been looking over my shoulder ever since the brawl." I can't bring myself to call it murder. After all, I didn't mean to kill the toad. It infuriates me that Onorio, Nico, and I face charges when the brutes who killed Lionello are free.

"I'll let you know when we set sail for Malta, but it will be several months at least. In the meanwhile, you should paint and continue to spread your fame so that when you reach

Malta, the Grand Master will be drooling at the thought of adding your illustrious name to his roster."

I take Fabrizio's advice, painting several large altarpieces. I even paint a *Crucifixion of Saint Andrew* for the Spanish viceroy himself, making as many friends in high places as I can. But I'm still wary whenever I'm out on the streets, jumping at every shadow, drawing my sword at every stray cat or dog. The Marchesa says I'm worth more alive than dead, but that's only true for the people who can afford to pay my ever-rising prices. To a beggar, an innkeeper, or a common soldier my corpse is worth more than they can imagine earning in a year.

Still, I can't stay inside forever, no matter how fine the Marchesa's palazzo is. I'm given a high-ceilinged studio with rich, buttery light pouring in from the tall windows and a comfortable bedchamber, but a house becomes a prison if you can never leave it.

When I'm absolutely desperate, I sneak out to the docks and sketch. I love the salty sea air, the screeching gulls, the gray foam of the waves. I paint the ships, the men working on them, the rocky cliffs of the shore. Or I sit and listen to the sound of the surf pounding in my ears and dream I'm back in Rome.

This afternoon the chill of winter drives me back to the palazzo, but I feel calmer after my time by the sea. In the front hall, I recognize a familiar walking stick and cape. My pulse quickens and I hurry to the big salon. The sight of the empty room makes my stomach pitch with disappointment. But he must be here somewhere. I try one of the smaller salons. Even before I walk in, I hear his voice.

It's Del Monte, sitting in a royal blue chair next to the

Marchesa, a tray of bread, cheese, olives, and sardines in front of them.

"Cardinal!" I whoop. "It's so good to see you again! What news from Rome?"

"Michelangelo." Del Monte nods and smiles broadly. "Sit down and I'll tell you all I know. But first let me say that you are greatly missed. And from what the Marchesa here tells me, greatly welcomed in Naples."

The Marchesa beams at me, her pet painter. "It's true. Everyone is clamoring for a Caravaggio! I think the Romans are jealous that we have you here and that may be just the thing to hasten your pardon."

"Is that true?" I ask.

"Let's hope so," he says. "The situation is complex. Giovan Francesco Tomassoni, Ranuccio's brother, has been cleared of any charges. The two Giugoli brothers fled to Parma. Onorio is in Milan. Nico spent the last six months in prison, but is free now, though the muscles in his arm were so savagely cut, he's lost the use of it."

"Poor Nico!" I gasp.

"He's staying with me for now and is well taken care of. As for you, many voices are urging the pope to pardon you and bring you back to Rome."

"Scipione?" I ask.

"Ah, the cardinal nephew." Del Monte snorts. "He's a complicated one, he is. I think he actually helped make sure you were punished with the Banda Capitale."

"But he collects my paintings!"

"Exactly! As soon as you were branded a capital criminal, the Papal Grooms couldn't wait to get rid of the altarpiece you'd made for them. Any guesses as to whom they sold it?"

"He said he'd already tried to buy it from them. I took it as a compliment."

"It was, but one that didn't help you. Scipione loves to collect art but he's notoriously cheap about paying for it. He prefers to have it stolen for him, like the collection of the Cavaliere d'Arpino that was confiscated for tax purposes, and a beautiful Raphael he procured in a similar way. And now he got your altarpiece, not exactly for groats, but certainly for far less than you would have charged."

I sit back, stunned. I'm a pawn on a great political chessboard. And everyone knows how the game is supposed to be played except me. I must become a knight as soon as possible and play the game according to my own rules.

"Don't worry, now that Scipione has the picture at the very low price he wanted, there's no reason to leave you with this terrible sentence on your head. As the Marchesa has told you many times, you're much more valuable alive than dead, especially to Scipione and to Pope Paul."

"What do you suggest I do?" I tell him about Fabrizio's advice to become a Knight of Malta.

Del Monte nods. "Why not? I'm sure the papal dispensation will come quickly now and the pardon shortly after that. Both Giustiniani brothers are Knights of Malta and will put in a good word for you. Fabrizio is right – you should paint something absolutely magnificent as soon as you get to Malta, something that will set tongues wagging and remind Rome of the cost of your banishment."

"Should I send something small to Scipione now, a gift to curry favor?"

The cardinal shrugs. "Maybe later, if the pardon takes

too long in coming. For right now, I'd continue exactly as you are, painting altarpieces that spread your fame, and getting that knighthood as soon as you can."

"I miss Rome," I sigh. "The sun on the ancient stones. The soaring dome of St. Peter's. The way the air itself seems lighter in the Pantheon."

"Of course you miss Rome. There's nowhere else in the world like it. But I've brought you something that might remind you a little of home." He gestures to the servant standing by the door who bows and leaves to retrieve my gift.

There's a strange clacking sound, oddly familiar. The door opens and Raven gallops in, toenails clicking on the marble floor. The dog jumps up, his paws on my shoulders, his tongue all over my face, his tail wagging wildly.

"Raven!" I pet his head, scratch behind his ears, stroke his back. When did his muzzle get so gray? What happened to the young puppy I found on the church steps? Raven is grizzled and thick now, his eyes watery and dim with age. My heart tightens seeing his mortality. I'd rather die young and strong than sink into that kind of decrepitude. "Good dog," I croon. "Good, good dog!"

"And someone else, as well," Del Monte says.

I push Raven down and look up to see Giovanni grinning like a monkey. He's not the boy I first hired either, but a handsome young man now. His curls are still golden, his face still alluring, but the signs of the pox mar his mouth and throat. I'm lucky to have escaped the disease myself. Poor Giovanni isn't so fortunate.

"Master!" he says. "I'm happy to see you're well. You still have your ear!"

"My ear?" I touch the scar that runs in front of it in

a long jagged seam. "Yes, I managed to keep it. Are you both here to stay?"

"If you'll have us," Giovanni says.

I smile and reach down to Raven's silky head, resting on my thigh. "Of course, so long as you don't mind a little sea journey. To Malta."

"We go wherever you go, signore."

LXVIII

It's summer by the time we get to Malta, the sun burnishing the waves copper. The island is a small scrap of rocky land with most of the population living in the walled city of Valleta. There are no trees, little green of any kind, but the city is rich in its variety of people: merchants, sailors, Turks, Greeks, Armenians, Jews, traders of every kind. The stone is all the same yellow-ochre, but the people wear a wide palette of colors, from dull gray armor to brilliant purple turbans.

Fabrizio must have sent word to expect me, because as soon as I step off the boat, I'm greeted by several knights dressed in medals, ribbons, and feathers and am led with great pomp to the Grand Master's court. Giovanni and Raven are sent to wait in the kitchen while I have my audience. Good thing, too, since the boy looks ready to puke and the dog is not much better. The sea journey didn't agree with either of them, but I found it bracing, strangely freeing to be tossed along the waves, no longer held to the earth.

Grand Master Fra Alof de Wignacourt has a stern mouth, but there's a trace of humor in his eyes. He sits in a ponderous chair, a throne really, and motions for me to come closer.

"Michelangelo Merisi da Caravaggio, it's truly a great pleasure to welcome you to Valletta. Everyone knows of your talent, but your praises have been sung highly by one I hold especially dear, Cardinal Scipione Borghese."

I'm still not sure whether to consider the cardinal a patron or an enemy, but I bow my head. "His grace has been kind enough to honor me with important commissions and I am most grateful to him."

"Much as I know Rome misses you and yearns for your return, I have important plans for you here. You'll be housed in the Auberge of Italy and study for your knighthood with the other aspirants. You're expected to follow some of the courses – those in the statutes, customs, and traditions of the Knights of Malta. Others you're excused from – those in seamanship, gunnery, and fencing – so that you'll have ample time to paint. Valletta has been waiting for someone of your genius to beautify it, to give us the artistic distinction we deserve to match our military prowess."

Translated, that means that Rome won't pardon me until the Grand Master has gotten what he wants out of me. I grind my teeth impatiently, but I have to admit it's not a bad trade. I'm guessing I'll have to spend a year of my life here in return for a title and a full pardon.

Too bad I can't take the classes I'd actually enjoy. Fencing and gunnery sound like fun. Studying statues, customs, and traditions, not so much.

My fellow knights-in-training are a mixed lot though all except me are blue-bloods. Many are younger sons, the ones who won't inherit their fathers' titles and so have to create their own. I'd say they're hot-headed adventurers, looking for military glory skewering Turkish infidels, but there are a few gentler sorts, more interested in the order's hospital mission, caring for the sick and poor.

I make quick friends with Francesco who enchants me with his stories about journeys to the Holy Land.

"You think Rome is a magnificent city – you should see Jerusalem! The stones are so steeped in history, I can hear them whispering to me. You feel like you're going back in time when you wander the narrow streets. There are snake charmers in the markets, dancing monkeys, and even better, dancing girls. You should go, Michele! The pictures you could paint!"

"Maybe, someday," I agree, though Malta is exotic enough for me.

Alonso becomes my other close friend. He's a trickster and likes to play pranks on the other students. He slipped a snake into one man's room, frogs into another's.

"We aren't allowed to drink or gamble," he complains. "What else can I do for amusement?"

"Someone will give you a black eye one day for your troubles. And you're not supposed to brawl either, so how will you explain that?" I ask.

Alonso shrugs. "I haven't been caught so far. You won't tell my secret, will you?"

"No," I laugh. "But Fernando suspects. He has it in for you since you put those flies in his soup."

Fernando is a short-tempered sort, but that's not his

worst fault. He's absolutely obedient to every rule, even the most minor, and he expects everyone else to be as well. If you don't address a knight with what he considers the proper amount of respect, he'll clout you on the ear. As if it's his job to make sure we all behave. He detests Alonso, and isn't fond of me, either.

"Why aren't you taking the same classes as everyone else?" he demanded when I first arrived.

"Is it any business of yours?" I ask. Fernando towers over me and he points an emphatic finger at my chest, but I stand up tall, eyes narrowed in anger.

"What kind of knight are you anyway? You aren't noble, are you?" His eyes bulge in rage and flecks of his spittle land on my beard.

"What business is it of yours?" I repeat, louder this time, harsher. Just try to pick a fight, I think. You'll be breaking one of your precious rules.

"I, I, I have a right to know!" he stammers.

"I don't think so," I sneer, staring him down.

We stand like that for a while, the air between us hot with tension. He may be taller, but I'm more stubborn. He falters, drops his gaze and rushes off.

Ever since then, he makes jabbing comments about my low birth whenever there's an opening in the conversation and even when there isn't. Normally, I'd whip out my sword and have at him. But now all my effort goes into proving myself worthy to be a knight. Which means I don't fight.

I'm not sure how long I can keep up this unnatural behavior, but Alonso and Francesco cheer me on. And every day, seeing Giovanni and Raven reminds me why I'm doing all this – so I can go home, back to Rome, where I belong.

Months pass and after painting several portraits (including three of the Grand Master), I receive the commission that will finally earn me my knighthood: The Beheading of Saint John the Baptist for the newly finished Oratory of San Giovanni Decollato (which means Saint John Beheaded). It will be my largest painting yet, filling the wall of the grand room that's both lecture hall and judicial court.

Most knights pay a generous sum to enter the order, but my payment will be made in paint. The Grand Master suggests the trade himself when he calls me in to discuss what kind of knight I should be named.

"This matter of which order you enter is delicate, Michelangelo," he tells me. "The easiest would have been the Knighthood of Magistral Obedience, since it's chiefly an honorific title and can be granted to anyone of high prestige, including a famous artist such as yourself."

"Then why not that order?" I ask.

"Unfortunately when I first became Grand Master, I abolished it as an empty title used to repay favors. It was supposed to be reserved for men of great achievement such as yourself, but had been granted to much lesser men in exchange for political or financial favors. I had to put a stop to it."

"Surely there are other orders," I suggest.

"The Knighthood of Justice is reserved for those who are fully noble, but if there's even a drop of blue blood in your heritage, we could try for the Knighthood of Grace."

Fabrizio had told me that commoners could hold that title. He forgot to mention I needed at least a trace of nobility. Once again I curse my father for not recognizing me as his son before he died. Is there any point in claiming Sforza as my father when I'm an unproven bastard? I glower at the floor, searching for a solution in the cold marble and finding none.

"There's a way around this. I have to ask the pope for special dispensation to grant a title to a murderer in any case. I'll simply ask for a second dispensation at the same time, one allowing the title of Magistral Obedience to be resurrected in this one case, given that you're a man of recognized exceptional accomplishments."

"You think that it will be granted?" I try not to sound desperate.

"I'm sure of it. You won't have as generous a stipend, but you'll still wear the Knight's uniform, still have room and board granted while in Malta. And most important, you'll have a title."

"I'd be most grateful," I murmur.

"Remember that responsibilities come with the title. You can't leave Malta without my consent, no more taverns, gambling, or brawls. I expect you to bring honor to the order in every way."

"Of course, your excellency." I've had enough fighting to last me a lifetime. That part of me is gone now, despite the temptation to smack Fernando. I'm too old for black eyes and bruised ribs.

It's cold, drab winter when the pardon is sent for and only a month later, I'm summoned to the Grand Master. I know it's too soon to expect an answer, but I'm edgy anyway, clenching my teeth in anxious misery. It's not that life on Malta is dreary. It's fine enough, and being accepted in the company of knights as one of them has its satisfactions.

But I'm not in Rome. Once I was in the very center of the world. Now I feel perched on its outer edge.

Wignacourt is standing by a window, reading a letter

when I'm led into the audience hall. He looks up and I search his face for any hint of good news. The eyes are sharp and commanding as always, the mouth set firmly. He would make a good pope, I think, less susceptible to the pleasures of the flesh than most and a brilliant diplomat and military commander.

"Thank you for coming so promptly."

"Of course, your excellency." No one keeps the Grand Master waiting.

"Rome has written back quickly. You have your dispensations, both of them."

"Really? Already?" I haven't dared to hope, and here it is, granted to me so soon. That must mean a pardon for the murder won't be long! "Then I can be named a knight?"

"As soon as possible! But you must finish *The Beheading of John the Baptist* first. Then you'll receive your investiture in front of your own masterpiece, very fitting for the occasion, don't you agree?"

My eyes swim with tears. Once all I cared about was having an altarpiece in Saint Peter's. Now this is what matters most to me – returning to Rome to claim my place as its greatest artist with all the rights and privileges a knight's title grants. I can wear a sword without being accosted by the sbirri. If I ever do get arrested, I'll be quickly released. And if I challenge that donkey d'Arpino to a duel, he'll have no choice but to fight me or be branded a coward. I thought that what I wanted was for Sforza to recognize me as his son, to grant me his noble name. But this, this is even better. My title is one I've earned with my brush.

I work on the painting in a feverish haste, a dreamlike intensity. Drawing on my memories of Tor di Nona, I paint a dark cavernous prison, forbidding and dank. In the center of the floor, John the Baptist lies, his hands tied behind his back like a sacrificial lamb. The scene is brutal, but John's face is almost calm, accepting of his fate. The executioner bends over him, holding down his head with one hand, a blade in the other. A servant leans forward with the gold basin meant for the blessed head while another servant holds her face in sorrow. The colors are muted, grays, browns, and dull greens, except for the bright red cloth draped over John the Baptist and the equally bright blood pouring from his slit throat.

As I finish painting the blood, I'm seized by a sudden impulse to sign my name, something I've never done on any picture before. But now I have a name I'm truly proud to display, so I put it there, as if my finger had been dipped in the blood to spell out "Fra Michel Angelo." The Knight Michel Angelo.

LXIX

Onorio Longhi
Private Letter, 12 July 1607

I hear the same rumors everyone else does – that the great painter Caravaggio killed a man over a tennis match, over a bet, over an unpaid debt. There are as many reasons as there are storytellers. But never the right one. Though when I think about that day, I can't for the life of me say what the reason truly was. A fight started, the way they do. Only this time, two men died. And now I'll never be able to return to Rome. There will be no pardon for this.

I write to my old friend, following his trail as best I can, but he never writes back. He's supposed to be in Malta now, studying for knighthood. That's rich! He'll finally get the title he's always craved, all while facing the Banda Capitale, the punishment that awaits a murderer. He always was a bundle of contradictions: brilliant, generous, loyal, quick to anger, moody, brutish, and incredibly talented. One thing you can say about Michele, he has the courage of his convictions, the stubborn heart necessary to paint his visions. I make my safe little drawings for buildings, design elegant facades, charming gardens, but none of it really matters to me. For Michele, his brush is the only thing that really matters. I envy him that.

LXX

The ceremony is shrouded in ancient ritual and secrecy, the way knights have been invested for almost seven hundred years. I feel sacred, blessed afterwards, both noble and pure.

In contrast, the reception afterwards is complete pomp, almost papal in its splendor. There's a feast, the tables so well laden they seem to sink under the weight of the many dishes. Musicians perform in one corner, but the buzz of conversation is so loud it's hard to hear what melody they're playing. No one is supposed to get drunk, but glasses are filled and refilled.

The summer evening is warm, so the windows are open to let in the ocean breezes. Flames flicker in wall sconces and in the elaborate candelabras positioned throughout the room. We're celebrating in the same place as the original ceremony, in the great hall where my painting hangs. It's an odd sensation, feasting like this in front of my own immense picture, in front of my own name, as if I'm present twice, once in my own body, then again in the painting.

Faces are rosy with drink, bellies filled with chicken simmered in plum sauce, roasted pig, and broiled fish crusted in herbs. We're all wearing our knightly habits, proud in our black mantles emblazoned with a large white cross. I have on a heavy gold chain as well, a gift from the Grand Master. He was so pleased with my painting he awarded me this chain, a sign of my favor above all others.

Alonso and Francesco, also newly named knights, sit on either side of me, still eating though they complain their stomachs can hold no more.

"Then stop stuffing your faces!" I say.

"But it's all so good!" Alonso smacks his lips. "Especially after a year of monkish meals. I'm eating like a knight now!"

Francesco holds up his goblet. "And drinking like a knight, as well!"

Fernando sees us and can't resist sniping, even now. "It's a mistake, Michele. Your title is a mistake!"

"Really?" I touch my chain. "The Grand Master doesn't think so. And look, he's about to speak." I'm not simply trying to distract the big brute. It's true. Wignacourt has stood up and pounds his staff on the floor to silence the crowd.

"This reception is in honor of all those who have studied so long and hard to be made knights, but I'm especially gratified that we now have in our esteemed membership an excellent painter who brings glory to our order. Today I can say that I envy no court, no kingdom for the artistic talents they may house, because no man is the equal of the artist we now call one of our own. This man, whose name and brush are so distinguished, so famous that the pope himself was honored to have his portrait painted by him, is none other than our own Michelangelo Merisi da Caravaggio! Michelangelo, stand here by me so that we may all applaud you and raise our glasses in a toast!"

Alonso pulls me out of my chair and I stride as forcefully as I can, given all I've drunk. I bow my head before the Grand Master, take his hand and kiss it, but he shakes me off and lifts his goblet, urging me to lift mine beside him.

"To Michelangelo Merisi da Caravaggio, the greatest artist of our time and now a Knight of the Magisterial Order!"

My ears ring with all the voices calling my name and I can't stop smiling. I notice Fernando sneaking out, and my smile stretches even wider. Who's not noble enough now?

The faces around me are a blur but the painting, my painting, is bright and bold before me. The powerful image is both intimate and utterly strange, as if someone else created it. There's my proof of nobility, right there, in front of everyone. And that's what will get me my pardon – when Pope Paul hears about The Beheading of John the Baptist, he'll want me for himself. And not even the Grand Master can deny the pope.

"Will we be going home soon?" Giovanni asks the next day. "Why stay in Malta now?"

"I'm waiting for the official pardon. I expect it any day. And if it doesn't come by the end of the month, we can go to Naples and wait for it there. At least we'll be closer to Rome then." I lean down to pet Raven. "You don't like it here?"

"I don't mind it, I suppose." Giovanni shrugs. "It's a bit odd, that's all, kind of like living with monks and soldiers at the same time. I like regular people better."

I chuckle. It's a good description of this place, though

there's much more opulence than you'd expect from a religious or military order. That's the noble part, the part that can't do without satins and silks, gold and jewels. Or drinking and gambling, which happen plenty for all the vows that are taken. Like in Rome, there's an entire neighborhood devoted to those pleasures – not that I would know anything about them personally. I've stayed away while working for my title, but I'm tempted now that I'm safely a knight.

I spend the next month as if I'm back in Rome – painting during the day, carousing with my friends at night. I fall back into my old habits quickly, but there's a difference now. I'm a knight and I hold myself as if my noble birth has finally been recognized. Wearing the white cross of a Knight of Malta across my chest, I look as blue-blooded as the next knight and I hold my head as high.

"When are you going back to Rome?" Alonso asks one night after we've already had a few glasses of wine and are weaving our way down the narrow streets.

"Don't go yet! We'll miss you too much!" Francesco bawls. Drinking makes him sentimental.

"As soon as the pope pardons me and sends for me, I'll have to go," I say. "But you could come with me."

"No, we can't! We have to follow the Grand Master's orders. We'll probably set sail for the Holy Land or Turkey or some god-forsaken place like that."

"You can hardly call the holy land god-forsaken," I remark. "You're the one who's always saying how beautiful Jerusalem is."

"Yes, yes I can – it's over-run by infidels now, so that's as god-forsaken as you can get! A beautiful, god-forsaken place!" Francesco wipes his nose on his sleeve, blubbering. He makes a maudlin drunk.

A tall figure steps out of a brightly lit tavern and shoves Francesco to the side. "Out of my way, you miserable wretch! Can't hold your liquor, can you?"

"Leave him alone!" I bark. "He's done nothing to you!"

"He's offended my sense of smell! And you're even worse – you sully the cross you're wearing!"

I pull out my sword. "Say that again, to my blade, you brute!"

"With pleasure!" The man steps forward into the light and I recognize Fernando. "You've no right to be a Knight of Malta! You're not really noble! The Grand Master is a blind fool, but I can see the truth and I'll right this injustice!"

I grit my teeth and slice the air in front of me. "Come no closer or I'll be forced to harm you!"

"Michele, no!" Francesco yelps.

"No talk of harm. Let's all go home now," Alonso says, but no one is listening.

Fernando has his own sword out and strikes, blade clanging on blade. "I'm not afraid. Come to your death!"

I don't answer. I'm too busy parrying. He has the advantage with his height, his longer reach, but I'm quicker and I dance around him, searching for an opening. Then I find one and drive my sword into his leg, the hit I was trying for with Ranuccio. Not too deep – I don't want to kill him, just teach him a lesson.

Fernando yowls and grabs his thigh. "You villain!" he roars. He sinks to the ground. "A knight has been hit! Help me!"

Alonso grabs my arm. "Go! Quick!" He runs on one side of me, Francesco on the other. Giovanni and Raven are in front, leading the way.

I should feel panic, but what fills my chest is dread. It's just like the time with Ranuccio, only this time I'm certain I didn't kill Fernando. I couldn't have. But still, everyone knows that fighting with another knight means expulsion from the order.

"Giovanni, go back there!" I yell. "Find out what happened to Fernando and if he knew it was me he fought with. Maybe it was too dark."

"He sounded like he knew it was you," Francesco says. "He said you weren't really noble. That's what he always says about you."

"No! I can't have earned a title to lose it after only a month!" I pull on my hair, furious with myself. "Curse my temper! I haven't fought in so long! Why tonight?"

Alonso and Francesco try to comfort me, but nothing can ease the loathing that rises in my throat. I've ruined everything, everything!

Toward dawn, Giovanni returns with his report. Fernando is fine. The wound was only superficial, but he's named me as his attacker and officers are coming to arrest me.

"I'll be arrested?" I quaver.

Giovanni nods. "There's some underground prison, like an upside-down bell, and that's where they're going to throw you. There's a hole at the top so they can dump you in, and once inside, it's impossible to escape. That's what everyone says."

Alonso nods miserably. "It's called the Birdcage. It's hewn out of rock, 11 feet deep, 12 feet in diameter, with a small opening at the top, like Giovanni describes. It's a living grave, broiling hot during the day, freezing at night."

"Are you sure that's where they're putting Michele?" Francesco asks.

"That's what the officers said."

"Which officers?" I ask.

"The ones right behind me."

As if on cue, there's a knock on the door and a military guard pushes open the door. My hands are chained behind my back and I'm shoved out of the room.

Raven runs up to lick my bound hands one last time. The guard turns to kick him, but Giovanni pulls him back.

"It'll be fine," he murmurs to the dog. "I'm here."

And I won't be.

Alonso and Francesco stand silently. There's nothing they can do. Nothing anyone can do.

I'm put into a boat and rowed across the harbor, led into a prison surrounded by massive walls with the sea on three sides, a moat on the other. Even if I managed to get out of the Birdcage, how would I escape the prison? I hang my head and allow the pent-up tears to run down my cheeks. I've done this to myself, brought myself to these depths.

The Birdcage is as miserable as Giovanni described except he forgot to mention the darkness. It's utterly black inside. Voices occasionally drift in from the grill over the hole in the ceiling, but otherwise I'm completely alone. The prison cell in Tor di Nona was heaven compared to this.

I don't know how long I'm there. It's impossible to have a sense of time without a rising sun, a starry sky. My stomach growls with hunger, but that could mean a couple of hours or a couple of days. I sleep when my eyes are too heavy to stay open. Wake up when a rat runs across my foot or the chill seeps into my bones or a sound from the outside world tantalizes me.

"Pssst! Signore! Can you hear me?"

Am I imagining things? Is that Giovanni calling to me?

"Giovanni?" My voice is hoarse from disuse. My throat burns with thirst, but I try again, louder this time. "Giovanni!"

"Here! I'm lowering a rope. Grab it and climb up."

I flail my arms out in the darkness until I feel the rope and clutch it. I reach my sore, tired arms up, try to heave myself up, hand over hand, but I'm too weak, too dizzy with hunger and thirst.

"I'm not strong enough! Can you pull me up?"

"It's just me, Giovanni. You have to do this yourself. It's your only chance, signore! Please!"

"You've gotten yourself into this mess," I berate myself. "Now get yourself out of it!" I try again, sweating with determination. But after a few minutes, I fall back down, exhausted.

I sit there, disgusted with myself. I refuse to die in a pit like this. I stand up again, find the rope, and start to pull myself up.

My muscles scream, but I focus on the small circle of light I can see now, a torch held by Giovanni flickering over the opening. One arm at a time, one leg at a time, I inch my way up the rope like a worm, stopping to catch my breath, but I don't let go. My hands are blistered and bleeding as I grip all the tighter. Just a little bit further. A little bit further. A little bit further.

The light grows brighter and I can smell fresher air now. Still dank and damp, but not as foul as in the pit. I pull myself steadily up until my head is out of the hole and I can feel Giovanni grabbing under my arms, helping to swing my body over so I can thrust a leg out of the hole, clamber the rest of the way out.

I fall back on the stone floor.

Giovanni pours some water down my parched throat. "We have to hurry, signore, they're waiting for us."

"Who? How do we get out?"

"Shhh!" he whispers. "Follow me." Giovanni takes one of my hands and pulls me along the corridor. It's strangely quiet and empty. He finds a small door and opens it. Just like that, we're outside in the sharp, salty sea air, standing on a small wooden pier. I swallow big gulps and feel the weariness drop away in the fresh night breeze. I'm suddenly alert, the hairs on the back of my neck prickling. Where are all the guards? There's not a lot of moonlight, but there's some, enough to catch a sense of something moving.

Giovanni crouches low to stay in the shadows along the wall's edge. At the edge of the pier he looks down. "Here they are," he says. And then he jumps, vanishing from the dock. I wait for a splash but instead there's a thump, as if he's hit solid ground. I creep to where he disappeared and look over the side of the pier. A boat sits low in the water. Giovanni is huddled at one end near another man holding oars. I drop myself off the pier and land in the boat, caught by someone's arms.

"Shhh!" It's Alonso. He sits me down, hands me some bread, and starts to row. The man at the other end of the boat rows in rhythm with him and they slice quickly through the water.

"Where are we going?" I whisper when it seems like we're far enough away.

"To the boat," Alonso says. "The one that's going to

Sicily. It's the Marchesa's son. He'll smuggle you that far. The rest is up to you."

"But how did you do this? Did Fabrizio help you?"

"He's not the only one. The Grand Master had no choice but to punish you, what with all of Fernando's loud squawking, but he was under orders from the pope to let you escape. That's how we came to be here. We get you to the big boat. Fabrizio gets you to Sicily. From there you're supposed to go to Rome."

"Am I pardoned?" I can't believe it. "Am I really free to return to Rome?"

"Yes," Francesco says. He's the other rower. "We have a document for you from the Grand Master, proof you've been pardoned and granted safe conduct. But you must be careful. Fernando has a lot of friends."

I look up at the velvety sky, the pinpricks of Orion's belt, the Great Bear arcing overhead. What do I care about Fernando? I'm free! And I'm going home!

LXXI

The boat trip is suffocating, hidden as I am in Fabrizio's tiny captain's cabin. I'm starving for fresh air, for the sight of the blue sky, the warmth of the autumn sun on my face. But I'll have to wait for that. Fabrizio huddles me out of the boat in the dark of night onto land in Sicily. He can't risk having any of the other knights see me.

"Good luck, Michele," he says. "The pope may have pardoned you, but Fernando has put his own price on your head. You must be careful."

"I will," I promise. "Thank you for all you've done – and give my thanks to your mother as well."

"Don't worry about your boy and the dog. The next time I set sail for Naples, I'll take them along. They can stay with my mother until you send for them."

We clasp hands, then he goes his way, I go mine. Except I have no idea where to go. I wander around the dark, empty streets until I find a courtyard where I can huddle and doze until morning. I'm still wearing the black tunic with the white cross of a Knight of Malta. Filthy and ragged as it is, I hope it will offer me some protection as I sleep.

A broom sweeping over my boots wakes me up in the pale thin light of dawn. An old woman is clearing the courtyard of dried leaves and she looks like she's trying to push me into the gutter along with them.

"Excuse me!" I say, stumbling to my feet. "Am I in your way?"

"Hmmmmph!" she snorts. "Go sleep off your drinking somewhere else! This is a decent house here!"

"I'm not drunk! I'm as decent as you are!" I comb my hair with my fingers.

She stops sweeping and glares at me. I've heard the expression "the evil eye," but I've never seen it so vividly as in that old woman's face.

"Sorry to trouble you," I mumble. "I'll leave you in peace, signora." I walk through the streets, but one way or another makes no difference to me since I have no idea where to go. I'm not even sure what city I'm in. I stop at a bakery, the rich scent of bread curling in my stomach. Fabrizio gave me some money, so I spend a coin on a roll hot from the oven and learn that I'm in Syracuse.

Syracuse! That's where Mario lives!

I ask everyone I meet if they know Mario Minniti, the painter. The first few faces give me blank stares, but the blacksmith grins a gap-toothed smile and draws me a crude map in the dirt to show the way. I climb up a steep hill and find the house. It's larger than I expected, the home of a successful artist. I knock on the door and a young servant followed by a hugely pregnant woman answers. The woman's face is thin, but her large dark eyes and rich black hair hint at lost beauty. Now she's pretty, but worn. I'm guessing this isn't her first child.

"I'm sorry to disturb you so early, signora, but I'm an old friend of Mario. Is he home?" I hold my hat in my hand, trying to look like a gentleman, not a tramp who's spent the night on the street.

"Mario," she bellows into the interior of the house. "Some friend of yours!" She leaves me with the servant and walks away, hurrying to a screaming child. Mario walks up, dressed more fashionably than I've ever seen him. Clearly he's done well. When he sees me, his eyes light up and he throws his arms around me.

"Michele! I can't believe it! You're here! Come in, you must eat. And you look like you need a good wash and change of clothes as well. What's happened? You must tell me everything!" Mario guides me into the large kitchen where a long narrow table is set with bread, butter, jam, cheese.

I sit down and start stuffing my face, letting Mario's voice wash over me, just like so long ago. He tells me of his family, two children with a third on the way, of his business, painting altarpieces in a light, breezy style. His studio is so busy, he has twelve apprentices, as many as Cesare d'Arpino had. I listen to my old friend, warmed to hear of his success. He's wealthy, respected and beloved, as he's always deserved. At least one of us has the life he planned on.

I watch the servants bustling in the kitchen, the apprentices coming and going, the sense of an enterprise, of people working together.

"Mario!" I burst out, interrupting him mid-sentence.

"You're the Cavaliere of Syracuse! Look at all your assistants, your list of commissions! You run a big studio, the kind of thing I've never done."

Mario blushes, becoming once more the young boy I knew so long ago. "I suppose it's true. If a man can't be king in the great city, why not king of a village?"

"Syracuse isn't a village!" I protest. "You're every bit as good as d'Arpino was."

"I know your opinion of him!" Mario laughs. "Are you trying to insult me?"

"You know what I mean. You're better than d'Arpino, better than you thought you were."

"Maybe," he admits. "And what about you? I know you don't like the whole studio system, but have you given in, bought a huge palazzo? Are you surrounded by student Caravaggios?"

"Never! Giovanni mixes my colors. He's enough of an assistant for me. I don't want crowds of hangers-on. You're the only man I could ever stand to paint with."

"Then tell me what brought you to Sicily. And everything that's happened since I left Rome. Like how did you become a Knight of Malta? Very impressive, even if the uniform looks a bit . . . ahem, worn."

It seems impossible to describe it all, but I do, from the Saint Peter's commission, to the fight with Ranuccio, to hiding in Naples, to Malta, to Knighthood, to another stupid fight, to the impossible escape, and now to Sicily, to Mario's house.

Mario listens, absorbed. He asks a few questions, but mostly he's quiet, taking in the whole complicated saga.

"And you say the pope has pardoned you? You can

go back to Rome?" he asks when I've brought my story to the present moment, sitting here, in my old friend's kitchen.

"Yes, but I'd like to go back in style. Clean myself up a bit. Perhaps there's a church that would love to have an altarpiece by the great Caravaggio?"

"Of course there is! There'll be a bidding war to see who can land you! I'll take care of everything! Oh, Michele, it's so good to see you."

As promised, Mario arranges a commission, a well-paying one to paint the Burial of Saint Lucy for the Franciscan church of Santa Lucia al Sepolcro. I stay with Mario in his large house, get my clothes cleaned, hair trimmed, stomach filled. By the time I finish the altarpiece, I feel my old self again. Since I was thrown into prison, but not defrocked, I still consider myself a knight and hold myself as a noble. I buy a new sword, fine boots, a hat to replace my much battered one.

But I look over my shoulder whenever I leave the house. Sudden movements startle me. I tell myself I'm not afraid, just alert, wary for any sign of Fernando or one of his friends. Still, I sleep in my clothes, my dagger at my side. Just in case.

Even in the backwaters of Sicily, Mario is up on all the latest gossip – stale in Roman terms, but fresh for Syracuse.

"So what have you heard about me? About the Knights of Malta?" I ask him at supper after I've delivered *The Burial of Saint Lucy* to ecstatic appreciation.

"Rome adores you as much as ever," he says, shoveling stew into his mouth. "Cardinal Scipione Borghese is eager for your return. He told the pope to pardon you, and you're right, word is that he's the one who urged the Grand Master to let you escape."

"I owe the man a lot, though he's also the one who allowed the Banda Capitale in the first place. All to get a painting cheaply!"

"He's a shrewd one, the cardinal. And greedy. He keeps his purse closed, especially when he can add to his collection in less costly ways."

"And what have you heard about the knights? Do you know if one named Fernando Roero, Conte della Vezza di Asti, has arrived in the city?" I keep my voice calm. I told Mario about the fight with Fernando, but not his full name and title. And I haven't said anything about my fears that he's following me, hunting me down.

"Fernando?" Mario shakes his head. "No, but I have heard that you've been defrocked, stripped of your knighthood. There was some kind of ceremony back in Valletta."

"No!" I pound my fist on the table. "They have no right! I'm a Knight of Magisterial Obedience! They can't take that away from me!"

"But Michele, you know that the punishment for fighting with another knight is expulsion from the order."

"But was the other knight expelled as well? He started it! They can't kick me out and not him!"

"Actually, I think he's been defrocked, too." Mario shrugs. "At least that's the gossip – that both of you have been expelled from the Knights of Malta."

I hold my head in my hands, quaking with rage. I refuse to be expelled! I'm wearing the cross of Malta and I'm calling myself a knight. Once I get to Rome, Borghese will support my claim and that will be the end of it. As for Fernando, he deserves to be kicked out, though that means he's free to go where he wants, to track me down. I'll have to be even more careful.

I wish I had Raven here with me. Old as he is, he could smell Fernando long before I see him. For a week, I stay home, avoiding taverns and inns. Then I get angry at myself for building my own prison. I'm not letting Fernando keep me locked up in my own studio!

I paint *The Raising of Lazarus* and *The Martyrdom of Saint Ursula,* my brushstrokes looser than ever. I paint with a fierceness, an intensity that overwhelms me. I feel as if the Angel of Death is whispering over my shoulder, telling me to hurry, to paint all I can before Fernando catches me. The big altarpieces are commissions. On my own, I paint three smaller paintings, gifts for Scipione Borghese, my way of thanking him for advocating for my pardon.

The first two are subjects I know will please him – a *Mary Magdalene* and a *Young John the Baptist.* The last one is for myself, the picture I need to paint. It's *David and Goliath.* David is pensive, almost sad that's he's had to destroy Goliath. He holds up the giant's severed head by its thick black curls, offering it to the viewer as if to say, "Here, see all the sins of the world in this face – I had to kill him."

David's face is my own, fifteen years ago, when I was young, newly come to Rome and ready to conquer the city, to prove my worth.

The face of Goliath is also my own, me now with shaggy curls and beard. I'm offering Scipione my head, not quite on a platter, but there, in all the naked honesty I can paint. He's given it back to me, taking the price off of it. I owe him this much, my head, my life, my sins to do with as he will.

I feel lighter when I finish the painting, as if I really have cut off my sinful head and grown a new, purer one.

"Come!" I call Mario. "Let's go to a tavern for once! I've finished my gifts for Scipione and I've booked passage on a small boat heading for Rome in three days. It's time to relax, to celebrate getting through all this. And it's been far too long since I've had an evening out."

Mario grins. "That's the old Michele I know and love so well!

It's July now, so the evening is warm. Still, we wear cloaks, hats, swords, and I slip my dagger in my belt as well. The weight of the steel blades is reassuring.

"I know just where to go," Mario says. "The Osteria del Ciriglio. The food is good, the wine high quality, and the ladies particularly lovely."

"Sounds perfect!" I agree. And it is. Mario and I are happily into our third glass of wine. I'm eying the women on offer, deciding which one to take to bed. There's a redhead who reminds me of Anna Bianchina. I point her out to Mario but he sees no resemblance at all. He's fixated on a voluptuous brunette.

"Do you mind if I leave you, Michele?" he asks. "Just for a bit?"

"Of course not, go!" I wave him off. "I'll see you in the morning."

"You don't mind going home by yourself?"

"Why would I?" I narrow my eyes. Has he noticed the way I look over my shoulder, the way I search the doorway whenever someone enters the place?

"No reason, nothing," he assures me. "I'm off then." He finds his girl and she leads him up the narrow stairs in the back of the inn.

There's a ruckus at the counter, some drunk pushing

around another drunk. Another fight breaks out in a corner when two men grab for the same woman. It's a normal night in Syracuse.

Except something sends a shiver down my spine.

I sense him before I see him. There he is – Fernando, his dagger already in his hand, and he's heading straight for me. I whip out my sword in one hand, my dagger in the other. The brute is even bigger than I remember. I charge at him, roaring, "Be gone, you devil!"

I push past stools and tables, knocking glasses on the floor, trying to defend myself from Fernando's frantic thrusts. I think I hit his arm, but he keeps coming at me. I feel something warm run down my neck, feel a sharp pain in my cheek.

"Noooo!" I bellow, throwing myself at him in a blind rage. I'm not dying now! I hack wildly and when I see a clear path to the door I take it, running like a fiend. I turn down one street, then another, looking over my shoulder, but he doesn't seem to be following me. Still, I don't stop until I'm back inside Mario's house.

I sink onto a stool, trying to catch my breath. Carefully I touch my face. There's an ugly gash in one cheek, almost slicing it off and a deep cut across my nose. I clean myself up gingerly and send the servant for a doctor. Too bad I didn't wait to paint my portrait as Goliath. I'd be so much more convincing now.

In the morning I wake up to see Mario sitting next to me, deep shadows under his eyes.

"Michele, what happened?" he asks. "All I know is that there was a fight, actually several that night, though yours sounds the worst."

"Did I hurt him? What happened to him?"

"The man who attacked you? Seems like he's fine. He was with three other men and they're still looking for you. It's not safe for you here anymore."

"It doesn't matter. I leave for Rome in two days. They won't find me in two days."

"They might." Mario lowers his eyes. "If you can travel, I think you should leave today. I'll find a boat for you, don't worry."

I touch my face, feel the bandages the doctor wrapped around me. They're sticky with blood, but the pain is a dull throb now, not a sharp stabbing.

"I'll go then. I don't want to get you or your family in any trouble." I take my friend's hand. "You've been very kind to me, Mario. Always. And I'm glad I came to see you, to see how successful you are. Your talent has finally been recognized."

Mario smiles. "I'm a craftsman, Michele, nothing more. It's a good life for me and I know I'm fortunate. But I'm not like you. I'm not a genius."

"The more luck to you that way!" I say. "And a lot less trouble."

Mario finds a small boat that's willing to take me to the coast by Rome for a price. I roll up the paintings for Scipione, pack the rest of my few belongings in a satchel. I carry the safe conduct in my purse, a document from Cardinal Gonzaga assuring me of my pardon and removing the Banda Capitale.

It's not quite the triumphant return I'd imagined, but I'm going home and that's what matters most.

The boat puts in at Palo, a tiny port near Civitavecchia. The sailors need fresh water and supplies, then we'll head for Ostia, the port nearest Rome. I get off with them, glad for the chance to stretch my legs, to feel unmoving ground beneath my feet after the long hours rocking in the boat. I walk along the pier, imagining how Rome will have changed, what will be different. Saint Peter's should be almost finished by now. Scipione's villa is probably built, ready for his growing collection. But the Pantheon will be the same. So will the way the golden Roman light caresses the stone walls and turns them into living, breathing creatures.

"You there!" a guard calls out to me. "Who are you and what's your business here?"

"I'm waiting for my boat to take on provisions," I say. "I'm Michelangelo Merisi da Caravaggio." What is it about me that always attract guards and police? Still!

"Then I'm arresting you!" Before I can draw my sword, the guard grabs my arms and twists them behind me, binding me with a chain.

"What are you arresting me for?" I yell. "I have a safe conduct, guaranteed by the pope himself! This is a mistake!"

"We'll see about that," he says, dragging me to the fortress castle overlooking the port.

I scream curses the entire way, insisting he look at the safe conduct, but the brute ignores me, shoving me into a cell where I scream all the louder to talk to someone with authority. I've yelled myself hoarse by the time the captain of the fortress has a guard lead me into his office.

"There's been a mistake," I say.

"Has there?" The captain fingers his mustache.

"If you'd let me show you my safe conduct, this can be settled quickly," I seethe.

"Fair enough." The captain gestures to the guard to unchain me.

I rub my sore wrists, then bring out the document signed by Cardinal Gonzaga. The captain reads it slowly, like the imbecile he is. Then hands it back to me and nods.

"There does seem to have been a misunderstanding. You're free to go."

"A misunderstanding?" I poke an angry finger at him, searching for a threat big enough to contain my rage, but there's nothing I can say. I snort in disgust and push my way out the door, out of the fortress.

The sun is high in the sky now – hours have been wasted in that cursed cell. I rush for the pier, but it's too late! The boat is gone!

"What happened to the boat that was here?" I ask an old man coiling a rope nearby.

"They left a while ago. Was it you they were looking for? They yelled all up and down the pier, but nobody answered. So they up and went."

"Did they say where they're stopping next? Maybe I can get there by foot before they arrive by sea."

"I think they said Port'Ercole. You can try hoofing it. It's not that far." The man points out the road to me and I set off. My satchel and paintings are on the boat, but I have my purse with some coins in it, so I don't feel desperate. Anyway, there's nothing for it but to get going.

The road runs through marshes with not many trees to offer any shade. It's hot and my cloak and hat feel heavy and suffocating. I drape the cloak over one arm, but I leave on the hat to shield the afternoon glare. I'm wearing the black tunic with the white Maltese cross and I imagine the knight's uniform provides some protection if there are bandits around. Insects buzz and birds trill, but otherwise it's quiet, a heavy, muggy silence.

I walk for hours. I walk until the sun sinks low and a cool breeze blows in from the shore. I walk until I see the distant lights of houses, of the port. I walk until I'm at the pier at Port'Ercole, but there's no sign of my boat. And once again I'm told they put in, called my name, and left.

It's dark now. I'm exhausted, hungry, and dizzy from the sun baking my head for so long. I take a room at an inn and collapse on the thin straw pallet. Am I going to walk the entire way to Rome?

My dreams that night are feverish and vivid. I'm with Del Monte that first time we met. I'm in San Luigi de' Francesi figuring out what to paint for the Contarelli chapel. I'm in bed with Fillide. No, it's Anna. Now it's Lena. I wake up in a sweat, my mouth parched. I gulp down some water from the pitcher by the bed and try to sleep but I can't. When I close my eyes I see the blade chopping off Beatrice Cenci's head. I see the flames devouring Giordano Bruno. I see Fernando lunging at me with both blades.

In the morning I'm so weak I can barely move. The innkeeper sends for a doctor. When I wake up again I'm somewhere else, a place with whitewashed walls and an open window letting in fresh air. Am I back in Santa Maria del Consolazione? A nun comes into the room and I expect to see the moon-faced girl who modeled for *The Fortuneteller*. But this nun is older, her face creased.

"Where am I?" I whisper, my throat rough and raspy. "I need to get to Rome."

"Hush, now," the nun wipes the sweat from my brow with a cool damp cloth. "You're in the infirmary. And you're not going anywhere until you're better." She hesitates, then asks. "Do you want to see a priest? For the last rites?"

Am I as bad as that? Am I dying?

When I wake up again the room is dark. I can hear frogs and crickets. That's a good sign, I think. I'm getting better. I'll leave soon, very soon. Thoughts drift in and out of my head. I wonder if everything would have been different if I'd been named Bernardo or Paolo, Guido or Alessandro. Anything but Michelangelo.

The name has been nothing but a curse, a burden too heavy for me to carry, even if that's the name I signed on my painting. But at least I'm not the other Michelangelo anymore. I'm Caravaggio, Rome's most brilliant painter. It will be as Scipione promised, when people think of Rome, they'll think of me...

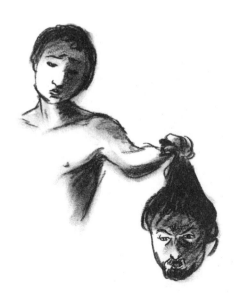

LXXII

Scipione Borghese
Personal Journal, August 1610

The news of Caravaggio's death travels fast. I hear it before the boat arrives in Ostia with his few belongings so there's time to send a servant to meet it and fetch me his things.

I had such big plans for him! Now all there will be lies here before me, his last three paintings. The Magdalene and the Saint John are classic Caravaggio's, gems of dramatic perfection. If ever a man knew how to capture the soul, it was he!

But the David and Goliath touches me the most. It's a raw cry of penitence, a pleading prayer for forgiveness. It will be the crown of my collection. The painter may be gone, but his pictures remain and I'll be sure to weave them into the fabric of the city. I'll keep my promise to him – Caravaggio's paintings will always be the beating heart of Rome.

Author's Note

Michelangelo Merisi da Caravaggio was in some senses the first modern artist. Unlike the other painters of his day, he worked alone, without a studio full of apprentices, despite his fame and fortune. At a time when artists worked from models and drawings, when ideal proportions regulated the look of artistic reality, Caravaggio painted from living people, blazing bright lights and rich shadows on his canvases. Compared to the pastel hues and thoughtful, careful drawing of his contemporaries, Caravaggio's paintings were shockingly bold. His style jolted people so deeply, he inspired a generation of followers all across Europe, from France to the Netherlands to Spain to Italy.

From his early days working in the studio of his rival, Cesare d'Arpino, to being "discovered" in an art dealer's window by the influential cardinal, Francesco Maria del Monte, to the height of his career, painting for the pope himself, Caravaggio blazed a unique path, defined by revolutionary ideas about art and society.

In his personal life, Caravaggio had the mercurial

temperament of an artistic genius, painting brilliantly by day, getting into fights by night. He was arrested dozens of times, for things as minor as carrying a sword without a permit to assault to libel.

His life, revealed in court documents and descriptions by his contemporaries, shows one man's rebellion against the staid art world and its strictures with his insistence on looking at the real world and painting real people. His saints have dirty feet, the models for his Virgin Mary were often prostitutes. At a time of great religious ferment as Catholicism was challenged by the Reformation, Caravaggio painted the sacred as the everyday and the everyday as sacred. Against the background of Rome reaching baroque heights as the papacy extended its power, his story provides an insight into European politics and strife in the time between the Renaissance and Early Modern periods.

Caravaggio's life was as dramatic as his art. Whenever he achieved greatness in a particular commission, an arrest for some petty violation would soon follow. Until the day when a brawl spiraled into killing a man. Condemned to death as punishment, Caravaggio escaped first to Naples, then to Malta where he worked to redeem his name as a Knight. Caravaggio earned his knighthood through his paintbrush, along with a pardon from the pope for his crimes, but once again, his hot temper landed him in a fight, this time with another knight.

Thrown into the notorious island prison, Caravaggio escaped, heading first to Sicily, where he was attacked, and then on a small boat back to Rome.

Though there has been endless speculation about Caravaggio's death, it's most likely that he died of a fever, probably malaria, in July 1610. He never made it back to his beloved Rome, but his paintings can still be seen in the churches they were painted for, San Luigi de' Francesi, Sant'Agostino, and Santa Maria del Popolo. Scipione Borghese's collection can still be admired in the Villa Borghese, including all the paintings mentioned as belonging to him in this book, from the early self-portrait as Bacchus to the last painting Caravaggio did, the soulful *David and Goliath*. Many of the paintings commissioned for churches can still be found exactly where Caravaggio put them: the three paintings in the Contarelli chapel of San Luigi dei Francesi (*The Calling of St. Matthew, Matthew Writing his Gospel, The Martyrdom of St. Matthew*), the two in the Cerasi chapel in Santa Maria del Popolo (*The Martyrdom of St. Paul, The Conversion of Saul on the*

Way to Damascus), and the final *Beheading of St. John the Baptist* in Valletta on Malta.

Caravaggio's style had so much influence that for decades after his death, his dramatic lighting and naturalism were copied, spawning a generation of painters called the Caravaggisti, followers of Caravaggio. Nobody remembers the painter's rivals, Cesare d'Arpino or Baglione, but the name Caravaggio is known far and wide. His deeply held convictions shaped a revolutionary style and his fierce determination changed the shape of art forever.

All the people and places in this book really existed, including Caravaggio's friends and models, his patrons, and enemies. Their personalities however are completely invented. The events depicted are taken from contemporary writing and follow the actual course of Caravaggio's life. The police reports, denunciations, acts of notary, and depositions are also all real, actual documents taken from the Rome archives, though the dates have sometimes been changed for dramatic reasons. Cardinal Francesco Maria Del Monte was not only Caravaggio's patron, but Galileo's as well, though the telescope he was given wasn't actually invented until 1609 (later than its mention here). For all of these details and so much more,

I'm indebted to Lisa Kaborycha, Italian Renaissance scholar at the Medici Archive. She also provided invaluable help in translating the police reports and other archival material.

The best way to get to know Caravaggio, however, isn't through anything written, but by looking at his paintings. Images reproduced on a screen or in a book give a sense of his art, but standing in front of the originals is the only way to feel their full power. Caravaggio is still the beating heart of Rome.

Time Line

September 28 or 29, 1571
Caravaggio born in Milan.

1577
Caravaggio's father, Fermo Merisi, administrator and architect-decorator to the Marchese of Caravaggio, dies in the plague.

1584
Caravaggio's mother, Lucia Aratori, who worked for the powerful Sforza family, dies.

1584-1590
Caravaggio is apprenticed to the painter Simone Peterzano in Milan.

1592
After some scuffles with police in Milan, Caravaggio leaves the north for Rome and becomes apprentice to Anteveduto Grammatica. Meets Mario Minniti and the two become life-long friends.

1593
Enters studio of Cesare d'Arpino, favorite painter of Pope Clement VIII. Mario joins him in the studio and acts as a model for Caravaggio. Paints *Self-Portrait as Bacchus* and *Boy with a Basket of Fruit* (later appropriated by Cardinal Borghese from Cesare d'Arpino for non-payment of taxes and still in the Villa Borghese in Rome).

1594
Gets kicked by horse, spends several months convalescing in a charity hospital run by the church, Santa Maria della Consolazione. Leaves Cesare d'Arpino's workshop with Mario and starts painting his own pictures, starting with *The Fortuneteller*.

1594
Sells paintings through picture dealer Constantino Spata, *The Fortuneteller* and *The Cardsharps* (both bought by Cardinal Francesco Maria del Monte).

1595
Enters household of Cardinal Francesco Maria del Monte. During his years with him, paints *Judith Beheading Holofernes, Saint Catherine, The Musicians, The Lute Player, Boy Bitten by a Lizard, Sacrifice of Isaac, Saint Francis of Assisi in Ecstasy, Bacchus*, and the *Medusa*.

1597
First scrape with Roman law, arrested for carrying a sword without a permit.

May 4, 1598
Another arrest: "I was arrested last night...because I was carrying a sword. I carry the sword by right because I am Painter to Cardinal del Monte. I am in his service and live in his house. I am entered on his household payroll."

1599
Meets courtesan Fillide Melandroni. Uses her as model for some of his paintings.

July 23, 1599
Gets first major commission, the Contarelli Chapel in

San Luigi dei Francesi, the *Calling of Saint Matthew* and the *Martyrdom of Saint Matthew*.

September 11, 1599
Beatrice Cenci executed in front of the Castel Sant'Angelo along with her step-mother and brother for killing her abusive father in self-defense.

February 17, 1600
Dominican friar Giordano Bruno burned at the stake in the Campo dei Fiori for his heretical views.

1600
Finishes paintings for Contarelli Chapel, hangs them to great acclaim, however *Saint Matthew and the Angel* is rejected and sold to the banker Vincenzo Giustiniani

Fall, 1600
Gets commission for the Cerasi Chapel in Santa Maria del Popolo.

1601
Finishes *The Crucifixion of Saint Peter* and *The Conversion on the Way to Damascus* for Cerasi Chapel in Santa Maria del Popolo. Paints a new version of *Saint Matthew and the Angel* for the Contarelli Chapel in San Luigi dei Francesi.

1601
Leaves household of Cardinal Del Monte for his own rooms, while still remaining under the cardinal's protection. A later legal complaint accuses him of breaking a hole into the ceiling, possibly for better light or to bring in large canvases.

1603
The painter Giovanni Baglione accuses Caravaggio and

his friends of libel. Caravaggio testifies, "In painting a *valent'huomo* [man of worth] is one who knows how to paint well and imitate natural objects well." Caravaggio is now one of the most famous artists in Rome.

September 25, 1603
Libel charges are dropped and Caravaggio, along with his friends, are freed from prison.

1604
Paints the *Entombment of Christ* for Santa Maria in Vallicella (now Chiesa Nuova) in Rome. The painting is one of the few Caravaggio's taken from the chapel it was painted for and now hangs in the Vatican Museum. Gets arrested for minor offenses several times – for assaulting a waiter who had served him with a plate of artichokes and answered sassily about whether they were dressed in butter rather than oil ("smell for yourself."); for throwing stones in the street in the company of, among others, a perfume maker and some prostitutes; and for telling a policeman who was attempting to release him, even though he was carrying a sword and dagger, that "you can stick it up your arse."

March 3, 1605
Pope Clement VIII dies.

April 1, 1605
Alessandro Ottaviano de' Medici named Pope Leo XI. He rules for all of twenty-six days, dying on April 27, 1605.

May 16, 1605
Camillo Borghese named Pope Paul V.

1605
Paints the *Madonna of Loreto* for the Cavalletti Chapel in

Sant'Agostino in Rome. Arrested yet more times – in late May for carrying his sword and dagger in a public place; on July 19 for defacing the house front of a woman named Laura della Vecchia, a crime known as *deturpatio*, often committed as revenge for an insult or affront; on July 29 for inflicting grievous bodily harm to the notary Mariano Pasqualone who wants to marry Lena, the woman who models for Caravaggio for the *Madonna di Loreto*. Caravaggio skips bail and flees to the coastal city of Genoa for the month of August. On his return he discovers that the landlady from whom he was renting his house in the Vicolo dei Santa Cecilia e Biagio, one Prudentia Bruni, has seized his possessions and changed the locks for non-payment of rent. He commits the crime of *deturpatio* against her, this time smearing excrement on the door of her house and singing obscene songs to the accompaniment of a guitar outside her window. In her deposition to the court, the landlady complains that Caravaggio had damaged one of the ceilings in her house. Paints *The Death of the Virgin* for Santa Maria della Scala, much admired by Rubens, but criticized by others, and taken down as scandalous.

1606
Paints *Portrait of Pope Paul V* and *The Madonna of the Serpent* for the Chapel of the Papal Grooms in St. Peter's. Up for only one month before being removed because it was considered "offensive."

May 28, 1606
Long-running tension between Caravaggio and Ranuccio Tomassoni erupts in a violent fight. Tomassoni is killed by a wound to his leg inflicted by Caravaggio. Caravaggio's

friend, Lionello, is also killed. Caravaggio flees Rome and is convicted of murder in absentia and sentenced to "bando capitale," meaning anyone who killed him would be rewarded.

Summer 1606
Caravaggio stays under protection of the Colonna family in Naples. While there he paints *The Seven Acts of Mercy* for the confraternity of the Pio Monte della Misericordia, *The Flagellation of Christ, The Crucifixion of St. Andrew.*

1607
Caravaggio travels to Malta and studies to become a Knight of Obedience of the Order of St. John. While there he paints the *Portrait of Alof de Wignacourt, Portrait of Fra Antonia Martelli, St. Jerome Writing,* and finally, as payment for induction into knighthood, *The Beheading of St. John the Baptist* for the conventual church of Valletta in Malta. The painting is still in the church, the only picture signed by Caravaggio.

1608
Caravaggio finally attains the title of Knight only to attack another knight and be thrown into prison, the inescapable "guva," a rock-cut cell in the fortress.

October 1608
With help, Caravaggio escapes from prison and makes his way to Sicily where his old friend Mario Minniti helps him get commissions for *The Burial of St. Lucy* for the Basilica of Santa Lucia al Sepolcro in Syracuse, *The Resurrection of Lazarus,* and *The Adoration of the Shepherds.*

1609
Returns to Naples, staying once more with Colonna family.

Paints *The Raising of Lazarus* for Sant'Anna dei Lombardi (later destroyed in an earthquake). Attacked by four men, most likely knights of Malta seeking vengeance, while in the Osteria del Cerriglio, Caravaggio is seriously hurt, his ear almost cut off. Recovers in the Palazzo Colonna.

July 9, 1610
Having heard news of a papal pardon for the murder of Ranuccio, Caravaggio boards a small boat for Rome, carrying a couple of paintings to offer to Cardinal Borghese in thanks, including the *David and Goliath*. When the boat puts in at Palo to reprovision, Caravaggio is arrested by mistake. By the time Caravaggio is freed, the boat has left and he continues to Rome on foot, making it to Porto Ercole when he collapses.

July 18 or 19, 1610
Caravaggio dies at Porto Ercole, probably from malaria or another disease, and is buried in an unmarked grave. He is 38 years old.

For a complete list of paintings and where you can find them and for original documents relating to Caravaggio's life, go to www.caravaggio.com

Bibliography

Carofano, Pierluigi. *Il Giuco al Tempo di Caravaggio: Dipinti Giochi, Testimonianze dalla Fine del '500 ai Primi del '700*, Pontedera, Bandecchi & Vivaldi, 2013.

Vodret, Rosella, editor. *Roma al Tempo di Caravaggio: 1600-1630*, Skira, Milan, 2012.

Spadero, Alviso. *Le Parole di Caravaggio*, Bonanno, Rome, 2012.

Atti della Giornata di Studi Francesco Maria del Monte e Caravaggio, Bandecchi & Vivaldi, Pontedera, 2011.

Franklin, David and Schutze, Sebastion. *Caravaggio & His Followers in Rome*, Yale University Press, New Haven, 2011.

Merlini, Valeria and Storti, Daniela, editors. *Michelangelo Merisi da Caravaggio: Chiuder la Vita*, Skira, Milan, 2010.

Macioce, Stefania, editor. *I Cavalieri di Malta e Caravaggio: la Storia, gli Artisti, i Committenti*, Logart Press, Rome, 2010.

Macioce, Stefania, editor. *Michelangelo Merisi da Caravaggio: la Vita e le Opere Atrraverso I Documenti*, Logart Press, Rome, 1996.

Carvaggio in Galera: Conversazioni sull'arte nel Carcere di San Vittore col Gruppo della Trasgressione, ARPANet, Milan, 2010.

Come Lavorava Caravaggio, Romartificio, Rome, 2006.

Macioce, Stefania. *Michelangelo Merisi da Caravaggio: Fonti e Documenti: 1532-1724*, U. Bozzi, Rome, 2003.

Spike, John T. *Caravaggio,* Abbeville Press, New York, 2001.

Hibbard, Howard. *Caravaggio,* Harper & Row, New York, 1983.

Samek Ludovici, Sergio. *Vita del Caravaggio dalle Testimonianze del Suo Tempo; Studio e Note,* Edizioni del Milione, Milan, 1956.

Sapio, Maria, editor. *Mario Minniti: l'eredita di Caravaggio a Siracusa,* Electa, Naples, 2004.